Brad knew he should leave, but he couldn't.

What was happening to him? He couldn't seem to be near Penny without his heart wanting to explode. Without his hands wanting to touch her and his lips needing to taste her. He seemed to lose all sense when she smiled at him. He had no willpower, no strength around her at all.

He *would* change. He would take himself in hand and control all those urges. Maybe it wouldn't be easy, but it was possible.

And absolutely necessary.

* * *

Dear Reader,

This month, Silhouette Special Edition presents an exciting selection of stories about forever love, fanciful weddings—and the warm bonds of family.

Longtime author Gina Wilkins returns to Special Edition with *Her Very Own Family,* which is part of her FAMILY FOUND: SONS & DAUGHTERS series. The Walker and D'Alessandro clans first captivated readers when they were introduced in the author's original Special Edition series, FAMILY FOUND. In this new story, THAT SPECIAL WOMAN! Brynn Larkin's life is about to change when she finds herself being wooed by a drop-dead gorgeous surgeon....

The heroines in these next three books are destined for happiness—or are they? First, Susan Mallery concludes her enchanting series duet, BRIDES OF BRADLEY HOUSE, with a story about a hometown nanny who becomes infatuated with her very own *Dream Groom.* Then the rocky road to love continues with *The Long Way Home* by RITA Award-winning author Cheryl Reavis—a poignant tale about a street-smart gal who finds acceptance where she least expects it. And you won't want to miss the passionate reunion romance in *If I Only Had a... Husband* by Andrea Edwards. This book launches the fun-filled new series, THE BRIDAL CIRCLE, about four long-term friends who discover there's no place like home—to find romance!

Rounding off the month, we have *Accidental Parents* by Jane Toombs—an emotional story about an orphan who draws his new parents together. And a no-strings-attached arrangement goes awry when a newlywed couple becomes truly smitten in *Their Marriage Contract* by Val Daniels.

I hope you enjoy all our selections this month!

Sincerely,

Karen Taylor Richman
Senior Editor

Please address questions and book requests to:
Silhouette Reader Service
U.S.: 3010 Walden Ave., P.O. Box 1325, Buffalo, NY 14269
Canadian: P.O. Box 609, Fort Erie, Ont. L2A 5X3

ANDREA EDWARDS

IF I ONLY HAD A...HUSBAND

Published by Silhouette Books

America's Publisher of Contemporary Romance

to ld, thank you for your grace, your courage
and your humor.
you are an inspiration.

 SILHOUETTE BOOKS

ISBN 0-373-24246-8

IF I ONLY HAD A...HUSBAND

Copyright © 1999 by EAN Associates

Look us up on-line at: http://www.romance.net

Printed in U.S.A.

ANDREA EDWARDS

is the pseudonym of Anne and Ed Kolaczyk, a husband-and-wife writing team who have been telling their stories for more than fifteen years. Anne is a former elementary school teacher, while Ed is a refugee from corporate America. After many years in the Chicago area, they now live in a small town in northern Indiana where they are avid students of local history, family legends and ethnic myths. Recently they have both been bitten by the gardening bug, but only time will tell how serious the affliction is. Their four children are grown, but remaining at home with Anne and Ed are two dogs, four cats and one bird—not the same ones that first walked through their stories but carrying on the same tradition of chaotic rule of the household nonetheless.

Penny's Journal

Dear Diary,

I was cleaning out a corner of the barn today and you'll never guess what I found—the secret box from our girlhood club, The Bridal Circle.

Boy, did the contents take me back! The picture of the "perfect" wedding dress I drew. Even the menu for my dream reception under a huge tent at the family tree farm. And the results of that silly personality quiz we took about our future husbands. I remember being so excited because it said I would marry a smart man! So, of course, I had to make up some stationery proclaiming me Mrs. Brad Corrigan.

That sure was a long time ago. Back then, we all thought we'd have to leave Chesterton to find the men of our dreams. After all, my secret girlhood crush, Brad, had left town with his family, and none of us girls in The Bridal Circle ever heard from him again. Well, the road out of town sure didn't lead me to any great happiness...until it brought me back to the family farm. Back home.

And as for Brad Corrigan, I'd forgotten all about him until I'd found this box. Well, almost.

Prologue

Penny lay back in the beanbag chair and stared up at the flickering lights of the TV dancing on the ceiling. Her slumber party was even better than she had hoped. She rolled over on her side and looked at her three very best friends in all the world.

"I think we should start a club," she said. "Just the four of us."

"Cool." Heather stopped taping a wedding picture of Princess Diana and Prince Charles into her wedding scrapbook. "What kind?"

"How about a Boys Are Jerks club?" Karin suggested.

"No," Penny said. She didn't think they were. "How about a—"

"Hey, Penny, there's somebody out in your yard," Dorothy said from over by the sliding patio doors.

"Really?" Karin cried indignantly. "I didn't think anybody was supposed to be out there."

"You think it's a burglar?" Heather asked, breathless suddenly. "Maybe we'd better call your dad, Penny."

But Penny was already scurrying with Karin over to the far side of the room where, next to Dorothy, they peered out at Penny's moonlit yard. The backyard sloped down into the daylily acreage and beyond that were the hardwood seedlings, but off to the side, between the greenhouses and the truck barns, they could see a figure.

"It's just Brad Corrigan," Penny said, though she felt her cheeks warm. Good thing they'd been working on their wedding scrapbooks by the light of the TV. Nobody could see her blush.

"Oh, is that all?" Heather sounded relieved. "What's he doing here?"

He probably came out to watch Dorothy, but Penny couldn't say the words aloud, as if saying them would make them absolutely undeniably true instead of just positively true. Still everybody—not just the ninth graders, but the whole high school—knew that Brad loved Dorothy even if they hadn't started going out or anything. And Penny was happy for Dorothy, really she was. After all, Dorothy didn't have her own home or family or nothing and kept getting moved from house to house by her social worker, so she deserved to have a handsome boyfriend. But why did it have to be Brad? Brad who was just the handsomest, smartest, most perfect boy around.

"You know, I think he's the smartest person in town," Dorothy said. "Even smarter than Alex Waterstone."

"And lots cuter," Heather said with a giggle.

Penny just watched as Brad walked across the yard and disappeared into the shadows by the garage. Even if he stopped loving Dorothy, he would never start loving her. Dorothy was always Dorothy—beautiful and sweet. Penny was always the scarecrow—tall, skinny and without a brain.

"What's he doing here at this time of the night?" Karin asked. "Is he coming out to do your homework, Penny?"

Penny's stomach tightened up. Besides knowing that Brad loved Dorothy, everybody also knew that Penny's dad hired

Brad to help Penny with her homework. Which usually meant Brad did it, because he couldn't even stand to talk to her long enough to explain it.

"Penny doesn't have any homework now," Heather said. "Summer school's over."

"Oh, right." Karin frowned out at the night. "So, why's he here?"

Penny still didn't say anything. Life wasn't fair. Some of the kids at school laughed at Brad because he didn't have much money or a dad, but Penny never ever made fun of him. And it wasn't 'cause her mom was dead like his dad. It was because she thought he was nice. In fact, this past school year when his locker had been next to hers, she'd brought extra stuff in her lunch just so she could slip some into his. Cookies, fruit, an extra sandwich. His mom made him the most pitiful lunches, mostly because she had the most pitiful jobs and couldn't afford more, but Penny loved helping him. Okay, so she thought one day he'd find out and love her back and it would turn out that he was rich and famous and only pretending to be poor to see who really loved him for himself. Of course then she'd have to be really smart and only pretending to be dumb because…because…

She sighed. This is where her dream always fell apart. Well, she could take Brad loving Dorothy, but not him coming over here to swoon over her. Not at her own slumber party. That just wasn't nice. She pulled open the screen door.

"Where you going, Penny?"

"Whatcha gonna do?"

"Give him a piece of my mind."

Nobody made a crack about her not having any pieces to spare, like the boys at school would have, but she hurried outside as if the taunt just hadn't caught up with her.

She raced across the yard ahead of the others and down the driveway toward the barns, ignoring the sting of gravel on her bare feet. The burning in her eyes got worse and the world turned blurry, but she just kept running. The worst feeling throbbed in the pit of her stomach. Or was it in her throat? She couldn't tell anymore.

She pushed open the potting shed door and saw Brad by the workbench. Even dressed in an old T-shirt and jeans, he looked cuter than all the hunks on the ''Dukes of Hazzard'' put together, but she wasn't going to let that stop her.

''What are you doing here?'' she demanded.

Brad started, spinning around. Penny didn't know what he was doing, but he sure looked guilty.

''Are you sneaking around and spying on us?'' she asked as the girls crowded around behind her.

Whatever Penny'd thought she'd seen in his eyes at first was gone and he was back to his old know-it-all self. ''Spying on you?'' he snapped. ''Why would I do something dumb like that?''

Dumb? That stung.

''I was just bringing over the birdhouses I made for your dad.'' He waved at the box on the floor.

Penny saw a few birdhouses on the workbench, and the box with more of them at his feet. She'd forgotten her father had asked Brad to put them together so Penny could paint them. A little misgiving quivered in her stomach. Maybe that was all he was doing here.

''You're delivering them now?'' Karin said. ''It's almost the middle of the night.''

''So?'' he said and then looked nasty at them. ''It's not like I waste my time going to stupid parties like some people.''

Stupid! Another sting. And just when she had almost been feeling sorry for him.

''Penny's party's not stupid,'' Heather said, slipping an arm around Penny's shoulders.

''Yeah, you're just jealous 'cause we're having fun,'' Dorothy said.

Penny tried to keep her anger going, but the birdhouses seemed to be staring back at her, in a lopsided way.

She took a step forward. ''What's wrong with these things?''

She picked one of the houses up and the roof wobbled. "The roofs aren't fastened down."

"They're not supposed to be." Brad certainly didn't have the same trouble maintaining his anger. He snatched the birdhouse from her. "They come off so you can paint the inside."

"Paint the inside?" she asked. "Why would I paint inside?"

Brad didn't say anything, just slamming the roof in place so it wouldn't come off.

She had annoyed him. She had no idea why, but she kind of liked the feeling. "Maybe instead of painting the inside, I should wallpaper it," she suggested with a smile. "And put in carpeting, too."

"That's stupid."

He called her stupid again! "Yeah, you're right," she snapped. "Tile would be better. So much easier for them to keep clean, you know."

"Where do you come up with all these dumb ideas?" he said. "Do you sit up all night or do they just come to you in a flash?"

Angry or hurt? She didn't know what she felt anymore—except that her stomach ached worse than when she'd had the flu last winter.

"Get out of here," she shouted at him. "Or I'm going to tell my father."

"I don't care who you tell." Brad said. "I'm not going to be here anymore. I'm blowing this stupid hick town. My mother and I are leaving tomorrow morning for California. There's going to be nobody left here but you stupid jerks."

He pushed past her, past them all, and left the shed, the door banging hard against the frame, then swinging back open on the night. Penny was scared, a deep-down-into-your-very-soul kind of scared and she rushed out after him. Afraid he was leaving and afraid that he wasn't. How could she ever look at him again? But how could she live if he was gone?

"You be careful of Penny's stuff," Karin was shouting after Brad as he trudged through the shadows up ahead. "If this door is broken, we're calling the police."

He turned for a final shot. "I'm going to come back one day and make you all really sorry."

Penny's heart was breaking into a million pieces and none of her dreams would ever come true, but she couldn't let him know that. "You'll be the sorry one," Penny shouted even louder. "You ever come around here again and I'll punch your lights out."

She could hear his steps on the gravel as he ran, then nothing. Just a dog barking in the distance and the crickets chirping their laughter. How could she feel so mad and hurt and sad at the same time? She wouldn't cry over him, though. Not now, not ever.

"What a dope," Dorothy muttered.

"A real jerk," Karin agreed.

"I kind of hope he does come back someday," Penny said as she hurried up the slope toward the house.

"You want to punch his lights out?" Heather sounded surprised and a little worried.

"No." Penny turned to face them, walking backward up the hill. "Because we're all going to be married and happy and not have any time to even talk to him."

Dorothy danced up to her side. "Right. Heather's going to run off and join the circus and marry a lion tamer."

Heather giggled. "And Dorothy'll go someplace really exciting and marry a prince and live in a big palace."

"Karin's going to be rich and famous," Penny said. "And marry somebody even richer."

"And what about you, Penny?" Karin asked. "Where are you going to go?"

Penny looked for a long moment over at the shadows where Brad had disappeared. He was long gone, she knew, but the ache in her heart was still there. She slowly turned her back on that part of the yard and smiled at her friends.

"Me? I'm going to go to college and become really smart and I'm not going to marry until some guy who knows ten different languages falls in love with me."

Dorothy laughed as she tucked her arm into Penny's. "Guess we're all going to show Brad Corrigan."

"We sure are," Penny agreed. "We sure are."

Chapter One

"Good evening, sir." The tollbooth attendant spoke loudly to be heard above the rain. "Need any help with directions?"

Brad Corrigan stared at her for a moment, but then realized the gray-haired woman must have noticed the Illinois plates on his rental car and the open map on the front seat. And jumped to the logical conclusion that he might need a little help.

"No, thanks. I'm familiar with the area. I grew up around here."

"Did you now?" The woman's smile broadened. "Welcome home."

Home? Brad couldn't help wincing.

It had been an August day just like today. Black clouds had filled the sky and lightning had danced to a crackling tune. It had been raining. Pouring, actually. Exactly like today. Coming down so thick that he couldn't see more than three or four car lengths ahead. Your ordinary Indiana summer storm.

He was in the front seat of their '68 station wagon, rain

dripping on his leg through the crack in the windshield. The car was thirteen years old and a real junker.

He and Mom were heading west to California. To start a new life had been the way she'd put it.

"Don't worry," she said as they chugged along Route 30, not even having the fifty cents for the toll road. "Once we get settled you can come back and visit your friends."

The angry shouting from last night at Penny's house seemed to be still hanging in the air for everyone to hear. He should never have gone over there with those birdhouses. No, he should never have made up that stupid poem and written the lines inside the houses for her to find.

Lots of the kids made fun of him for not having new clothes or for working odd jobs to help his mom make ends meet, but Penny and her friends never did. So, why had he wrecked it all by trying to be romantic? They were probably all laughing at him right now. He would never ever do that again.

"I don't have any friends here," he'd told his mother. "And I don't care if I ever see this place again in my whole life."

It hadn't been home then, and now, eighteen years later, it still wasn't. Oh, he wouldn't be the butt of jokes anymore. Not once somebody found out he could buy and sell this town a couple of times over. He wouldn't tell, but they'd be able to see the signs for themselves. The expensive clothes. His limited edition Rolex watch. And someone was bound to have read about him in some publication.

Not that he needed or wanted anybody's approval. He had all he needed in his bank account. All he wanted in his stock portfolio. The rest was all nonsense, children's games. He was a man, took care of himself and put no burdens on anyone. And quite happily alone, thank you. He had learned his lesson eighteen years ago and hadn't forgotten it.

A horn sounded behind him and the tollbooth attendant's smile seemed edged in concern. "Are you all right, sir?"

"Me?" Brad laughed. "Sure. Of course. Just steeling myself up for the traffic of downtown Chesterton."

"You're going into Chesterton?" Her voice had taken on a

pleading quality. "Could I ask you a big big favor? Would you drive Junior into town? It wasn't raining when he came out here to visit me, and I'd hate to have him walk back in the rain."

Brad looked ahead. The rain was coming down so hard, he could barely see Route 49. It was a terrible day to drive; even worse to walk, though Chesterton was less than a quarter mile up the road.

"Sure," he told the woman. "No problem." It would be good to have some company, someone to talk to actually. "Where—"

But the woman was opening the half door of the tollbooth and letting a huge black German shepherd out. As Brad watched in semihorror, she pulled open the back door of the car and let the dog hop inside. He could feel the monster's breath on the back of his neck.

"Now, you behave, Junior," the woman told the dog, then closed the back door before turning to Brad. "Drop him off any place near Centennial Park, if you would. He knows his way home."

Was it his imagination or had the dog's breath gotten hotter and closer?

"And don't you worry about him none," the woman said. "He's as sweet as can be—unless you have a beer and don't share."

"Uh, I'll remember that," Brad said. With a wave at the dog, the woman went back into her booth and Brad pulled forward carefully. He glanced into his rearview mirror. Large canine teeth were all he saw.

"Hey there, Junior. How's it going?" He could see the head-lines now—Former Chesterton Resident Chewed to Death Just Outside City Limits. Lot of good his fat bank account would do him then.

Brad glanced forward again, but saw little except the rain rushing down his windshield. No visibility in front of him and the jaws of death behind him. Great. If he had to ride with the jaws of death though, he'd rather have them where he could keep an eye on them.

"So, Junior," he said. "Want to ride in the front seat?" Sure. Like the dog could—

Junior hopped into the seat next to him, scrunching the road map as he settled himself down to stare out the front window. Okay. The dog threw a quick glance at Brad, then looked forward again with a slight growl.

"I know there's a stop sign up here," Brad said and came to a complete stop—since it looked like Junior was a stickler for such things—before he eased his way onto Route 49 and rolled on north toward Chesterton.

"I am tired, but not so bad I'd ignore a stop sign," Brad said, then gave a mighty yawn and found the dog staring at him. "Hey, give me a break. It's got to be forty-eight hours since I had some sleep. If I had bedded down in Chicago like I should have, you'd be walking home in the rain."

Home. There was that word again.

Home was where you hung your hat. And he had no intention of doing that in Chesterton. Besides—yawning again, he shook his head to clear the cobwebs—he didn't even own a hat. Not unless you counted that beat-up old hat Ray Bolger had worn in *The Wizard of Oz* that Brad had bought in auction a few weeks back; he didn't think the paperwork was complete yet for the donation to the Smithsonian's American Classics exhibit.

"You really ought to wear a hat, you know," Penny told him. "You'll get heatstroke and collapse and die."

He yanked up a thick wad of chickweed from beneath the fan of iris leaves. "I'm not going to die," he muttered. Not unless he had to keep talking to her. Not unless she moved her foot six inches and brushed his hand.

"You didn't bring one, did you?" she asked.

The heat of her nearness burned him hotter than the blazing July sun. "I hate hats," he said as if he had hundreds of them at home and rejected them all.

He'd be okay if she would just go back to deadheading the

*spent daylilies over in the next yard. Then he could watch her
from a distance and his body could be all fiery just from looking at her, but he wouldn't have to fight the roaring in his ears
to make sense of her words. He'd be able to think then, and
would come up with something clever to say when he left the
nursery at the end of the day.*

"Thad's got a bunch. You can use one of his."

*He hadn't wanted one of her brother's hats. She'd touch it
and it would forever wear that soft sweet smell of roses from
her soap and he'd never come up with the right words to say.*

*"I hate hats," he said again. "I never wear them. Not even
in the winter."*

And he still didn't. Of course, living in Los Angeles was the
reason, not that silly statement. Once he'd left Chesterton, he'd
left behind all the silly statements he'd made. And he'd made
quite a number of them to Penny Donnelly.

"Lordy, but I had it bad for her," he told Junior. "I wasn't
able to say a coherent word around her from about fourth grade
on. In ninth grade, I made friends with her best friend, Dorothy.
That way, I could be close to Penny and still have somebody
to talk to."

Junior thumped his tail twice in admiration, not an easy feat
while sitting in a bucket seat. Obviously the dog recognized
genius and Brad found himself warming to the beast.

"You know, I once vowed I'd come back and make them
all sorry. But I'm not. I'm over all that. I'm just back to drop
off some probate papers, pick up a few boxes of my uncle's
old belongings and put his house up for sale. Don't care if I
see anyone or not. Shows what happens when you grow up,
huh? The old emotions lose their power over you."

Junior didn't look impressed this time, as if he were thinking
all those things could have been done long distance.

"All right, so they could have been," Brad acknowledged.
"But I was out this way already and it seemed just as easy."

It sounded insane when Brad said it aloud, but Junior was
kind enough not to point that out. Damn, Brad thought with a
shake of his head, what in the world had he been thinking of?

He'd been in Omaha for the past week—a two-hour plane ride and an hour's drive from Chesterton, Indiana. Hardly "out this way."

"Lack of sleep," he told Junior. "I wasn't thinking clearly. But it doesn't change anything. If I can get to Matt Harris's office before seven-thirty tonight, I can drop off those legal papers he sent me. Hey, with luck, I might even find a real estate office still open, too, and get the house put on the market. That would leave picking up the boxes from the old house which should take about ten minutes, tops. I could still sleep in Chicago tonight. At worst, I do it all tomorrow and be out of here by lunchtime."

Junior grunted and gave his head a shake. Skepticism or an itchy ear?

Exhaustion or insanity on Brad's part? Jeez, he was one of the highest paid computer network consultants in the business with part ownership of almost a dozen companies around the country. A software firm in Tacoma. A bakery chain in Orlando. Hell, even the rental car company this car was from. And what was he doing? Rationalizing his actions to a dog. He needed a vacation. Maybe once he left here, he would take one.

Peering ahead, he frowned. The downpour seemed to be increasing and his visibility was getting worse. Damn, maybe getting out of Chesterton wasn't going to be as fast and easy as he had hoped. He glanced at his watch. A few minutes before seven. He still had time.

"Looks like we may have to pull over and wait this out. Keep your eye out for some place to stop, will you?"

Junior yipped slightly as lights from a strip mall flashed in the murk up ahead, along with a sign that said Sam's Place. Scary, Brad thought. It was almost as if the dog understood. But he patted the dog's shoulder, not about to argue. "Good job, Junior."

Brad turned into the parking lot and pulled around a Dumpster, putting the car beneath the widespread branches of an old oak that looked as if it had been there before the Potawatomi Indians. He shut off the motor and looked at Junior.

"I'm going to grab a quick bite to eat. You want to wait in the car or come inside? I don't remember Sam as being too particular."

But as soon as Brad opened the door and stepped out under the slight protection of the oak branches, Junior jumped out of the car and took off, trotting toward downtown Chesterton, a few blocks west. So much for his company.

"You're welcome," Brad called after him, then raced for the tavern's rear entrance. The town hadn't changed at all—still filled with snobs who thought they were too good to spend a little time with him. Well, he didn't care.

Brad stepped into a short corridor and went past the bathrooms and the kitchen, but stopped short as he entered the dining room. Gone was the dark, dingy hole-in-the-wall he remembered coming to for Sunday dinners once a month with Uncle Hal. This place was light and cheery with not a speck of duct tape on the bar stools. Maybe Junior was right to leave—Brad wasn't sure the dog would have been welcome here.

Brad took a seat at the bar, ordered a hamburger out of habit and a soda, then sat there, watching the clock above the bar. He should have ordered a sandwich. It would have been quicker. He drummed his fingers on the bar and stared at a poster for *The Wizard of Oz* festival in town next month.

Lordy, were they still having that? He wondered if it was still such a big deal, with people coming from all over the country to dress up like the Tin Man or the Cowardly Lion and exchange Oz memorabilia. It actually had been a lot of fun when he'd been a kid—and a good weekend to earn extra money by working parking crews and cleanup the week after. And none of the thousands who came to the town for the weekend ever seemed to mind that Chesterton had no connection to Oz or—

The front door of the tavern opened, letting in some laughter mixed with thunder. Brad idly glanced in the mirror and saw a couple about his age, in their early thirties—a man in glasses and a tall blond woman.

His system suddenly froze up. His muscles, his nerves, everything turned to stone. She'd been the prettiest girl in their class; now she was the most beautiful woman in the world. Her pale blue dress made the most of a perfect figure. Taller than average, she moved across the room with an easy grace, so that the soft blond curls falling down onto her shoulders swayed gently.

Brad watched as they passed. His eyes took in her ringless left hand, and then the familiar-looking man with her, holding her arm while he smiled at the waitresses they passed.

And just like before, she needed protection from the cretins.

It was the last night before the freshman science fair projects were due and Brad was walking down the road from Penny's house. He'd just spent the past two hours finishing up her science fair project, while trying to work up the nerve to ask her to the spring dance next week. When he was finally done with her project, though, he still hadn't thought of the right words to say and had just left. Rats. He might as well resign himself to being a monk. At least he had plenty of practice with this vow of silence stuff.

Brad stopped as Alex Waterstone came driving his car around the bend in the lane. "What are you doing here?" Brad asked him.

The high school junior looked smug. "I'm going to see Penny, if that's any of your business ."

Brad got a whiff of aftershave and knew in an instant—Alex was going to ask Penny to the dance. Alex, who was the wildest kid in Chesterton or any of the surrounding counties. And sweet innocent Penny—who didn't know not to trust guys like Alex— would accept.

"She's not home," Brad said. "She went out."

"On a school night? Her father never lets her go out on a school night."

"Always a first time," Brad said.

Alex looked surprised and then a touch belligerent. Damn.

If Alex'd been some little twerp, Brad would have just pounded some sense into him, but Alex was as big as Brad. He needed to try a different tactic.

"Actually her dad grounded her," Brad said. "He got mad because so many guys were calling her and coming over."

"But that's not her fault," Alex said.

Brad shrugged in his most worldly-wise way. "Try telling that to her father." *He stopped and frowned.* "No, don't. It'll only make things worse for her. Best thing is just to lay low and let it blow over."

"You think so?"

Brad nodded. "She'll like you all the more for it, I guarantee."

Alex didn't look pleased, but put his car in reverse. "Will you tell her I stopped by the next time you see her?"

"Be glad to."

Brad watched as Alex roared back down the lane spewing gravel in his wake, then started walking again himself. When the right guy came along, one that treated her right, Brad wouldn't stand in his way. But until then, he was not going to let some wild reckless cretin break her heart.

Brad drained his glass and walked over toward the hallway where Penny had disappeared. Amid posters advertising the Oz festival, tarot card readings and the fire department's all-you-can-eat spaghetti dinner was a small sign. Tonight, in Sam's Place, there would be poetry readings by local poets. Including Dr. Alexander G. Waterstone III.

Damn. Well, the probate papers would have to wait until tomorrow. Alex Waterstone might have lost his wild streak but he was still a cretin. And a man just didn't let the cretins have the upper hand. Ever.

"Ah, gentle Penny. Would you be caring for some libations?"

Penny tried to smile at Alex as they stopped in the middle of the meeting room, but her stomach was dancing a tango inside her. "Libations" were the last thing she wanted, unless she wanted to distinguish her first ever poetry reading by up-chucking in the middle of her "Ode to the Yellow Brick Road."

This nervousness was crazy. Working on the Oz festival's publicity committee had made her used to public speaking. Of course, public humiliation was another story.

"No, thanks," she said and tried to wipe the rain off her new blue knit dress. Why had she ever agreed to this? Reading her own work was a millions times scarier than reciting festival facts that she'd known since she was a kid. "I'm just fine."

"You look pallid. Beautiful as always, but pallid."

Pallid? Would she ever be able to speak like that? "Protective coloration. Just so people can find me on this dark carpet when I pass out."

He patted her hand. "There's no cause for apprehension. You'll do quite respectably and the feedback will be vital in fine-tuning your work."

Easy for him to say, he wasn't trying to earn an invitation to speak at that symposium in Washington D.C. next winter. "One Hundred Years Later: *The Wizard of Oz* in Retrospect." But come to think of it, maybe upchucking on her poem would be the best idea yet. She'd been crazy to think that she—a sometime student of American Literature with a C plus average at nearby Midwest University—could be included in a group of renowned scholars. It was crazy to begin with. She should stick to running the tree service.

"I think I'll confirm the refreshments with the staff," Alex said and handed her a stack of programs. "Why don't you find a place for these?"

How about in the trash? But she just smiled at him. "Sure. I can do that."

"Penny!" Dorothy's voice was almost a squeal as the short brunette hurried into the room. "Oh, hi, Alex." Her voice had dropped about twenty degrees. "How are you?"

"Quite satisfactory, thank you. Quite satisfactory." He nodded at Penny. "I'll be back momentarily."

She waved slightly. A clap of thunder shook the building,

sounding loud even inside the quiet of Sam's. Maybe they should have canceled this. Or postponed it, anyway.

Dorothy was watching Alex leave with a sour look on her face. "That guy seems to have lost all the spark he had when we were kids. I don't know what you see in him."

Penny winced and spread the programs out on a table near the door. Dorothy had started this discussion about six weeks ago and hadn't let up since. But Penny just wasn't up to it tonight. Not when she was about to prove that she was every bit as dumb as the world thought.

"He's very nice," she said. "I happen to prefer this quieter Alex."

Dorothy just gave her a look. "Are you still on that the-man-I-marry-will-speak-ten-languages kick?"

"Are you still on that I'm-going-to-marry-a-prince-and-live-in-a-palace kick?"

But rather than get annoyed, Dorothy just laughed. "Guess neither of us has grown up yet."

But Penny had. Her ten-language criterion for a husband proved it. She'd outgrown that silly notion of marrying for love about the same time Brad Corrigan had moved away. Good thing he had, too. Who knows what kind of dangerous fantasies she'd still be clinging to if he was around?

And hopefully Dorothy had outgrown her silly ideas, as well. She had happiness staring her in the face if she'd just stop and realize how perfect Tom "Toto" Tollinger was for her. The trouble was, over the years, Dorothy had written her dream in stone. She couldn't see that a policeman could be a prince and that a walk-up apartment could be a palace, and Toto had let himself be convinced they were just friends.

But Penny was going to change that. Dorothy had been her best friend since fifth grade and Penny was going to make sure Dorothy got that home she'd longed for forever, if it was the last thing Penny did. Well, getting Dorothy settled and herself a spot at that seminar. She wasn't letting anything stand in her way of achieving either.

"Jeez, there aren't many people here," Dorothy observed.

Four to be exact. "The only good thing about the evening."

"Must be the storm," Dorothy observed.

"Or the threat of my poetry."

Dorothy just laughed again and dug in her purse. "I brought my camera." She waved the offensive contraption in Penny's face. "I'm going to write this up for the *Duneland* and Debby promised me the front page in next week's issue."

"Great. Now everyone who misses me passing out in the punch will still get to see it."

"You've got no reason to gripe. You're so damned photogenic no matter what you're doing. I don't know why you stopped modeling." Dorothy looked over her shoulder. "Hey, there was a major hunk out in the hallway when I came in. Maybe I should see if he wants to come in."

"Oh, do. A major hunk is just what this evening is missing."

Dorothy grinned wickedly. "That's what I've been telling you since you started dating Alex."

Penny forced a smile and an offhanded laugh, but was inwardly cursing herself. Damn. She had to be careful about what she said if she didn't want Dorothy to be suspicious.

As if on cue, Alex came back into the room just then, followed by a waitress with a tray of finger foods. Penny gave him a big smile and hurried over to his side. "Everything all set?" she asked and took his arm in hers.

He looked a little surprised but just nodded. "Indeed it is. The *fromage* and crackers are coming in now and the punch will be ready in a few moments. Still apprehensive?"

"Not with you here," Penny replied, and ignored the look of nausea Dorothy gave her.

Dorothy wouldn't understand why she was doing this. None of them would. But then none of them had had to endure the years and years of teasing that she had.

"Penny! Penny! Is this where the poetry reading is?"

Penny turn around to find an elderly couple in the doorway. "Mr. and Mrs. Jamison. What a surprise."

"We had to come see you," Mrs. Jamison said as they came into the room. "You're getting to be quite the star."

"First on television and now here," her husband added.

Penny felt her cheeks flush slightly. "Channel 22 always does a promo piece on the Oz festival," she said. "Anyone on my committee could have answered the questions."

"But not looking so cute while they did it, I'm sure," Mrs. Jamison assured her.

Penny just smiled and tried not to feel discouraged. Someday people would praise her brilliance, not her looks.

Alex patted her hand as if he understood. "If this evening goes even half as well as that one did, we'll be asking for her autograph pretty soon."

Mrs. Jamison nodded. "Her grandmother is so proud."

"She told us Penny's an expert on *The Wizard of Oz*," Mr. Jamison said. "And is going to make some kind of speech at a big conference about it."

The flickering of the lights hopefully kept Penny's grimace from showing, but it was hard not to groan aloud. Good old Gran. She saw one paper Penny got an A on and was certain Penny was on the dean's list. Penny mentioned once that she'd sure like to speak at that symposium and her grandmother had her as the keynote speaker. But if that's what it took to make Gran proud of her, that's what she was going to get.

"Why isn't she here?" Mrs. Jamison asked, looking around. "She said she would be."

Penny shook her head. "Her hip was really bothering her today and I thought she really should stay home, especially with the storm and all."

"What's it been? A month since her surgery?" Mr. Jamison asked.

"Just about. Why don't you sit down over here?" Penny showed the Jamisons to some seats. "I'll get you some punch, all right?"

She was sure Alex was eyeing her strangely when she came back to the refreshment table. "I didn't tell my grandmother that," she whispered. The lights flickered again. Good. Maybe they'd go out and stay out. No, she didn't really want that.

She needed to perfect these three poems about the allegorical implications of Oz so they could be sent to that literary journal Alex talked about. The abstract of her paper on Oz had been sent to the selection committee already, but he'd said it would help if she had other publications on the subject.

"I never suspected you had," Alex said and readjusted the program array a fraction of an inch.

She tried not to let Alex's precision annoy her. "Gran just gets these ideas in her head...." Penny sighed. Gran getting the ideas was one thing; Penny letting her keep them was a whole different issue. "But she's so damn proud of me, I couldn't tell her the truth."

"You're going to be so proud of me," she told Brad as they put their coats into their lockers. "I know my verb forms."

"That's good," he mumbled.

"Go ahead, ask me one."

"I believe you."

No, he didn't. She could tell. "Ask me one," she insisted. "Ask me a hard one." Infinitive wouldn't count.

"Past tense of sit," he said.

She frowned at him. "That's an easy one. I want a hard one."

He gave her a look that said she was nuts. She wanted a look of awe and respect. One that said they were equals.

Fine. She would pick for him—the absolute hardest. "Past participle of lie," she said. "Has laid. The book has laid open all day." She knew by the look in his eyes that she was wrong. "I mean, have laid. Er, has lay."

"Has or have lain," he said.

"Oh."

He just stood there, his deep blue eyes filled with pity. He was going to say something nice, something consoling. Something she hadn't wanted to hear. It wasn't going to be how proud he was of her. Nobody was proud of her, not the way Daddy was proud of Thad when he got another honor roll ribbon. Penny just turned and walked into the classroom.

Penny swallowed hard to get past the lump of regret and wistful thinking lodged in her throat, and glared at Alex.

"That's why I hired you," she whispered sharply and jabbed a finger at his chest. "You're going to help me get invited to that symposium and my grandmother's going to have a real reason to be proud of me."

"Perchance, Penny." His voice was low. "We should be exploring other—"

"You don't think I can do it."

He shook his head. "Now, now, I never said that, but perhaps studying the allegorical themes of—"

"You want someone else to take that old dead elm down— and maybe your phone and power lines along with it?"

"Penny, we are drawing notice."

Penny turned slightly and saw that all eyes were on them. Not that there were that many people here, but she didn't need anybody to get suspicious. The last thing she needed the town to know was that she had hired herself a tutor.

She smiled and tried to turn her jabbing finger into a lover's pat. "Don't forget we've got a deal," she whispered, then patted him on the cheek with what she hoped looked like affection. "I have to get the Jamisons some punch."

She moved over to the punch bowl, with a bright smile that should fool even the most curious of watchers, and filled two cups. Maybe she'd take them a little plate of this cheese spread and some crackers, too.

"Penny!" Dorothy squealed beside her. "You'll never guess who's here."

"A reporter from the *Tribune*?" Now that would be something.

"No."

"A camera crew from WNDU?" Too much to hope for, she knew, but… She carefully lifted the cups of punch.

"Turn around."

Penny turned and came face-to-face with a tall, dark-haired man. A clutch of panic gripped her stomach. His blue eyes were intense, sending shivers right down into her toes.

An all too familiar reaction.

It couldn't be. He was gone. Gone for good.

"Isn't this the coolest thing?" Dorothy was gushing.

"Penny?" Brad said.

No, no, no, she wanted to shout.

But suddenly, the building shook. The earth crackled and a roaring explosion deafened them all. Lightning had hit—and close by. Then the lights went out, throwing the room into total darkness.

Chapter Two

It was pitch-black inside the restaurant. Brad Corrigan wasn't making a sound, but the smell of fruit punch hung heavy in the air. Penny moved the cups in her hand slightly. They were empty. Damn.

"Golly, that was loud," Dorothy said. "What do you think happened?"

"Just remain calm," Alex called out from somewhere near the door. "No reason for anyone to panic. Just a little weather mishap, I'm sure."

That was it, Penny told herself. She'd been startled by the lightning and thunder, not by Brad's presence. And maybe she hadn't gotten him with the punch. Maybe she only thought he had been that close to her. She probably had dumped it on the floor. She took a deep breath. "So, what are you—"

Above the general murmur in the darkness, she heard laughter. Laughter that teased at long-sleeping memories. Laughter that tied her heart into knots and did somersaults in her stomach. Brad's laughter.

Damn it. She was not going to feel that way about him again. She wasn't twelve anymore. "What's so funny?" she demanded.

"You sure do keep your promises, don't you?"

"What? What promises?" Dorothy asked.

Good question. "I have no idea." Penny knew she sounded stiff and unfriendly but this was supposed to be her big night. She was supposed to discover acclaim for her poetic insight into the journey to Oz, not rediscover an old crush that had been idiotic and juvenile. "You'd think this place would have some emergency lights or something."

Even as she spoke someone from the restaurant's staff came in with candles—a mixed blessing. Now she could safely move away. But now she could also see Brad Corrigan right before her. Lean, sharply cut face. Strong nose. Those intense blue eyes.

And a huge, cherry red stain on the front of his shirt.

Good gracious, she *had* dumped it on him!

"You were always one to keep your word," Brad was saying. "That's one of the things I always liked about you."

One of the things? What hurt was he trying to inflict now? He had never liked anything about her. Good thing it no longer mattered.

"Heavens!" Dorothy cried, gently touching Brad's stained shirt. "What in the world happened? Are you hurt?" She grabbed up some paper napkins from the table and began to dab at the stain.

The light in the room was pretty bad, Penny admitted, but even in the deep shadows, the punch hardly looked like blood.

"Only Penny keeping her word," Brad said.

"Penny keeping her word?"

Dorothy looked from Brad to Penny, even as she ministered to the man as if he were on death's doorstep. Penny had never seen Dorothy that concerned about Toto.

"What is he talking about?" Dorothy asked Penny. "What promise?"

"I have no idea." She looked down at the empty cups in

her hands, then held them out to Dorothy. "Dorothy, could you take these? I really ought to go—"

"Come on, Penny," Brad cajoled. "Don't you remember what you said? How if I ever came around here again you'd punch my lights out?" Brad waved down at his shirtfront. "Looks like you did. Just a different kind of punch and everybody's lights, not just mine."

Dorothy started to laugh. "That's so funny. I can't believe you remembered that. It was at Penny's slumber party, right?"

He nodded. "Just before I left town."

"You remember, don't you, Penny?" Dorothy asked.

"I guess," she replied with a shrug. What she did remember was that he'd vowed to come back and make them sorry. Or had he just come back for Dorothy? He had loved her then; maybe he still did. Penny's mouth was as dry as sand.

"Dorothy, I really need to check with Alex and see what's going on," Penny said and shoved the empty punch cups into her friend's hands. "Will you take care of these?"

"What's the big deal?" Dorothy asked, but she did stop fussing over Brad to take the cups. "We can just leave them here." She took two steps over and put them on the refreshment table.

But Penny just smiled at her as if that task had been beyond her ability. "Thanks so much. Want to come with me to talk to the manager?"

Dorothy frowned at her. "No. Not really."

Penny sighed, biting her lip to keep from snapping at her friend. What did Dorothy think she was doing? How could she just forget about poor Toto like this?

"Why don't we all go see what's going on?" Brad took Penny's arm. "Maybe a show of force will convince the heavens to turn on the power again."

Dorothy laughed as if she'd never heard such wit. Penny just wished there was some way to make him let go of her. Some way short of making a scene, that is. She didn't like the way warmth traveled up her skin from his touch. She didn't want to feel that tingling in her fingertips when his hand moved slightly. And she definitely didn't want to suddenly find it hard to breathe just because he was back.

"Ah, Penny, there you are," Alex came over, a frown marring his normally pleasant good looks.

Dare she hope he was going to help her out?

"I just spoke to the manager," Alex continued. "She said she called the power company and the lightning took out a transformer. They won't have electricity until sometime after midnight so the bar has to close. Health regulations."

"Oh, what a shame," Penny cried and moved away from Brad and over to Alex. "We're going to have to postpone this."

"Yes. Or cancel it all together. I know you wanted to read your poems but I'm not sure we can afford—"

"Let's not decide now," she said quickly, putting her hand on his arm. Jeez, he wasn't thinking at all! She knew they couldn't afford to wait much longer before sending her poems in to that magazine. But he didn't have to say so and announce he was her tutor and this was all a plan. "I'm too disappointed to think what to do."

"You were reading, too?" Brad asked her.

"Yes, I was."

"Penny was one of the stars tonight," Alex stated and frowned at Brad. "Have we been introduced?"

"Of course, Alex," Dorothy said. She took Brad's arm, pulling him close to her. "You remember Brad Corrigan. He used to live in Chesterton."

"Certainly." Alex sounded much more gracious than Penny felt as he offered Brad his hand. "How good to see you again. Have a little mishap with the punch?"

"Just a slight one," Brad replied as the men shook hands.

Alex seemed friendly but Penny sensed a wariness on Brad's part. Or was it just a physical awkwardness since he had Dorothy hanging on him and was drenched in punch?

Alex eased himself away from Penny with a regretful nod. "I'll just announce the bad news and then we might as well go."

"All right—" she caught Brad watching her strangely "—honey," she called after Alex quickly, hoping it sounded even half-natural.

"So, what are you doing here?" Dorothy asked Brad. "You back to stay?"

"Heck, no," Brad said. "Just here for a brief visit."

If he was going to add more, he didn't have the chance as the Jamisons and the few others who had come for the reading began to leave.

"What a shame," Mrs. Jamison consoled Penny and gave her a hug.

"You let us know when you're doing it again," Mr. Jamison said.

They left, led by the waitress with a flashlight and followed by the other guests. Silence reigned loud and long in the little candlelit meeting room. Penny didn't know if it was just disappointment at having her evening canceled or worry over Dorothy's apparent fascination with Brad, but she was suddenly exhausted.

"I guess we might as well go on home," Penny suggested. "We can figure out what to do tomorrow."

By the light of the candles, they made their way to the back hallway—lit by an emergency light—more or less in pairs. Her and Alex, Dorothy and Brad. Though she and Alex were leading the way, she was all too conscious of the pair behind her, Brad's arm around Dorothy's shoulders as they laughed and talked. And what did Dorothy just say about—

"Penny?" Alex called. "I say, Penny."

She jolted into attentiveness. "What?" she said and smiled up at him. Dorothy and Brad weren't the only ones who could laugh. "I'm sorry, sweetie. What were you saying?" She leaned in closer, more provocatively.

"I was merely commenting that the storm has likely produced an abundance of work for you and your crews. We may not be able to get together tomorrow as we had planned."

Laughter pealed out from behind them again, somehow setting Penny's teeth on edge. She tried hard to purr as she smiled up at Alex, hanging on his arm for all she was worth. "Hey, a little work's not going to stand in my way. I always have time for you."

Alex gave her an odd look, as if to ask what in the world she was doing. A good question, actually. Pretending they were dating in front of crowds was one thing, but this private show was a little much.

They came to the parking lot door and went out under the slight overhang. By the illumination of the outdoor emergency lights, they could see it was still raining. And that the parking lot was a lake.

"My car's right over here," Dorothy said. "I'm gonna run for it. See you, Penny, Alex. Brad, great to have you back even for a few days."

With a quick wave at Penny and Alex and a peck on the cheek for Brad, Dorothy was on her way, running the few yards along the building to her car. Penny wasn't so lucky. Her truck was on the other side of the lot and the lake.

"If we hurry along this side of the water, we shouldn't get our feet too wet," Alex observed, pointing to the west side of the puddle.

"Okay," she said. "I'm game." She turned to say goodbye to Brad. "It was—"

But suddenly she found herself being swept up off her feet and into his arms. "What are you doing?" she cried. "Put me down."

"You can't walk through the puddle in those shoes," he said.

"I say," Alex interjected. "If she doesn't want—"

"Just lead the way, will you?" Brad told him.

"Brad, put me down now," Penny insisted.

But no one seemed to be listening. Alex was leading the way through the puddle and past the van parked near the back door. Brad was following, his arms holding Penny tightly. Securely. Possessively.

Gracious, she was hallucinating! Next she'd be thinking the rain running down their faces was romantic. "I really can walk," Penny objected, trying to keep that touch of panic in her heart from showing up in her voice. "This is ridiculous."

"It's nothing," Brad said. "Better than you walking on broken glass or something."

The concern in his tone touched her—and that was annoying. She didn't want to be touched by him, not literally or emotionally. Neither did she want the urge to wipe the rain from his face or brush his damp hair back from his forehead.

"I have shoes on," she snapped. "And if I really needed to be carried, Alex could have done it."

Alex looked a little stunned at that. "Oh, right. Certainly. Absolutely." He tried to cover up his surprise with a smile. "Want me to take her?"

"No." Both she and Brad spoke in unison.

Penny glared at Alex and then at Brad. "Would you put me—"

But Brad and Alex had stopped and were staring around the corner of the building. She turned to look in that direction, too.

The huge old oak tree that had stood at the edge of the parking lot had been hit by lightning. She could smell the scent of burned wood in the air. And in the hit, a massive branch—with a trunk as thick as her waist—had come down, just narrowly missing her truck while strewing leaves and branches all over.

"Holy cow!" she murmured.

Brad seemed to lose some of his fire and she was able to slip down to her feet. Warm puddled rainwater washed over her feet as the three of them walked over to the fallen tree. There was a car underneath, she realized. Or what used to be a car. Boy, somebody was in for a surprise.

Dorothy pulled up in her car beside them, rolling down her window. "Wow," she said. "That must have been that huge crash we heard. It get your truck at all, Pen?"

Penny shook her head. "Not so's you'd notice."

She frowned as she looked at the smashed car beneath the branch. By the light of Dorothy's headlights, she could see an Illinois license plate. What would someone from Illinois be doing around here tonight? And where were they while their car was being totaled? The restaurant had emptied and it was only—

Oh, damn. "Is this your car?" Penny asked Brad.

"Not exactly." He walked over to the side and peered under the greenery.

Suddenly Penny took in his faded jeans and worn loafers as well as the fact the car had to have been five years old at least. Five hard years old. Those scratches with rust in them hadn't happened tonight. Yet, obviously, the car was still being paid for. Times had been hard for Brad when he was growing up in Chesterton and it looked like they hadn't changed much for him in the past eighteen years.

"Damn. I'd better get..."

Brad was muttering to himself as he moved some smaller branches over to get closer to a back side window. The large branch had to weigh close to a ton, but it was perched precariously and wobbled as Brad tried to edge his way in.

"Hey," Penny cried and pulled him back. "Be careful. This whole thing is unsteady."

"I have to get some stuff."

"You don't need anything that badly," she told him. "I'll come by tomorrow with a crew and we'll get the branch taken care of."

He frowned at her. "You'll take care of it?"

"She runs Donnelly Tree Service now," Dorothy called from her car. "Come on, Brad, get in. I'll give you a ride to your motel."

"Marvelous idea," Alex said, trying to wipe the drops from his glasses. "Then we can get out of this deluge, too. Come, Penny. Let's get in the truck."

But Brad didn't move. "You all go ahead," he said. "I have to get my bag out of the back seat. The window's broken and some papers I need are getting wet."

"But you'll be stranded out here," Dorothy said. "You get your stuff. I'll wait for you."

"No."

The three turned to stare at Penny. Maybe her words had come out a little too strongly, but all Penny could hear was the warmth in Dorothy's voice. All she could see was Toto's love going down in flames. And for what? So Brad could avenge old hurts?

"I'll give him a hand and then give him a ride," Penny told Dorothy. "Maybe you can drop Alex off. It's right on your way."

"Uh, okay," Dorothy said, not sounding too thrilled.

Penny ignored it. "You don't mind, do you, sweetie?" she asked Alex.

"I would just like to escape this downpour," Alex muttered and climbed into Dorothy's car.

He shut the door a little more solidly than necessary, but Penny waved brightly as they drove off, then walked over to her truck. Her dress was soaked, her hair hanging in straggles down her face. Not the way she had envisioned her evening would be ending.

"You don't have to stay," Brad said as he went back to his car. "I can handle this."

"No, you can't," she snapped as she pulled open the back of the pickup truck. Why did he have to come back, anyway? He was going to spoil everything, she just knew it. "Get away from that mess before you make it even more unsteady."

Surprisingly Brad did as he was told though he didn't look happy about it. "You know, he's not right for you."

She pulled a pair of coveralls from the back of the truck, but paused to glare at Brad. "What are you talking about?"

"Alex," he stated. "I'm not saying anything against him. He may be a heck of a nice guy. But the two of you just don't click."

"My personal life is none of your business."

She stepped into the coveralls, pulled them up over her dress, then zipped them shut. She kicked off her sandals and pulled on her steel-toed work boots.

"Jeez, you really do run the tree service," he said. His voice was quiet, awestruck.

What, did he think she was too dumb to have her own business? She gave him a quick frown, then put her safety goggles on and a hard hat. That done, she pulled the small chain saw from the back. His look of amazement increased.

This was really the pits. She was supposed to be praised and respected tonight for her poetry and what happened? Same old, same old. When she was modeling, she was admired for her looks. Now that she ran the tree service, she was admired for her chain saw.

She pulled on the rip cord and the motor erupted, drowning out the wet sounds of a rainy night in Indiana. "Want to step aside?" she said.

Brad watched in total amazement as the chain-saw-wielding Penny lopped off one small branch after another to uncover the broken side window. He'd thought she'd looked sexy before, but that was nothing as ravishing as she looked in her hard hat and work clothes. He swallowed hard, trying to get his dry mouth to work, but had no luck. He felt as if he were on fire. The rain must be sizzling as it hit him. He needed to be doing something, not standing here like a statue.

"Want me to do some?" he shouted over the roar of the saw.

She just gave him a look that was answer enough so he came over and pulled the cut branches away.

"You don't need to do that," she shouted to him. "You shouldn't be this close without a hard hat."

"I have a hard head," he told her.

She didn't laugh or even smile. Maybe she hadn't heard him. Maybe she didn't think he was funny. The idea shouldn't bother him, but it did.

He definitely needed to be careful, but not of those branches. No, he needed to be careful that he didn't get snared by Penny's smile. A day here while he took care of business and checked Alex out—that would be all right. He could stay safe for two days even.

But if those probate papers got wet and had to be redone,

he could be stuck here for weeks in legal red tape. No man was that strong!

The way to the window cleared, Penny reached in, pulled out his duffel bag, and gave it to him. "That it?" she asked.

"Yes. Thank you." The bag was pretty wet, but a quick check said the probate papers inside were still dry. Relief washed over him. "I hadn't meant for you to go to all this trouble. I thought I could just reach into the car and fish it out myself."

"No problem." Penny put the chain saw into the back of the truck, and tossed her hard hat in after it, but left her work clothes on as she went around the driver's side.

Brad opened the passenger side of the truck, put his bag on the seat, then stripped off his stained shirt. The rain hitting his chest cooled him and he was tempted to leave his shirt off, but one look at Penny's red cheeks changed his mind. Surely she wasn't embarrassed by his shirtless state. It couldn't even be him affecting her—she'd never given him the time of day when they'd been kids. Maybe running that chain saw was harder work than she'd made it look.

After pulling a clean shirt from his bag and slipping it on, Brad put the bag on the floor and climbed into the truck. He took a deep breath as he closed the door. He hadn't noticed that pickups were so small before. He could barely move without brushing her arm. Barely breathe without being aware of her faint flowery scent. Time to get moving.

"You been dating Alex long?" he asked.

She started the motor then shot him a look that would have withered and dried up a tall oak. "I thought we'd agreed my personal life was none of your business."

He hadn't agreed to anything. "He shouldn't have left you to tackle the tree," Brad said. "He's really turned into a wimp. I'm surprised."

"He's a professor of literature and a poet. And what would he have done with the tree?"

"Been there with you."

She backed out of the parking spot and headed toward the

road. "Gotten in the way is more like it. He was better off going with Dorothy. What motel are you staying at?"

"Don't have one yet. You can drop me off wherever's convenient." He waited until she'd pulled out on the road. The rain wasn't coming down as heavily, but with the streetlights off, visibility wasn't great. "He didn't kiss you."

"And I didn't kiss him. Your life must be pathetic if you notice things like that. Did you have dinner yet?"

His life was not pathetic. It was ordered. Secure. Stable. Anyone would notice when a beautiful woman goes unkissed. "I'm not hungry." And he wasn't, even though he hadn't gotten to eat his hamburger at Sam's.

"Yeah, right." She drove along in silence for what seemed like hours. A few blocks later they turned off onto the county road that went by her house. "You can come home with me," she said suddenly. "The weather's just too lousy to be driving you all over creation. There are leftovers in the refrigerator and we've got plenty of empty bedrooms."

"Okay." He didn't mention that they'd passed a motel where they'd turned last. As long as he was stuck here an extra night, he might as well see if Penny was serious about Alex. And if the jerk was in any way deserving of her. Brad doubted it. Alex had gone from wild to wimpy and neither sort was right for Penny.

They drove in silence down the county road, then turned into the long gravel driveway. Brad closed his eyes, letting his body greet each and every bump like an old friend.

This had been his second home when he was a boy.

Home. There was that stupid word again, but he pushed his irritation aside. He was tired, that was all. Exhausted. Two days—forty-eight hours—without sleep was catching up with him. That was why he was reacting to the word *home.* Or the sight of Penny again.

He should have just picked some motel out of the air and had Penny drop him off there. Sleep was all he needed and he'd be himself again.

"Dorothy's looking good," he said. It would be a safe topic.

"Yes." Penny's voice sounded stiff. "She's a Realtor here in town. Won Top Seller of the Year twice now."

"Oh, really?" Maybe he'd give her a call about selling Uncle Hal's house. "Or should I say, realty?"

She gave a short laugh, not so much of humor as annoyance, and pulled the truck up to the house. Without a word they got out. The power was on and so the porch light threw shadows out into the yard. A birdhouse swung from a nearby tree and a wind sock danced in the storm. Brad looked around at the barns and the fields beyond, breathing in the scent of the rain-soaked earth. It smelled so good. About as far from Los Angeles as he could imagine.

Except Los Angeles was what he preferred, of course.

"Come on, let's go in," she said. "It's fixing to pour again."

He stood there a moment and watched her walk up the porch steps. Her coveralls were baggy, her hair was wet, yet she looked more beautiful than he could ever have imagined. She was an adult now, not that kid he'd had a crush on. Yet his heart was pounding just as it always had around her.

He should never have come back here. Junior had been right—there wasn't anything with his uncle's probate that couldn't have been handled by mail, phone, fax, E-mail or whatever.

"You coming?" she called from the back door.

"Yeah, sure."

All right, so she still held some sort of magical power over him. It didn't matter. He wasn't a kid anymore. He was an adult and well able to control his reactions. He could fight that strange hold Penny had over him. He could fight any hold anyone had. He had for the past eighteen years, hadn't he? Swinging his duffel bag over his shoulder, he walked boldly up the porch steps and into the old farm kitchen.

The first thing he noticed was the old woman in the dining room doorway. A big smile in a lined face. A mass of gray hair. She hadn't changed a bit. Then he noticed the cane, an

aluminum job with a four footed base. Well, some things might
have changed, but nothing important.

"Bradley? Bradley Corrigan?"

"Aunty Em," he murmured as he dropped his bag inside
the door and took her in his arms.

Emma Donnelly was Penny's grandmother but the kids had
all called her Aunty Em. She'd always had a kind word and
something on the table for a hungry boy. He let go and took a
step back.

"Still as beautiful as ever," he told her.

She cackled. "An honest man. Now, that's what I like." She
looked over at Penny and frowned. "Those don't look like
poetry-reading clothes, honey. What happened?"

Penny had gotten a towel from the small bathroom off the
kitchen and was drying her hair. A fire exploded in his belly
at the sight. She shouldn't be allowed to do such things. Or
she should wear warning labels. He made a show of slipping
off his wet shoes.

"The power went out and lightning hit that old oak behind
Sam's," Penny replied. "Part of the tree fell on Brad's car. I
had to cut a few branches so he could get his bag out the
window."

"Alex help?" Aunty Em asked.

Penny's lips tightened as she turned and headed toward the
back stairs. "I'm going to go change into dry clothes," she
said, then looked at Brad. "Bathroom's there if you want to
dry off. I'll fix you some dinner when I come down."

"I can start it." The old lady walked slowly over to the
refrigerator and took out some containers. "Beef stew okay?"

"Wonderful." It was possible to breathe now that Penny had
left the room. He got a towel from the bathroom and dried off
a little, then came back into the kitchen. "What should I do?
Set the table?"

"You still remember where everything is?"

He did. He wasn't sure how or why, but he did. Plates in
the cabinet next to the sink. Silverware by the stove and glasses
next to the pantry. It was as if he had never left.

"So, how is Mr. Donnelly?" he asked.

"Joe died about five years back," Aunty Em said. "Car accident when he was in Florida."

"What a shame. He was a good man." A man who put the need for dreams above the need for money. Brad finished setting the table in silence. "So, Penny runs the company now."

"And doing a right good job at it, too," she said. "She's a big shot in the Oz festival. Was on TV last week. Maybe you saw it."

"Uh, no," he said. "I don't see much TV. But Dorothy mentioned it."

"Did she? Such a sweet girl."

"Seems as nice as ever."

"She is. So, Brad, you got a wife?"

Brad just stared at the old woman, startled by the abrupt change of directions. "No, ma'am."

"Hear that, Penny?" Aunty Em said.

Brad was even more startled and turned. Sure enough, there was Penny at the foot of the stairs, dressed in shorts and a T-shirt. He hadn't heard a sound, though Aunty Em certainly had.

"Yes, I can hardly control my excitement," Penny said dryly and went over to the stove. She peered into the pot, then over at Brad. "Want any bread or salad?"

"No, the stew is fine." Some air would be nice, though. Just enough so that he could breathe again.

He sat down at the kitchen table, feeling the weariness wash over him. This had all been a monumental mistake. He should have stayed over in Chicago and driven out here for the day. Coming as he had in the evening had been asking for trouble. And he'd found it.

He just had to steel himself, though. Get a good night's sleep and in the morning he would be fine. He would be himself again, in control.

"You want to get Brad something to drink?" Aunty Em said to Penny as she dished up the stew.

"Sure. What'll you have? We've got milk, coffee or tea."

"Milk would be fine."

Aunty Em brought his plate over to the table. "You want anything else, give Penny your orders. Time for me to lay these old bones to bed." She paused to pat his arm. "It is good to see you again, boy."

"And great to see you, too." He dug into the stew. It was better than he remembered her food being, and he remembered it as being great.

After Aunty Em had shuffled down the back hallway to her room, silence rushed in to fill the void.

"So you're a bachelor?" Penny said after a few moments.

He looked up as he nodded, surprised to see a grimace on her face. Why would Penny care whether he was single or not?

"Where do you live?"

"Wherever I hang my hat." No need to get into his hatless state. Actually, he had a condo in L.A., but he hardly ever spent time there.

"Doesn't that make holding down a job hard?"

He could have said no, since it was for his consulting work that he traveled. Or he could have said it made no difference since he had two million in the bank and several more millions of dollars worth of common stock. But something wouldn't let him tell her and he just went on eating.

He wanted her to see on her own that he was doing well. He wanted her to notice the limited edition, gold-and-platinum Rolex on his wrist or the custom-made shoes he'd left over by the door. Or remember she'd seen him written up in the paper when he'd invested several million dollars in Rented Dented Car Rentals, now the third largest car rental chain. Mostly he wanted her to realize he wasn't that poor nobody anymore.

"Saw your essay in the paper, boy." Mr. Clevinger said as *he put the potted daylily on the counter. "Bet your mom's proud of you."*

"I guess, sir," Brad mumbled and checked the price tag. *"That'll be $5.00."*

Why hadn't Mrs. Hartman told them the winners would be published? He would never have written all that stuff if he had known.

"Five even?" The man pulled a ten-dollar bill from his wallet. "Tell you what, boy. How about if you keep the change? Don't want you worrying that you won't be able to buy your momma something special for Mother's Day."

Brad looked at the money with anger and disgust, unable to meet the man's eyes. He knew Mr. Clevinger was only being nice, but his stomach turned at the thought. He didn't need charity to buy his mom a present. He didn't need anybody's help to make a better life for his mom one day.

Brad took the ten dollar bill and made change, pushing the five back at the man. "Thanks anyway," he said. "But I already got her something."

"Then get something for yourself," the man said.

"I don't need anything."

Mr. Clevinger looked Brad up and down, then shook his head. "Looks like you could use a new pair of shoes," he said. "Or stop and get yourself a good meal before you go home so you don't eat your mom out of house and home."

"We've got plenty of food and my shoes are fine," he said but the man had picked up his daylily and headed toward his fancy car. The five-dollar bill was still on the counter.

Brad wanted to throw it away. He wanted to give it to someone else, but mostly he wanted to scream at the idea that his mom couldn't take care of him or that he couldn't take care of her. They didn't need anybody's charity. They didn't need anything from anybody.

But in the end, he slipped the bill into his pocket, feeling miserable and worthless. A nobody who wasn't even allowed pride. But the money would pay for Mom's gas for a week and he didn't have the right to throw it away. He learned a lesson, though—leaving a person with no pride was worse than leaving him with no money.

Brad just shrugged and turned his arm so that his Rolex caught the light. "I get by."

She nodded. "Want any more stew?"

"No, thanks. I'm full."

He got to his feet and picked up his dishes. Okay, so she

didn't know watches. No big deal. It didn't matter. He wasn't here to gain anyone's approval. Through the kitchen window over the sink he could hear the rain, slamming sheets of water against the house and rattling the roof. He was glad he wasn't outside, on the way to some motel.

"The dishes can go in the dishwasher," she said and pulled down the appliance door for him before she started washing the saucepan in the sink. Once he'd loaded his dishes, she turned. "Come on. You can have Thad's old room."

He grabbed his bag and shoes, then followed her up the stairs, all too conscious of the provocative sway of her hips in front of him. On the other hand, a motel would be a thousand times safer.

"I don't want to put you to any trouble," he said.

"Giving you a room for the night is easier than driving in that mess outside."

She stopped at the top of the stairs and opened the door to a bedroom that looked a little spare. Outside of a collection of baseball pennants hanging on the wall, only a few mementos remained of the boy who had grown up here.

"Do you need pajamas?" she asked, starting to open some drawers. "I think there might be some here. If not, I'm sure there are some in Will's room."

"Don't worry about it." Brad leaned against the door frame. "I never bother with them."

"Oh." A soft glow filled her face and, looking away, she shut the drawer sharply. "Well, I guess you have everything then."

He had, and for a couple of years now. But then all of a sudden, he felt a little voice mocking his certainty. A little voice asking if it wasn't loneliness that he felt late at night when he was all alone.

A little voice he wanted to drown out. "I'm sorry your poetry reading got canceled," he said. "I would have liked to have heard some of your work."

Penny's cheeks flushed even more as she looked down at

her hands. "Thanks. If there's nothing else you need, I'll let you get to bed," she murmured and tried to scuttle by him.

"Pen." His hand caught hers and she stopped, her eyes flying up to meet his.

Up close, he could see fleeting flashes of the girl she used to be. A shyness in her eyes. A determination in her jaw. But it was all wrapped so beautifully in this womanly package, she almost seemed a stranger.

"I'm glad things are working out so well for you," he said and leaned over.

He'd only meant to brush her cheek with his lips, but she moved at the last moment and his lips touched hers. And it was like the storm had consumed him. Thunder crashing in his ears. Lightning charging in his belly. And the wind swirling around, keeping him from moving.

His arms ached to pull her close. His hands wanted to touch and caress. His lips just wanted to taste her sweetness forever.

She pulled away. Her eyes were wide, but with what emotion he couldn't say. But then, he'd never been able to read her at all.

"Good night," she whispered, then left.

She was down the stairs and out of sight before he had a chance to breathe. He closed the door slowly then sagged against it.

He definitely should have done that probate stuff by mail.

Chapter Three

Penny was furious with herself by the time she reached the kitchen. What in the world was wrong with her? Letting Brad kiss her like that—and practically falling into his arms for more!

"That poor boy." Gran was standing by the table patting Einstein, their tabby house cat.

"I thought you were in bed," Penny said.

"No job. No family. No home."

"Everybody has a home," Penny murmured. "No matter how small or simple."

"A place to hang your hat ain't a home."

Penny needed to get to sleep. This was a busy time for them, and cleaning up the storm damage would make it even busier.

"First thing we have to do is get that boy a job," Gran said.

"Business is good most places. So he should easily—" Penny gave her grandmother a hard look. "How do you know he doesn't have a job?"

Gran looked about the kitchen before reaching down to pat Einstein.

"And that home is where he hangs his hat?"

"I heard you two talking." Gran continued petting the big orange tabby. "You know how you're always talking so loud."

"We weren't talking loud. Besides, I thought your hearing wasn't all that good."

"Must've had my hearing aid turned up too high." Her grandmother straightened up. "Best get me to sleep. Way it's storming out there, you know we're gonna have ourselves a whamdoozer of a day tomorrow."

"You don't wear a hearing aid. Remember? You said only old people wore them."

"Gonna be trees and branches blown down all over town."

Penny'd been down this path before. Gran would stall to-night, but if she went off to bed without answering Penny's questions, she'd plead a poor memory tomorrow.

"I heard you go down the hall," Penny said, remembering the thump of her grandmother's cane on the wooden floor. "And then I heard your bedroom door close."

"How could you hear all that when you had a guest to en-tertain?" Gran said, turning away from the table and Einstein. "You're never going to get yourself a fella if you don't get more sociable."

"Are you playing detective again?"

"I'm not playing." Gran stopped to glare at Penny. "I'm working hard to get my private investigator's certificate. The Institute of Advanced Careers is a real school even if the courses are all by mail."

"Did you plant any bugs in the kitchen?"

"Why would I want to do that?" Gran asked. "There are enough bugs around here without me growing any."

"I'm not laughing."

Her grandmother shrugged. "I was just doing my lessons."

"Isn't that illegal without a court order?"

"Oh, wonderful." Her grandmother snorted. "I'm trying to establish myself in a new career and you're going to throw me in jail. And how am I supposed to get my PI license with a record?''

Penny closed her eyes a moment. It was getting late and Gran was right—tomorrow would be a busy day. And she did not want to argue. ''Get your bugs out of here, Gran. Please.''

Her grandmother glared at her for a moment, before shuffling back to the kitchen table. She bent down and removed a gadget about the size of a half dollar from under the table.

''Is that the only one?'' Penny asked.

Gran stomped over to the sink and removed a similar gadget from beneath the cabinet. Then she walked over to the cat picture on the wall by the door and pulled out another one from behind the frame.

''I hope that's all,'' Penny said.

''Of course.'' Her grandmother gave her a look of childlike innocence. ''There aren't any more in the kitchen.''

Penny listened to Gran shuffle down the hall toward her room, then walked over to turn off the light. Her hand suddenly froze in midair. Oh, Lord. She didn't want to think where else her grandmother might have placed her bugs.

Dorothy stared at the Eiffel Tower through the flickering glow of the candles as she sipped her wine. Paris in the summer. Paris in the rain. Paris any way at all was perfect. The city of romance where love would sweep her off her feet. *Très magnifique.*

She leaned back on her futon and sighed. This is how it would be someday. Except that it wouldn't be a poster of Paris that she was staring at, but the real thing. One day when she had enough money saved to leave Chesterton.

A knock at the door interrupted her thoughts, but it was just as well. Mulling over the state of her savings account wasn't going to bring her dreams any closer. Selling a few more houses before her visa expired was what she needed. Either that or she was going to have to apply for an extension. Again.

She looked through the peephole. It was Toto. What a nice surprise.

"Bonjour," she said as she pulled the door open. "What are you doing here so late?"

"Just checking up on you," he said. "I saw the candles from the street as I was driving by. Hoped that you hadn't left them burning and gone to bed."

"Nope." He was such a worrier, went from teenager to old fuddy-duddy in one day. Sometimes she missed the old Toto, the one with passions and fire. "Want to come in? I just opened a bottle of wine."

But he shook his head. "No, I'd better not. It's getting late. Don't want anyone to get the wrong idea."

As if anybody cared, but she knew enough not to argue. That was Toto, a minister's son worried about what the world might think. "Did the storm do much damage?"

"Enough. How was the poetry reading?"

"Got canceled. The power went out."

"That's too bad. Penny must have been disappointed."

"Oui."

He glanced around the empty hallway, then shrugged. "I'd better go. It's time to hit the sack. Gotta be back on the streets by five."

"Okay. *Merci* for checking on me."

"No problem. Just part of the job." With a curt nod, he turned and left.

"Bonne nuit," Dorothy called after him, then closed the door.

She and Toto had dated through high school. They'd even been voted the Most Romantic Couple for the Valentine's Day dance their senior year, but then they both had grown up and apart. That happened a lot, she guessed, and they'd been lucky they'd recognized it. Some people just stayed together out of habit or fear of looking for someone new. They'd been smart and had chosen friendship.

Though sometimes, just sometimes, she wished things had been different.

Brad awoke to the sound of trucks just below him. Oh, great. It was morning already, six-thirty to be exact. His muscles ached with stiffness and his body felt as if it had been run over by a bulldozer, but he stretched and sat on the edge of the bed. He must have dozed off somewhere around five. Not bad, considering he hadn't thought he was going to sleep at all, not after kissing Penny.

He'd forgotten how early the day started here. And it felt even earlier since his body was still on Pacific time.

Still, there was no sense in going back to bed. A busy day lay ahead of him. Maybe he could hitch a ride into town with one of Penny's trucks.

After a quick shower, he hurried down to the kitchen. Aunty Em was there—and had a place set at the breakfast table for him. He gave a quick longing glance out the window at Penny and her crews, then sat down at the table. He couldn't disappoint the old lady. Besides, what could he do in town at this hour anyway?

"Looks like Penny's busy this morning," he said.

Aunty Em concentrated filling his coffee cup. "Lots of storm damage. It'll bring in a nice piece of change but I'd rather see her relax a bit. She's been working hard. Too hard."

"It must be tough running a business. Are her brothers around to help?"

"No. Thad teaches at Stanford and Will's a doctor at the Mayo Clinic, but it ain't just the business. It's school, too." She opened the refrigerator. "I got cold pizza, leftover stew or black bean burritos. Or are you one of those health freaks that likes bran flakes for breakfast?"

Cold pizza, leftover stew or black bean burritos? "Well, actually…"

She put a container of yogurt on the table. "Once Penny gets her mind set on something, there ain't no derailing her."

He opened the yogurt with some relief and tried to keep track of the conversation. "So, Penny's taking some business courses?"

Aunty Em sat down across from him, cold pizza on her plate. "She's studying English literature." The old woman shook her head, a bemused smile on her face. "Doing real good in it, too. Getting high grades. Talking at meetings and stuff."

Brad slowly stirred his yogurt. "So, why do I think there's a problem?"

"Because there is. And it's called Alex."

He stopped stirring. From out in the yard came the sound of another truck's engine. He had the feeling he should run out and catch that ride to town while he still could. Before he put himself in a trap. But he didn't move.

"Have they been going together long?" he asked.

"No. Two months, maybe."

"That's not very long. Maybe it'll die out on its own."

Aunty Em shook her head. "I was hoping, but so far she's only gotten worse about him, if anything. He's turned into such a stuffed shirt. They don't do any of the things together that she likes—tennis or biking or horseback riding. All they do is poetry. Stuff he likes."

Brad tried to force back that little flicker of worry. His days of watching over Penny were over. Finished years ago. He had his life and she had hers. "Penny's an adult," he said. "She's got a right to choose her friends. And while Alex might not be our choice for her, we can hardly object. He's not racing across the seawall anymore, is he?"

"Not that we know of." Aunty Em frowned at Brad thoughtfully. "How would you like a job?"

Brad froze, his hand midway to his mouth. A job offer was the last thing he'd expected her to say. Maybe he had misunderstood. "I beg your pardon?"

"I need help with my business," the old lady said. "I got me a private detective agency."

He hadn't misunderstood apparently, but all he could do was stare at her.

"Well—" she made a face "—I will as soon as I get my license. And I'll get that as soon as I get my certificate."

"Your certificate?" This conversation was making no sense.

She leaned forward. "I want you to be my legman. On account of the two legs I got ain't all that good."

Brad tried to speak, but no words would come. Maybe because no words were in his brain anymore. He should have had that cold pizza or one of those black bean burritos. Maybe they would have jolted him into wakefulness.

Aunty Em had a private investigating business and wanted him to work for her? Maybe he hadn't really arrived in Chesterton last night, but had stumbled through some time warp or something.

"Uh, I'm not going to be here for long," he said. "Maybe only for today."

She sat back, looking surprised. Confused. Worried. "Oh." She picked at her cold pizza for a minute. "I thought you would help. You used to kind of watch out for Penny. I knew that, so I thought I could count on you."

Her voice was quiet, her tone mournful. Nope, no time warp. He remembered now. This was pure Aunty Em. She was playing him like a violin. He knew it but he still couldn't keep the guilt from creeping in.

"Alex seemed like a nice guy," Brad said. *Liar,* a little voice inside him shouted. He hadn't liked Alex years ago and hadn't liked him last night.

"Not in my book," Aunty Em said with a sniff. "He doesn't treat her the way a fella's supposed to treat a lady."

Brad felt his heart wavering but he was not going to cave in. His life was elsewhere now. Chesterton and its residents weren't his responsibility, not in any way, shape or form. "If Penny's happy with him, that's all that matters," he said briskly.

"Who says she is? Maybe she don't know any better."

Brad went back to eating his yogurt. "Penny always had more common sense than anyone I ever knew."

"That was before she got smart." Aunty Em sat up taller, looking him in the eye. "You remember what an idiot Thad was? Boy was as smart as they come in schoolwork and would get lost walking up the stairs to his room. It seems in our family you either got common sense or book smarts, never both. Now that Penny's got herself book smarts, she's lost all her common sense.''

''I find that hard to believe.''

''You think he's right for her?''

''Well...''

''Did he act like a man in love last night?''

''No,'' Brad had to admit.

''Did he even act like a gentleman or did he run home so he wouldn't get wet?''

''Penny told him to go,'' Brad said.

She snorted. ''Would you have gone home just because Penny had told you to?''

This was insane. Penny did not need his help. What's more, she wouldn't want it. She would kick him clear across the county if she thought he was interfering in her life.

But Aunty Em had always been so good to him. Always fed him when he came to work here. Even gave him stuff to take home to his mother and did it without taking away his pride. He owed her. And she was genuinely worried. Maybe there was some simple way to relieve her worries. There had to be. And what could it cost him—an extra day or two? No big deal.

''What would you want me to do?'' he asked.

''Dig up stuff on Alex. Anything you can find.''

''How would I do that?''

''See who his friends are. Find out what the heck he's up to. Just follow him.''

''I can't,'' Brad replied. ''I don't have a car.''

''You can use my old Jeep. My hip's got to heal another month before the doctor says I can drive anyway.''

Oh, man, she was making this difficult. ''I don't know anything about surveillance or investigating,'' he told her, shaking his head.

''I can teach you,'' Aunty Em replied.

''I've got to take care of Uncle Hal's estate,'' he said. All right, so he was grasping at straws.

She just grinned at him. ''That's a perfect cover. Penny'll never get suspicious.''

* * *

"Easy there," Penny called out to the crew pulling the branch off Brad's car. "We don't want to wreck it any more than it is."

Carl, her crew chief, snorted. "Can't do it any more harm. It's totaled already. A few extra dings ain't gonna damage its resale value."

"Yeah, I suppose." She had been half hoping that it was repairable, but she knew it wasn't. It looked like a giant had slammed his fist down on the roof, mashing in the top and breaking all the windows. Maybe Brad had insurance, though, and would get a new car. Yeah, right. At best he'd get a new junker out of it.

She watched for a moment longer, then went over to her truck to check the schedule. She had to stop trying to take care of him. He wasn't poor anymore. He didn't need her to bring him an extra sandwich or cookies for lunch.

Swatting away a pesky mosquito, she pulled her clipboard off the dashboard. They should be done here soon and they could get on to—

"Hey, Penny," Carl called. "You know where Corrigan is?"

Damn. Had word gotten all over town that she'd taken him home last night?

"I'm not sure," she said carefully. "Why?"

"There's personal items here in the trunk," Carl said. "What should we do with them?"

Penny hesitated. Their policy was not to deal with personal items, yet she couldn't afford to let one of the crew go running off after Brad. If anybody had to go, it ought to be her, but she wasn't any too anxious to see Brad again. She'd acted like a fool enough last night; she wasn't ready to risk another mishap. Fortunately, a police car came rolling around to the back of the tavern before she had to make a decision. She saw the call number and breathed a sigh of relief.

"It's Toto," Penny said. "He'll see that Brad gets his things."

"Great." Carl turned on his heels and strode toward his crew. "Come on, guys, let's hustle. There's still a lot to do before the sun sets."

Penny walked over toward the police car. "Hi, Toto."

"Hi, Pen." He got out of his car and stretched. "Storm work keeping you busy enough?"

"Too busy." She paused. "Did Dorothy tell you about Brad Corrigan coming back?"

He looked surprised. "Brad Corrigan?"

"I assumed you had talked to Dorothy last night and that she told you."

"I did, but she didn't." Toto frowned. "Maybe she forgot because she was busy practicing her French again. I think she's thinking about moving to Paris. Like soon."

Not if you'd ask her to stay! At times Penny wanted to shake some sense into the two of them, but she just said, "I doubt it."

"It's all she's ever talked about since we graduated from high school."

"And how many years ago was that? If she wanted to go, she would have gone," Penny said and took a giant leap forward. "Maybe you need to give her a reason to stay."

Toto looked stunned. "Why would I do that?"

"Do you want her to go?" Penny asked.

"That's not the point," he returned, his words coming quickly. "We're just friends. Nothing else. Just good friends. I wouldn't want to stand in the way of her dreams."

"Uh-huh." But was Brad that altruistic?

They watched as her crew cleaned up the last of the debris, sweeping sawdust off the parking lot surface onto the dirt beneath the trees.

"Boy, that car's a wreck," Toto said.

"It's Brad's."

"Oh, yeah? He wasn't in it, was he?" Toto sounded worried.

"No, he was in the bar with us. We're just cleaning up the mess. He's got some personal stuff in the trunk, though. Can we just give it to you?"

"Sure." He took a deep breath. "So, was she excited about him coming back?"

Penny swallowed hard. How did she play this? "I don't know," she said. "You know Dorothy. She's so friendly, it's hard to tell what she's really thinking."

"Yeah. He was probably glad to see her. Didn't he used to have a crush on her?"

Damn Toto anyway. How could she light a fire under him so he'd fight for Dorothy? She frowned at the wreck of Brad's car. Even if he wanted to leave, he couldn't now. Not without a car.

"Guess I should write up an accident report," Toto said. "He'll need it for insurance."

She watched as Toto filled out his form, walking around to secure the license number and the vehicle identification number. He looked through the broken front window.

"Not much inside," he said. "Just some maps on the front seat and nothing much in the glove compartment."

"We got a bag out of the back seat last night."

Toto nodded. "You know where he's at?"

Penny shrugged. "He stayed at my place last night, but I have no idea where he is now. Aunty Em might know." Penny looked over at her crew, already leaving for another location. She had a mile-long list of damage sites to assess. "I have to run, Toto. We have a lot to do after last night's storm."

"Okay," he replied. "I'll drop by the farm when I'm done here. See if I can find Brad and give him his stuff."

"Fine. Great." She hurried toward her truck. "Thanks for all your help."

And don't bother to let her know where Brad was. She didn't care.

Oh, yeah? So why did her heart just skip a beat?

"We should paint the damn thing," Aunty Em said.

Brad looked from the old, rust-spotted Jeep to her. "I think it's beyond a new paint job."

"Lordy, boy," Aunty Em exclaimed. "I ain't trying to pretty it up any. I mean as a disguise."

"A disguise?"

"Everybody in the county knows that there vehicle is mine," she said. "Alex'll make you in a minute."

Hadn't she heard anything he'd said earlier? "I really have to take care of that probate stuff," he reminded her. "I don't know that I'll have time to tail Alex and—"

"Then I guess you'll be walking to town."

Brad sighed. He didn't really need Aunty Em's Jeep. Hell, he could buy a fleet of them just on his credit card alone, but he didn't want to hurt the old woman's feelings.

"Well, like I said, I'm not experienced in tailing people but I'll do my best."

"Can't ask no more of anyone than that," Aunty Em replied as she handed him the keys. "And make sure you hang back. I don't want him spotting you."

Brad nodded as he hopped into the driver's seat. "I'll be back in a bit." He turned the ignition, almost jumping out of the seat when the motor caught. "Holy catfish. You got any muffler left on this thing?"

She just waved as he put the vehicle in gear and made his way down the lane. The old Jeep wasn't exactly a surveillance vehicle. Hell, Alex would have to be stone deaf not to hear him coming. It would be believable then when Brad had nothing to report.

But by the time Brad'd hit the edge of town, the noise and fumes were giving him a headache. Figuring he'd be doing everyone a favor, he pulled into the Muffler in a Minute Shop.

"Can you put a muffler on this thing?" he asked the attendant and handed him a hundred dollar bill. "Quick?"

"Sure thing."

Brad saw another mechanic in back and took out another hundred. "How about if you check the brakes while he does the muffler?"

"How about we change the oil, too?"

While the old Jeep got fussed over in the service bay, Brad walked over to a bench and sat down, staring at the traffic.

"Go away, Brad," Penny said. *"I'm doing my homework."*

"I just want to help."

"No, you don't," she snapped back. *"You want to do it for me."*

He bit his lip and looked down at the floor. He did want to help her but he could never explain things to her. His tongue would get so twisted up that it was just easier to do it himself.

"I don't want you doing my homework. It's my responsibility. I'd rather flunk on my own than get an A because you did the work."

"Penny, let the boy help you," her father interjected. *"That's what he comes here for."*

No, he came because he had to. Because he couldn't stay away. But all Brad could do was stand there and stare at her.

"Fine," she said and threw her pen down. *"Here. Do it. I don't care."*

That had all been handled so badly back then. Did she still resent him for the help he tried to give her? But look how well she was doing now. She obviously didn't need his or anyone else's help anymore.

No, not with her homework. But he wasn't all that sure about her ability to judge character. She'd been a softie back then, always falling for some hard luck story. He doubted that she'd changed. Somebody needed to look out for her, but it didn't have to be him.

But then who would?

And who would once he was gone again?

He'd found no answer to either question by the time he left the repair shop about a half hour later. The old Jeep was running much better, but he couldn't say the same for himself. Determined not to think about Penny anymore, he drove to the lawyer's office.

There weren't many cars in the parking lot. Great. He should be in and out of the office in the blink of an eye. Review the documents, sign them and fly.

"Hi," he said, smiling at the receptionist. "I'm here to see Matt Harris."

"You'll have to come back Monday."

He looked around the empty office. "Are you telling me I need an appointment?"

"Nope," she replied. "He's not here. He went up to Michigan on vacation. Won't be back until Monday."

Oh, hell.

"Can I help you with anything?"

He looked at her a long moment. She could probably witness his signature. There wasn't any reason to stay to see the lawyer. But he found himself shaking his head. "No. No, that's okay. I'll come back Monday."

Sanity returned by the time he had the Jeep back on the road. That was the stupidest thing he'd done in a long time. He should have just signed the damn papers. What was the big deal about talking to the attorney? He'd talked to lawyers before. And on the phone no less.

He drove around a few minutes, not really ready to return to the nursery and Aunty Em. Or the reminders of Penny. No, he needed to find a shady place to sit and think.

And as long as he was out, he might as well see what was going on with Alex. Give him something to report to Aunty Em.

Chapter Four

"I'm sorry I didn't make your poetry reading last night," Heather said. She shifted the calico cat in her arms to her other shoulder. "I did try but only got a few blocks from home." She smiled apologetically. "You know me and storms."

Penny completed her walk around the fallen tree in Heather's front yard. She thought they could get the tree out and not damage Heather's prize rose bed any more than it already was. "You didn't miss anything," she said as she made some notes.

"Don't put yourself down," Heather scolded. "I bet it was great."

Penny looked up. "No, really. You didn't miss anything. The power went out and it got canceled."

"Oh. What bad luck for you." Heather put the cat down, then stepped carefully into the mud of her flower bed to pick up a birdhouse that had fallen from the tree. She put it on the porch, out of the way. "Are you going to reschedule?"

Penny shrugged. "Maybe. Depends on the demand for that meeting room. Alex was going to check." She glanced over at

Alex's house next door. "I suppose I could drop by and see if he found out anything. You think he's home?"

"Don't ask me," Heather replied. "The man's a recluse. I never see him. And even when I actually see him, he rarely talks to me. I think I need to speak in iambic pentameter or something."

"Maybe he's afraid you're going to try to give him a cat."

"I've never approached him about one."

"He must be the only person in town, then."

Heather looked hurt. "I can't help it if there are so many that need rescuing. If people wouldn't dump their pets when they get tired of them—"

Penny laughed softly. "Heather, honey, I'm teasing you. I just think Alex is kind of shy."

"He wasn't when we were in school."

"People change," Penny said.

After all, she had, hadn't she? She was running a business now and going to school…and still trying to prove she was smart. Okay, bad example. Had Heather changed? She was always scared of her own shadow and now she was a kindergarten teacher, living in her grandparents' old house and…hiding at home when it thundered and lightninged. Dorothy was still dreaming of finding her prince in some exotic location. And Brad still had his crush on Dorothy—she was all he talked about last night. Jeez, hadn't anybody changed?

"I'll have a crew over tomorrow to take care of this," Penny said and tucked her pen under the clip on the clipboard. "I know it's a mess but we've got more critical sites to take care of first."

"Sure. Whenever you get to it is fine with me." Heather walked out toward Penny's truck with her. "You know, speaking of cats, I've got the prettiest brown tabby that needs a home. She's kind of wild, but would make a great barn cat for you."

Penny knew better than to argue. "Sure, need me to pay for her spay?"

"No, Sarah's going to cover it…" Heather stopped to stare

down the street. ''Boy, for a minute there I thought that was
Aunty Em's Jeep down the block. But she's not driving yet, is
she?''

Penny glanced to where Heather was looking, a reflex action
more than anything. ''Nope. She's got another month before
the doctor's going to let her.'' Her eyes narrowed as she looked
again, closer this time. ''It does look like her Jeep,'' she said
slowly, then frowned. ''It's Brad Corrigan.''

''Brad Corrigan?'' Heather repeated, confused. ''He's
back?''

''He's back and I would guess Aunty Em loaned him her
car.'' Penny tossed her clipboard onto the front seat of her
truck, then marched over to where the Jeep was parked.

Brad must have seen her coming because he smiled at her
as she approached. It did nothing to ease her suspicions.

''Hi, there.'' His smile was as wide as Indiana was long.
Damn. Eighteen years and all it did was make him handsomer.

''What are you doing here?'' she asked.

''Came to take you to lunch,'' he said.

''Lunch? I don't have time for lunch,'' she snapped. ''I've
still got a dozen calls to make.''

Brad just shook his head. ''Even poets have to eat. How
about if we go to a drive-through, then I'll take you to your
next stop while you eat?''

The idea of taking such a break was tempting—and for that
very reason she wouldn't. She had a weakness where Brad
Corrigan was concerned and she needed to stay away from him.
''That's crazy. I've got my calls laid out in order. It would
take too much time to drive back here for my truck.''

''So, I'll drive you all afternoon.'' He looked past her suddenly. ''Hey, is that Alex? I didn't know he lived around
here.''

Penny turned. Sure enough, Alex's car was backing out of
the drive. She waved when he looked her way and she hurried
over when he stopped. Hopefully, Brad would take the hint and
leave.

''We still on for tonight?'' she asked Alex.

"But of course. Unless you need to reschedule."

She shook her head. "I've got an Oz festival meeting tomorrow night, so it's got to be tonight. You said I need to have my paper ready if the seminar committee should ask to see it."

"They won't before the end of the month and that's a couple of weeks away. We needn't rush if you're too busy."

"This is important."

"Then tonight it is. Sevenish?"

"How about eightish?"

He nodded and then drove on.

Penny turned. Brad was still there, leaning up against the driver's side of the truck. Down the block, the Jeep stood with its hood open.

"The engine died," he said. "I guess I'm going to have to bum a ride off of you anyway."

She wasn't surprised. Somehow as soon as she'd seen him down the street, she'd known she wasn't going to be able to avoid him. She climbed into the passenger side of the truck and grabbed up her cellular phone.

"I assume it needs to be towed."

He just shrugged and got into the driver's seat. "Why don't I come back and take a look at it later? Is Bill's Barbeque still around?"

"Yeah."

She put down the phone as he pulled away from the curb and took out her list of calls. She didn't intend to phone anyone at the moment, but it was better than staring at Brad. Her eyes forgot her resolve and her gaze wandered to him anyway.

He'd been the cutest guy in high school when he'd left and had only gotten better. He looked toughened by life, but it was a good toughening. He looked strong, both inside and out, and dependable. Someone you could climb a mountain with.

She looked away and stared at the passing houses. Not that she needed that kind of help. There weren't any mountains in this part of Indiana. There weren't any mountains anywhere in Indiana.

"So, why did you come back?" she asked suddenly.

"To clear up my uncle's probate."

That sounded simple, but Brad had always been able to make the most complex things sound simple. And she couldn't forget his arm around Dorothy last night.

"Do you have to handle that kind of stuff in person?" she asked. "I would've thought you could do it by mail."

"I could have," he admitted as he pulled into Bill's drive-through.

The words killed Penny's appetite. He was here for Dorothy. She'd known it. A sick feeling took up residence in the pit of her stomach. Well, she was just going to have to stop him, that was all. Dorothy belonged with Toto, whether she knew it or not.

He got their order of barbequed chicken sandwiches and soda, then pulled back onto the highway. "So, where's our first stop?"

His voice did funny things to her heart. It was deep and rough, yet somehow like velvet. She could imagine it whispering words of endearment to a lover. She could hear him—

Lordy, but she needed to get hold of herself. "Look, you don't need to do this," she said. She had to think of a plan, but obviously that wasn't possible with him around. "Why don't you take me back to the Jeep? Maybe I can get it started. You must have probate stuff to take care of."

"Not really. Matt Harris was my uncle's lawyer."

"And he's up at his cabin in Michigan," she said, her hopes crashing.

Brad grinned at her. "So, I have nothing to do until Monday."

Nothing to do but go after Dorothy—who shared office space with Matt. "You need to get your car taken care of."

"I did."

"And get your personal stuff from Toto."

"That's all set up."

She was feeling panicky for no reason. He was only talking about three days. What could happen in seventy-two hours?

She could protect Dorothy for that long. Dorothy was her friend. She'd protect her forever.

He glanced at her list, reading it in a split second. "First stop is the Rogers' farm on Country Road 112." Brad was intent on the road and his sandwich, but managed to look over at Penny. "How about dinner tonight?"

"What?" That was dumb. Made it sound like she'd never been asked out to dinner. "I mean, no thank you. I have a previous engagement."

"You have a date?" he asked.

"That's none of your business," she said and unwrapped her sandwich. She might not have much of an appetite, but at least she wouldn't have to talk if she was eating.

"With Alex?"

"You don't listen very well," she snapped. "What did I just tell you?"

He turned onto a county road and headed east. "He's not right for you."

Who did Brad think he was? She took a couple of bites, hoping he'd change the subject if she refused to answer.

"You need somebody with a little backbone. Alex used to have some but it looks like he lost it."

She took another bite and chewed it determinedly.

"Poetry is fine, but there's more to life than a rhyme scheme."

He would get the idea. He wasn't dense. She took another bite and stared out the window as she ate it.

"Just because he's got a couple of degrees, it doesn't mean he's a great catch."

The sandwich was gone. She had no choice but to talk. "You may not have noticed, but in the eighteen years you've been gone, I grew up. I'm now a mature, adult woman. Fully capable of running my own life and making my own decisions."

"Where are you guys going?" he asked. "Does he take you to nice places?"

"Which part of 'mind your own business' don't you understand?"

"I just want to make sure you're happy."

If that didn't take the cake! Those eighteen years might never have happened. He was still secretly in love with Dorothy and still into bossing Penny around. Nothing had changed with the man.

"You're not my father or big brother," she said.

"I'm not applying for either job."

He sounded annoyed with her, just as he had as her tutor. As if he were irritated with everything she did. As if she were the biggest bother in the whole world.

"We've all done quite well without your help," she said sharply. "I'm doing just great in all my courses—with me doing my own homework." Well, she was completing her own assignments, and she wasn't failing anything—so that was doing great, for her. "And the business is so successful, I'm thinking of buying the MacKenzies' land to our north and expanding the nursery."

"That's great."

"And Dorothy and Toto are really in love," she added quickly. "I've never seen a couple so in love. I expect they're going to get engaged on her birthday next month."

"That's swell."

He turned into the Rogers' yard as he said it, his voice even and relaxed now.

Damn. She'd screwed up. She should have thought this through. Now he knew that there was nothing official between Dorothy and Toto. He probably thought that made her fair game.

Damn. Damn. Damn. Maybe she was as dumb as everybody used to say she was.

Toto opened the door to the Yellow Brick Road Bar and Grill and he and Junior stepped into the bar's cool, dark interior. The dining room was nearly full, but there were a lot of open seats at the bar. While Junior headed straight toward an empty stool, Toto followed more slowly, greeting friends, letting his eyes get used to the dim lighting, and letting the heavy burden of circumstance weigh on him.

What was Brad Corrigan doing back in town?

"The usual?" the bartender asked as Toto seated himself.

Toto nodded and within moments, a tall glass of Mountain Dew was before Toto and a bowl of near beer was in front of Junior. Then the bartender walked away, letting them be. Leaving Toto to stare at his image in the mirror as he sipped his drink and listened to Junior eagerly lapping his nonalcoholic beer.

All the clothes in Brad's suitcase had been casual ordinary-looking stuff, until Toto'd looked closer. Labels he'd never seen in the stores in Chesterton or Michigan City but that reeked of wealth. And then there was that expensive, fully equipped microcomputer that had been in Brad's trunk.

But if Brad could afford that kind of equipment and those kinds of clothes, why was he renting his car from a cheapo outfit like Rented Dented?

It all came back to the first question. What was Brad Corrigan doing back here anyway? Staying over to Penny's house and leaving Dorothy all dreamy like some junior high girl.

Toto didn't think he liked it. He knew he hadn't liked that look in Dorothy's eyes last night. She hadn't spoken French for ages now and he thought she'd gotten over that. He thought she was happy with life here and their friendship. And that maybe they could start moving into something else. But now he wasn't sure and that worried him.

Maybe he'd gone a little overboard, but Toto had done a little checking. Brad had a driver's license from California. No record of moving violations. A credit check showed he had no financial problems. Actually he didn't owe anybody money, although he did have an American Express card with no limit.

So, what was he doing here? And how could Toto make sure it didn't involve Dorothy?

Brad had expected the Yellow Brick Road Bar and Grill to be filled with a comfortable blend of scents from beer to fried food. What he hadn't expected was to see a big German shepherd sitting at the bar with a police officer. A familiar-looking German shepherd.

"Junior?" Brad said.

But it was the police officer who turned around. "Brad?"

It was Toto. His face was round like it had been eighteen years ago, but the body had firmed up. The blond hair was in a short military cut now. He got to his feet, hand outstretched. "Hey, long time."

Brad shook his hand. "Real long." Junior continued slurping something from a bowl in front of him. "Junior with you?"

Toto looked at the dog, then at Brad. "You know him? After being in town less than twenty-four hours? Damn, that dog has more of a social life than I do."

"I gave him a ride from the tollbooth yesterday," Brad said.

"That was you? Mom said she asked somebody to bring him in."

"That was your mom? I didn't recognize her." Brad was embarrassed. He'd always liked Toto's mom. Had so much time passed, had he changed so much that he didn't remember old friends?

"Guess she didn't recognize you, either." Toto motioned to an empty table, apparently unconcerned about the lack of recognition. "Hey, let's sit down. Have something to eat."

"Sure."

Toto picked up his glass and Junior's bowl and moved them to an empty table as Brad waved the bartender over for a beer. Brad and Toto had been good friends when they were kids. He'd always been able to trust Toto's read of things. Surely that would still be true today. He'd ask him a few questions, get some reassurance about Penny and Alex and then hit the road. He could always mail those probate papers. Brad took his beer and met Toto and Junior at their table.

"So, Junior's your dog?" he said.

Toto nodded. "Actually, he's a retired police dog. Took a bullet in his back leg about a year ago so he lives with me now." He patted the dog, who was scrupulously cleaning out his bowl. "We used to be partners. The precinct got him from an outfit in North Carolina and they'd found out about Chesterton and *The Wizard of Oz* festival so they named him Toto. But when he got here, the sheriff said it would be too confusing to have two officers named Toto. I had seniority so we all called him Junior."

"Lucky he agreed."

"True." Toto took a long drink of his soda. "What brings you back to town?"

"Just handling my uncle's probate."

"Ah." Toto nodded slowly. "Heard you saw Dorothy last night."

"At the poetry reading. It was great to see her again. She's just as nice as ever. But I couldn't believe how different Alex is now. And that he was there with Penny."

"Yeah, they've been dating for a couple of months now. He seems like a nice enough guy."

Brad frowned. *He seems?* Didn't Toto know? After all, they did live in the same town. "I never liked him. Thought he was a show-off."

Toto just laughed. "We were all kind of nerdy back then, weren't we?"

"Dorothy wasn't." And neither was Penny. "How does he treat her?"

It seemed to take Toto a moment to get back on track. "Oh, you mean Alex and Penny? All right, I guess. I never paid much attention."

Brad felt his annoyance growing. What kind of a cop was Toto if he didn't notice the little things around him? "I just thought someone as beautiful as Penny deserved better."

"She is gorgeous, isn't she? You know she was a model in New York for a few years?"

"Really?" Was that it? Did Alex consider her some kind of trophy girlfriend?

"Yeah." Toto nodded. "She entered some contest in Chicago and got offered a contract by some big New York firm.

She did real well. Made the *Sports Illustrated* swimsuit issue one year.''

"Why'd she come back here?"

"Her dad died and Aunty Em was alone." Toto shrugged. "And I guess she was tired of life in the fast track."

Up at 5:00 a.m. to clean up storm damage wasn't exactly living in the slow lane. "She seems to be doing well," Brad said.

"She's really turned that business around. Went from one crew to three. Making money hand over fist."

Maybe that was it. Maybe Alex was after her money. Or the land the farm was on. This close to Lake Michigan, that property would be worth a pretty piece. Brad bet the bum had an armload of debts and was going to try to con his way into her bank account.

And they had a date tonight. He wondered how far along Alex was in his campaign to weasel money out of Penny.

It was just as well that Matt Harris wouldn't be back until Monday. That would give Brad more than enough time to take care of a schnook like Alex. He'd sent him packing once and he could do it again.

"I just thought of something," Brad said as he got to his feet. "I can't stay for dinner, after all. Can I get my stuff from you?"

"Yeah. Sure. It's out in the car."

Toto got to his feet, called Junior to follow, and led Brad out to the parking lot. The early evening air still held the muggy warmth of the day and Brad felt a closeness, a tension. As if the air were scarce and he had to fight for every breath.

"I'm parked over there," Toto said.

Brad followed, frowning at the cars crowded into the lot and then at the darkening sky. How was he ever going to find her? Chesterton was a small town, but not so small that he could cover all the restaurants and bars before it got dark.

"You don't happen to know where Penny and Alex would have gone tonight, do you?" Brad asked.

Toto was unlocking his car trunk, but stopped. "Tonight?

Probably at the Pizza Prince. I think they go there on Thursdays a lot.''

The Pizza Prince every Thursday? What kind of a date was that? It was bad enough that Alex was a schnook. But a cheap schnook on top of that?

Penny made a face as she looked over Alex's notes. ''So, you're saying the paper stinks, basically?''

Their pizza lay off to one side, practically untouched. But then, they didn't come to the Pizza Prince for the great pizza but because it was always deserted on Thursday evenings and they wouldn't be overheard.

''Not at all,'' Alex said. ''I just thought you needed to strengthen your argument that the wizard was a tragic hero. Maybe insert some more references from classical works.''

No matter what Alex said, the paper looked the same as her schoolwork had all along—covered with red ink. ''This is hopeless, isn't it?'' she said. ''I'm not going to be invited to speak at that symposium.''

He took her hand in his and gave it a gentle squeeze. ''If it's important to you, then you should try. I don't know whether you'll get invited after all your work, but I do know that if you don't do the work, you definitely won't get invited.''

She smiled at him and reached over to plant a quick kiss on his cheek. ''You're right, as usual. I need to quit griping and start revising. What do you think about adding more biographical data from Baum's life?''

''That would work and—''

''Well, look who's here.''

Penny looked up, her heart practically stopping. It was Brad.

''Hi, Brad,'' Alex greeted him. ''How are you?''

What in the world was he doing here?

What did it matter? Penny scrambled to gather up her notes and shove them into her folder before he could see them. This was the most unbelieveably rotten timing.

''Hi, Brad,'' she said once her things were hidden.

''I can't believe the coincidence,'' Brad remarked as he sat down at the table with them. "I was in the mood for some good old Pizza Prince pizza and who should I run into but you two?"

"Was Pizza Prince here when you were still living in town?" Alex asked.

"No, it's only been here five years," Penny replied.

"Really?" Brad just leaned back in his chair with a bright smile. "Imagine that."

Penny had a number of things she'd like to imagine. Brad being chased out of town by Junior. Brad being soundly trounced by Alex. Brad crawling on his knees to tell her he loved her. Now, where had that image come from?

"How did you get here?" Penny asked him. "I thought the Jeep had died."

"Nope, started right up again. Just like magic. Hey, aren't you eating this?" Brad asked.

"The Jeep sounds like a tank approaching," Penny said. "I didn't hear it."

Brad smiled as he helped himself to a slice of cold pizza. "Guess it just needed a little exercise to get rid of the roughness. Hmm, this pizza's the best." He looked around as if captivated by the Formica decor. "You guys don't mind that I joined you, do you?"

Penny just sighed. Why was he so damn good-looking? No, that wasn't it. Alex was good-looking and did nothing to her heart. Was it just habit? Maybe her heart had a serious defect and she was particularly susceptible to blue-eyed charmers.

Alex was watching her with an odd look in his eyes. She wasn't sure what he was trying to tell her. That she should be more welcoming? No, it wasn't a scolding kind of look. It was more thoughtful, more wondering. Probably he was just wondering how she wanted to play this. Which was a good question. How did she want to play this? Should she ask Brad to leave or just tell him?

But one look at Brad's smile and she seemed to have no choice but to give in. The man was just outrageous. "No, it's fine," she assured him with a sigh. "And help yourself to the pizza. We got to talking and it got cold."

"Nothing wrong with cold pizza," Brad said.

"True enough," Alex said and took a piece himself. "In fact, I think some of the things that have been left to age are the sweetest and truest."

Penny helped herself to some pizza, without having the slightest clue as to what Alex was talking about. "Was just about to say that myself," she agreed anyway. "Nothing like aged soda. Nice and flat."

Alex laughed and leaned back in his chair. "So, Brad. What have you been doing with yourself?"

Brad shrugged. "This and that."

"Nice watch," Alex said with a nod toward Brad's wrist.

"Thanks." But Brad moved his arm so Penny could barely see the watch.

She frowned. Why had Alex done that? She had caught a glimpse of Brad's watch before—gold in some parts and silver in others where the gold plating must have worn off. He couldn't even afford one of those expensive Timex sport watches like she had. It wasn't like Alex to call attention to something like that.

"Did you get your stuff from Toto?" she asked quickly. "Was anything else damaged?"

"Looked fine." He didn't seem to realize she'd been trying to change the subject. "Say, was that your truck out front, Penny? I saw it when I pulled in, but I didn't think it could be. Where I come from, a man drives a lady when he takes her out."

Penny just blinked at him. So much for trying to ease his discomfort! "It didn't make any sense for Alex to drive all the way out to the farm," she informed him. "Not when we were going to a restaurant just a few blocks from his house. We always meet here on Thursday."

"A gentleman doesn't do what's sensible. He does what's right."

"Oh, give me a break," Penny said. "Since when does driving a few miles out of the way become right, and saving time and gas become wrong?''

''What—he doesn't make enough money for the gas out to your place?''

''He makes plenty of money. He just doesn't choose to waste it.''

''How can ensuring your safety be wasteful?''

Laughter interrupted them. Alex was laughing harder than she'd ever seen him laugh before. He was laughing so hard he didn't seem able to talk. Penny just glared at him.

Finally, wiping his eyes with his linen handkerchief, he got to his feet. ''I hate to miss any of this debate, but I really must get home. Penny, it's been a delight as always. Brad, can I assume you will see her safely home?''

Penny stared at him, unable to form a response. Unable to even figure out what her response should be. To laugh with him? To tell him off? To fire him as her learning coach? She ended up not saying anything, just watching him stop at the counter to pay the check and then walk out.

''Well, that should tell you something,'' Brad said.

She spun to frown at him. ''What? That you're rude and boorish?''

''At least I have a sense of responsibility.''

''Oh, spare me your lectures.'' She went over to the counter and got a pizza box for the leftovers, then tossed the remaining pieces into it. Gran would be in seventh heaven. Breakfast for the next few days. ''You have no right to come barging in here and bossing people around.''

''I didn't boss anybody around. I merely made a few comments.''

''That you had no business making.'' She grabbed up her folder, her purse and the pizza box. ''I'm leaving. And I'd prefer if you didn't follow me home. I just might give in to temptation and run you off the road.''

''I can't help it if I have a different set of standards.'' He got to his feet.

She gave him a look. ''I mean it. Don't tempt me.''

He stood a moment and glared at her, meeting her angry look square on. "Fine. I wanted to talk to Dorothy anyway. Can you at least tell me where she lives?"

Dorothy? Damn. Her anger vanished, replaced by a sick feeling in the pit of her stomach. Just because he hadn't mentioned Dorothy, she was letting herself forget the real reason he was back in Chesterton—to get his true love. He was so clever, he wouldn't mention her on purpose, just to fool everyone. That's what he had done in the past, too. And she had known. Everyone had known.

But she was smarter now. "Dorothy's not home," Penny said and tried to think quickly. "She's never home on Thursday nights."

He shrugged. "Fine, I'll talk to her tomorrow."

Damn. "You can't."

"I can't?"

Penny took a deep breath, letting her brain scramble for some semblance of rationality. "That's not exactly what I meant," she said and smiled at him, hoping to dazzle him.

He didn't look particularly dazzled. "What did you mean, then?"

She clutched the pizza box. "Well, since it looks like you're going to be around for a few days, I was kind of hoping you could give me a hand."

"Sure," he said, his voice easy though his eyes were still wary. "With what?"

With what? With what? "Uh, with the office." Yes, that was it. She hurried on. "We've been so busy with the storm damage. Gran usually does just fine with the regular office work but she had hip surgery last month and still has to take it easy. And the air conditioner broke in the trailer and it's way too hot for her to be out there."

She hoped she hadn't overdone it, but the look on his face assured her she hadn't. Those blue eyes were just overflowing with worry and concern. She felt just a twinge of guilt.

"Why didn't you say earlier?" he said, taking her arm and

walking with her to the door. "You must be exhausted, car-rying the load of the business and worrying about Aunty Em."

"I guess. Sometimes anyway."

They headed outside, trading the cool air-conditioning for the muggy warmth of the summer night. His hand on her arm felt good, felt right. Felt all too reassuring.

A slightly larger squiggle of guilt tried to raise its head but she refused to notice it. Gran had had hip surgery and it was unfair to expect her to handle the deluge of work. None of that was a lie. Penny wasn't doing this just to keep him away from Dorothy. Well, not entirely.

They stopped by her truck. She was close to him, close enough to breathe in the woodsy scent of his aftershave. Close enough to feel dwarfed by the breadth of his shoulders. The night was suddenly soft and embracing, the warmth a caress.

Penny swallowed hard. "I really appreciate your helping us out," she said. For some reason her voice came out quiet and breathless.

"No problem. That's what friends are for."

Friends. But that slow warmth growing inside her didn't feel exactly friendly. And she'd never felt such weakness in her knees around friends.

The stillness seemed to hit him, too, because he didn't move away. Shadows covered his face but she knew he was watching her, reading her heart and for the moment she didn't worry about what he might see. She didn't think at all, just reached up slightly and let her lips touch his.

The kiss the other night had been an accident, this was de-liberate. But it was a fire all the same. It was scorching and electric and consuming. The heat raced through her, a blaze that she had never known, so strong and so demanding. She leaned closer to him, his hands came up slowly to take her shoulders, to pull her even nearer.

But all she felt pressed against her chest was the solid wall of the pizza box.

Lordy, what was she doing?

She pulled back, trying not to gasp audibly for breath. Hoping he couldn't hear the frantic pounding of her heart that seemed to drown out all thought. ''The pizza's getting cold,'' she said. ''I'd better get going.''

''Sure.'' He let go of her shoulders.

For a split second, her knees protested, her heart screamed to lay back in his arms, to rest in his embrace. But two split seconds later, her head was in control again.

''I'll see you later,'' she said.

''In your rearview mirror.''

''Right.'' Oh, Lord, she'd forgotten. He was coming home now. She was going to have to face him in the bright light of the kitchen.

For a moment she was tempted to tell him where Dorothy lived, but the temptation passed. No, she could face him, in bright lights or no lights, and he wouldn't read a thing in her eyes.

Not that she used to love him. Not that she used to dream of him. Not that her heart still melted when he looked at her.

Certainly not that.

Chapter Five

"So, that's the setup," Penny said.

Brad looked around the trailer that was the nursery's office. If he had nightmares, this place would figure largely in them from now on. Although it was barely eight o'clock, it was already like an oven inside. The floor fan did nothing but move hot, stale air around.

The desk was piled high with papers, some yellowing with age. The map on the wall was dotted with colored pins, and the computer in the corner was an antique. He'd been in worse, though.

He turned back to Penny, standing tall and beautiful in jeans and a T-shirt. She looked uneasy here in the trailer's close quarters, and not because she thought that stack of work orders was going to fall on her. No, she looked as if last night's kiss had kept her as sleepless as it had him.

He had spent long hours dreaming of kissing her, but that had been years ago. A lifetime ago. Yet he'd been in town barely thirty-six hours and already he'd kissed her twice. It was almost funny, this success that came only after he'd vowed he was never letting himself get close to anyone again. That he was never letting his heart get so tied up by anyone as it had been tied up by Penny all those years ago. He forced himself to concentrate on what he'd come to Chesterton to do.

"Any questions?" Penny asked.

"Yeah. What's Alex's appeal?"

She just stared at him. That obviously wasn't the question she had expected. "What brought that up?"

"I'm curious," he said. "I could see why the girls liked him in high school when he was wild and exciting, but he's dull and lifeless now. What do you see in him?"

"I don't see why I have to explain anything," she snapped. "I might be curious about you but you don't find me asking personal questions, do you?"

"You could." The tightening of her lips egged him on. "We'll take turns. Ask me anything you like."

She looked torn. She looked like she wanted to turn on her heel and stomp out of the trailer. But she also looked like she had thought of a question.

"Why haven't you ever married?" she asked.

At least it was an easy one. "Some people aren't the marrying sort," he said, but not about to tell her why. No need to relive those awful times of desperate longing for her while he'd lived here and then the even worse loneliness of being without her once he'd moved. "I like being on my own."

"Don't you get lonely?"

"I have friends."

"But that's not the same."

"Exactly," he said. "You don't have to open up every facet of your soul to a friend. You can share what's shareable, and keep private what's not."

"Such as?"

"That's your third question, you know," he said, just to remind her this was a trade, but then he went on. "There are some things you just don't share with others. Things like your feelings. Your fears. Your dreams."

She sat on the edge of the desk, shaking her head slowly. "But those are the very things you want to share in a relationship. Sharing those is what makes it a relationship." She looked at him a long silent moment, her lips twisting thoughtfully. "You know what I think? I think you got so used to hiding those things when you were a kid, you just don't know how to share them now."

"I think it's my turn to ask the questions. What's Alex's appeal?"

She wanted to leave, he could see that, but she just raised her chin slightly and looked Brad straight in the eye. "He's smart."

"He's smart?" Brad couldn't believe she'd actually said that. "What kind of a reason is that to find someone attractive?"

"Better than finding them attractive just because you did when you were a kid."

He felt a twinge as that arrow hit its mark. She had known about his crush on her back then, and she obviously sensed that he was finding it hard to be around her now.

"What happened to dating for companionship?" he asked, hoping he sounded unaffected.

"And that's your third question." She got to her feet with a bright smile and picked up a clipboard off the counter. "Nothing's happened to dating for companionship. It's just that some people are more companionable than others." With a wave, she opened the door. "Have a good day."

He sank into the desk chair. He thought he had been so circumspect as a kid, making friends with Dorothy and working at the nursery just to be near Penny. Yet all the time she had known. She had known that he had loved her. A sick feeling settled in the pit of his stomach.

He wasn't worried that she had laughed at him, Penny wasn't like that. No, that sick feeling was more a fear of something worse—that she had felt sorry for him. That she had pitied him.

He turned on the computer, more as a distraction than anything else. It worked, distracting him plenty. The system was older than Santa Claus and slower than frozen molasses in January. He backed the chair up and looked at the unit more closely.

He could fix this thing in no time. Penny would go back to using an abacus before she'd let him buy her a new unit, but she didn't have to know. Not if he just added a few chips for speed and some for memory. And a nice big hard drive. It would pay her back for letting him stay here. It would show her—when she discovered it long after he was gone—that he wasn't an object of pity.

Brad reached for the phone book and flipped through the listings of computer accessory stores. He made a few calls, found what he wanted at a store in Chicago, and arranged for them to deliver it to the nursery before noon. Good old smart Alex's response probably would have been to write her a poem about it.

The crack should have made him feel better, but didn't.

A framed picture of Penny and her dad on the wall caught his eye and he walked over to look at it. It had been taken back in junior high school when their class had put on the *Wizard of Oz* at the town's festival. Work hadn't left him time to be in the production, but Penny had played the Scarecrow and had been wonderful. Her father had sure adored her.

"You're a smart kid," Mr. Donnelly said to Brad after he'd gotten the garden sprinkler working again. *"How are your grades in school?"*

Brad didn't know what the man was getting at and answered cautiously. "Pretty good."

"Want to earn some extra money?"

"Sure." Dumb question.

"Penny's been having a bit of trouble with her schoolwork this year. I thought maybe you could give her some help."

Help her? Talk to her? Sit with her? The idea was as terrifying as it was inviting. "I suppose," he said.

Would he be able to breathe, though? What would he wear? Not these old jeans and shirts that he wore to work in the gardens here. She'd see the holes in the knees and the mismatched buttons.

"I hate seeing her struggle like she does," Mr. Donnelly added. "She spends so much time on her work and it doesn't seem to help, then she gets upset. I hate seeing her cry." He fixed Brad with a sharp gaze. "I don't want her crying over her schoolwork any more. And I'm willing to pay you to make sure she doesn't."

Brad looked back at him, trading steely glance for steely glance. "She won't cry over her grades again, sir."

The man sighed, his gaze softening. "I'm just a silly old man, I know," he said. "If Penny's mother was still alive, she'd know how to handle the tears. But I don't. I just can't bear to see her cry."

Brad swallowed hard. "I know what you mean." His voice was rough and uneven as he fought against opening a sliver of his soul. "And I won't let you down. I'll take care of Penny."

It had been a promise and he always kept his promises.

The trailer door opened and Brad turned around. It was Carl, Penny's crew chief. He dragged his hefty frame into the stuffy trailer, shaking his head as he closed the door behind him.

"Man, it's hot in here," the man said. "What happened to the air-conditioning?"

"It broke," Brad said. "That's why I'm working here instead of Aunty Em."

"Better you than me. First call I'd make would be to the repairman."

"I imagine Penny already did." Brad went over to get the job list he'd made up, then stopped. "I'm kind of puzzled about something. How come a beautiful woman like Penny isn't married?"

Carl shook his head. "Why don't you ask me something easy like why dogs bark or why the sky's blue? Damned if I know."

"I don't think this Alex's the one for her," Brad said.

"Don't recall her asking my opinion."

But Brad wasn't going to let him off the hook that easy. "You've worked for her since she left modeling. You've got to have some idea."

The older man shrugged, then gave a half smile. "My Millie says that Penny's always been trying to prove something."

"Prove something?"

"Yeah, that she's as good as everybody at stuff."

Brad sighed. "Yes, I can see that."

"You want my advice? You go for it anyway," Carl said.

Brad frowned at the other man. "Go for what? You mean Penny?" He laughed. "No, no. I wasn't asking because I was thinking of myself. I travel light and I travel fast. No commitments to slow me down."

Carl took the job list from Brad's hand. "Then all these questions, they're just for some scientific study?"

"I like her," Brad said. "She's a friend."

"Uh-huh." Carl grinned as he walked over to the door. "Ain't no such thing as a man and woman being friends."

Still grinning, he left, letting Einstein into the trailer at the same time. What was this, Brad wondered, Grand Central Station? The cat promptly marched over to sit in front of the fan.

"I've got it figured out," Brad said.

The big orange tabby flopped on his side and flicked the tip of his tail.

"It's easy to see the situation here. Penny's always felt that people looked down on her because she had trouble in school. So, she must feel that by dating Alex everyone will respect her more."

Einstein's tail went motionless and his unblinking yellow eyes stared at Brad.

"Am I right or am I right?"

The cat just stared.

"One flick of the tail for yes, two for no."

Einstein's tail flicked twice.

Making a face, Brad shook his head. "What do you know?" he said. "If you were so smart you wouldn't be in Chesterton.

You'd be in Egypt or Thailand. One of those places where they worship you guys as gods."

"You talking to cats now, boy? Sad. Real sad."

Brad looked up. Aunty Em stood in the doorway with a pitcher in her hand.

"The saddest thing is that he answered." Brad got to his feet, then took her arm to help her in. "What are you doing out here anyway?"

"Just thought I'd see how you were getting along." She came around over to the chair and sank into it, putting the pitcher on the desk. "Brought you some lemonade. Thought you were probably dying of thirst by now."

"Just about." He found a bag of paper cups under some catalogs on top of a file cabinet. "Want a glass, too?"

"Sure." She waited until he'd filled two glasses and returned to his seat behind the desk. "So, what have you found out?"

He paused, glass at his lips, and stared at her. "About what?" he asked.

She made a face. "About Alex? What else? You were on surveillance yesterday, weren't you?"

He took a long drink of the lemonade before he answered. It was cold and refreshing, but just the mention of Alex's name left a bad taste in his mouth. "I didn't find anything out. I watched his house for a bit and then he drove away."

"Didn't you follow him? Lordy, boy, you sure aren't good at this. Haven't you ever watched any TV?"

"Penny was there," he explained.

"She made you? Damn." She took a sip of the lemonade and then stared thoughtfully into the glass for a long moment. "I never thought you'd be so incompetent."

"I'm not incompetent," he replied sharply. "I just think we have a better chance of talking Penny out of this relationship, rather than digging up dirt on Alex."

"We'll never do it," Aunty Em said. "She's got this crazy notion about the man she's going to marry. And Alex fits the bill."

"What's her crazy notion?" He was almost afraid to ask.

"The man she marries has to speak ten languages."

"What!"

"I told you it was crazy, but she's got it fixed in her mind for some dang reason. And you know Penny. She's not going to budge."

Brad felt his stomach twist with worry. "I don't suppose we could give Alex the ten-language test."

"He'd probably pass it."

"Then I guess we'd better dig up some dirt."

"But don't do it from here. I swear she knows everything that goes on around this place. Sometimes I think she's got more bugs hidden than I do." Aunty Em got to her feet. "Dang, it's hot in here. Can't imagine what happened to the air conditioner. It was working fine yesterday."

"It was?" That was odd. He went over to the window unit to take a closer look. "The plug's partially pulled out." He pushed it in and cool air rushed into the room.

"Imagine that," Aunty Em said and settled back into the chair. "So, now you can go investigate Alex and I can take care of the office."

Dorothy walked about twenty feet, going from her air-conditioned car into an air-conditioned building, but that was enough to break a sweat on her brow. It was awful this afternoon. Maybe she should move to London, not Paris. London was cooler, wasn't it? But it was rainy, too. Did she want lots of rain that would make her hair go frizzy?

She closed her eyes. A little cottage with a mass of flowers in the tiny side yard. An apartment on the Seine, looking out at the Arc de Triomphe. A villa in the south of France, in the wine country.

"Hi, Dorothy. Hot enough for you?" a voice said.

She opened her eyes. She wasn't in the south of France or the north, either. No, she was in Chesterton, Indiana, where the conversation always revolved around the weather. Still she smiled at the receptionist who manned the front desk for her shared office space.

"Another couple hours of this," Dorothy said, "and you'd better not go out in heels."

"Tell me about it," Nancy agreed. "My sister-in-law went to the grocery store on Sheridan and her heel sunk about two inches into the blacktop. Twisted her ankle."

"Wow. Gotta be careful. Any messages?"

"Not really." Nancy handed her a stack. "Just the usual two or three thousand."

"Thanks," Dorothy said.

"Real estate business must be good, huh?"

"It would be if all these messages were sales," Dorothy replied with a laugh.

"Oh, and you've got a guy in your office," Nancy said with a wink. "A hunk. He said he wanted to make a few calls on his cell phone so I said he could wait for you there."

"Okay. No problem."

She went down the hall to her office, flipping through the messages, then stopped as a man's deep voice rumbled softly out toward her. Brad?

Pausing at her half-open door, she could see she was right. It was Brad, but why would he be calling from here? She paused a moment, torn between giving him the privacy to finish his call and knowing she had the right to enter her own office. Trouble was, his voice carried awfully well.

"I want a thorough check," he was saying into his phone. "Payment records, existing debt, any problems in the past. The whole schmear."

Penny had said things didn't seem to be going well for Brad, but the man in her office didn't sound as if he were down on his luck. No, he seemed confident and comfortable giving orders. She took a step into the room and closed the door softly behind her.

"I'll call you back in a day or two for the results." He said a curt goodbye, then broke the connection. As he slipped the phone into his pocket, he must have sensed her presence because he spun around. "Dorothy."

"Hi, there," she said with a grin and walked around to her

desk. "Don't tell me. You want to buy a house and aren't sure if your credit's any good."

A smile slipped easily onto his face and he leaned back in his chair. "Actually, I want to sell a house. My uncle's old place. That's why I'm here."

"Oh, yeah? That big Italianate house on Second Street? That place is gorgeous. Run-down, but gorgeous."

"Maybe even bring in a decent commission for you," Brad said.

"Maybe," she agreed.

"Matt Harris has the keys if you want to take a look at it and figure out the asking price."

"I'll do that. Nancy can get the keys from Matt's office for me, I'll take a walk through the house tomorrow morning, and work up some figures for you by early next week." She made a note on her calendar and then let a silence settle over the room for just a moment. "Who are you running a check on?"

He frowned. Someone who hadn't seen him operate at an executive level might have been impressed. She wasn't and kept up her stare.

"Alex," he finally said.

"Alex?" That wasn't what she had expected. Alex? The milquetoast poet of Chesterton? A million questions danced in her head. "Why? Are you some kind of spy or private investigator or something?"

Brad grimaced. "No, but Aunty Em thinks she is. She's rooked me into trying to find some dirt on him. She's convinced Alex is all wrong for Penny."

"Well, he is," Dorothy agreed. "I'm glad someone else sees that, too. You need any help, you just ask me."

"I will," Brad said and got to his feet. "Do I need to sign any papers about the house?"

"Not until I work something up. I'll give you a buzz when I've got something ready."

She walked with him to her door, relief making her almost light-headed. If anybody could make Penny see the light, it would be Brad. He would keep Penny from making a terrible mistake.

He'd opened the door, but before he could leave she threw her arms around him, giving him a big hug. "I'm really glad you're back."

His arms came around her. Tightly for just a moment. "It's good to be back," he told her. "It really is."

Dorothy let him go, watching with a smile as he winked at a grinning Nancy and left the building, then she turned back toward her office, her smile deepening. She'd always known. Even way back when they were kids and everyone thought Brad loved her, she'd known he only had eyes for Penny. He'd only made friends with her to be close to Penny. It hadn't bothered her at all; she rather liked being a part of his secret. And now she was again.

Brad was going to save Penny from Alex. That was the greatest thing she'd ever heard. The most romantic thing that had happened in Chesterton since Penny had put extra sandwiches in Brad's lunch.

Dorothy's smile faded slightly. That was probably why things hadn't worked out with her and Toto. Between Penny and the sandwiches, and Brad saving Penny from Alex, Chesterton's quota of romance had been used up.

The note on her calendar caught Dorothy's eyes and an image of Hal Corrigan's house briefly appeared in her mind. The commission on that sale would be enough to get her to Paris where romantic things happened all the time.

Penny felt as if she must have melted away twenty pounds in the day's heat. Normally, that would have left her dragging, but she was so pleased that she'd found a way to keep Brad away from Dorothy that even the heat wasn't bothering her. Okay, so it was a little mean to loosen the plug on the air conditioner, but she hadn't known it would get this hot today. And he was young and healthy.

She pulled open the trailer door and stopped. Cold air rushed out at her. It matched the cold clutch of fear that took hold of her stomach. She took a step inside and found Gran sitting at the computer, looking at pictures of various badges on the computer screen.

"What are you doing?" Penny asked.

The old woman didn't even glance Penny's way. "Surfing the Net. Brad showed me how."

Penny looked around. She and Gran were the only ones here. Rats. She came up behind her grandmother and watched as she flipped through some web page selling investigative equipment. Oh, great. That's all Gran needed—a source on the web to buy her stuff from. But then Penny looked closer at the computer and frowned.

"How'd the computer get that fast?" she asked.

Gran shrugged. "Brad said something was set wrong."

Brad again. Penny sank onto the corner of the desk. "Where is he, anyway?"

"Gone."

Penny's heart fluttered and she wasn't sure if it meant she was happy or sad.

"Went to see about putting his uncle's house up for sale."

"Oh." He hadn't left town yet. Not that she didn't want him to. She wouldn't be able to relax until Dorothy—

Damn. "What Realtor was he going to use?" Penny asked.

Gran frowned over her shoulder. "I don't know. Dorothy, I would imagine. Why?"

"Oh, no reason." She took a deep breath, hoping her agitation didn't show in her eyes or voice. "Hey, I just remembered a call I forgot to make. I'll be back in a little while."

She hurried out the door and back into her truck, putting it in gear and squealing out toward the road. Damn that Brad Corrigan. She should have known he would manage to spend time with Dorothy somehow. Damn her own belief that she was smart enough to trick him. She had never managed to get the better of him and never would.

She turned a corner, then hit the brakes as she saw the flashing lights at the railroad crossing ahead. Double damn. A train, and at a crossing that sometimes got blocked for an hour. She picked up her cell phone and dialed Dorothy's number.

"Chesterton Realtors."

"Hi, Nancy. Is Dorothy in?"

"That you, Penny?" Nancy asked. "She's on the other line. Want to wait?"

"Sure." Not much Penny could do unless the train—which turned out to be a slow-moving freight—suddenly sped up. "Hot enough for you?"

"I hope you're not wearing high heels."

"Ah, I'm working," Penny said. "So I'm wearing my boots."

"You know my sister-in-law Jenny?" Nancy continued. "She was walking across the grocery store parking lot and got her heel stuck in the asphalt. Twisted her ankle real bad and has to use crutches."

"That's too bad."

"It could be worse. Jenny's mad because it's her right ankle and it hurts too much for her to drive. She has to get other people to drive her around."

"Sounds like a bummer," Penny said. "I wouldn't—"

Wait! What a perfect idea!

"Oh, Dorothy just hung up," Nancy told her. "I'll put you through."

"And I just remembered something," Penny said quickly. "I gotta run. I'll call Dorothy later."

She put the truck into gear and made a U-turn, heading for the drugstore on the south side of town. An elastic bandage, some crutches, a pained look on her face, and she'd be all set. A sprained ankle was perfect, absolutely perfect!

"So, did you peek in his windows?" Aunty Em asked.

Brad sighed and concentrated on slicing the tomatoes for the salad. "No, I didn't look in Alex's windows," he said. "I didn't want to get arrested. I figured that would slow up the investigation."

"Yeah, you're right," the old lady said. "But you could go through his garbage. That's not illegal."

Brad ignored the suggestion. "You know, it's just possible that he has nothing to hide," he remarked.

"Baloney. Everybody's got something to hide."

Everybody? Did she think he was hiding something? Brad heard the pickup come up the lane. "Here's Penny now."

He put the salad on the table as he went to the screen door to look out.

"About time," Aunty Em grumbled as she pulled the broiler pan out of the oven. "Tell her to get her butt in here for dinner if she wants to eat before her meeting."

Penny had pulled the pickup to a stop, but was slow in getting out. He frowned and went out onto the porch. Maybe she was tired. It had been awfully hot today. Maybe she— Good gracious, she was on crutches!

"What happened?" he demanded as he hurried down the steps.

"Just a little accident," she said with a laugh as she closed the truck door and hobbled along. "I twisted my ankle."

The screen door banged behind him. "Penny!" Aunty Em cried. "Are you all right?"

"I'm fine," she assured them.

Her smile was bright, but Brad could see the effort it was taking to maneuver the crutches. And it hurt him.

"There's an easier way to do this," he said and took the crutches from her, leaning them against the truck while supporting her with one arm. Then he swung her up into his arms.

"This isn't necessary," she protested. "I can use the crutches."

"You need to rest that ankle," he said.

She felt so good in his arms, not heavy at all. It was like carrying silk. Or flowers. Or fire. A certain warmth ate at him. He carried her up onto the porch, through the kitchen door Aunty Em was holding open, and set her down in a chair.

And took a deep breath to ease the tension out of his heart.

"Mmm. Dinner smells good," she said. "Just let me wash up—"

"Just you sit there," he said. "I'll get your crutches and bring you into the bathroom."

. She frowned at him as she tried to stand. "You'll do no such thing."

"Stop arguing, Penny," Aunty Em said. "Brad, you go get the crutches. I'll keep her here."

Brad hurried out into the yard, grabbed up the crutches and went back up the steps. He should have gone with her in the truck today instead of staying in the office and then stopping in to see Dorothy about the house. If he had been with Penny, this wouldn't have happened.

"I'm not helpless," she was saying to Aunty Em. "I don't think I'm going to be able to drive for a few days, but I can move around the house."

"Of course, you can't drive," Brad said and leaned the crutches against the wall. "You shouldn't do anything but rest. At least over the weekend."

"I don't need to rest for two days," she said. "I'm fine."

"You're not fine." He bent down and picked her up again. The fire came back, harder and stronger, but he denied its presence. This was about helping, not wanting. "This bathroom okay, or do you want to use the one upstairs?"

"How about the one in the next county?" she said, trying for a sarcastic sugary sweetness but falling short. "I hope you aren't planning on staying in there with me."

"I can if you want," he said.

"I don't."

"Penny, be nice," Aunty Em scolded. "We're lucky Brad is here to help us."

"I know, I know." She did manage a smile. "And I have a big big favor to ask him."

He put her down just inside the bathroom door. "Whatever you want," he said. "You should know that."

She leaned against the doorpost, looking both frail and amazingly fit. "I wondered if you could drive me to my meeting tonight?"

"You're not thinking of going?" Aunty Em argued. "For goodness' sake, you can miss one and the festival won't collapse."

But Brad just looked at her eyes, at the soft green that did the craziest things to his knees. And at the stubbornness in her jaw that said if he didn't drive her, she'd try to drive herself. "Sure," he said. "I'd be happy to."

"And can you drive me around on the job tomorrow?" she asked.

There was a little tremor of worry and hope in her voice that tied his stomach up in knots. "You really ought to stay off that ankle," he forced himself to say.

"The more you use it, the longer it'll take to heal," Aunty Em added.

Penny's eyes got watery and her lip trembled as she looked up at him. "We just have so much work because of the storm," she said. "And the money will go a long way toward getting Gran's other hip fixed."

"Land sakes, girl, I told you I don't want them messing with my other hip. Give me a chance to get used to the one they just fixed."

But Brad barely heard the old woman. All he heard was the need in Penny's voice and the way it made his heart pound loud enough to drown out his better judgment. "I'll drive you as long as you need me to," he said. "A few days. A few weeks. A few months."

Penny smiled and straightened up enough to close the door. "You're such a sweetie. I'll feel so much better with you right next to me."

Why did he feel then that he was suddenly in danger?

Chapter Six

After an hour or so of Aunty Em's and Brad's fussing, Penny was ready to confess. She didn't think she could stand one more sigh from Aunty Em or one more scurry to help from Brad. If she wasn't doing this for such a good cause—getting Dorothy and Toto together—she would have caved in, just to save her sanity.

But she soon realized there were other—worse—threats to her sanity. Like riding into town with Brad that evening.

He was so gentle and so concerned, it tore at her heart. First she felt like a rat for pulling this trick on him, and just about the time she convinced herself she'd had no choice—and that it was his own fault for coming back with designs on Dorothy—Penny began to wonder what it would be like to have someone care about her like this for real.

All in all, she'd never had a more depressing ride into town and when Brad pulled her truck into a handicapped spot in the library parking lot, she was ready for a fight.

"You can't park here," she snapped.

"You're handicapped."

"I am not. And I don't have a permit to use this space."

"What do you think those crutches say?" he argued. His voice was all patient, which annoyed her even further. "While you're using them, you're *permitted* to park here."

Damn. Since when had he taken sensitivity training? No, that was unfair. He'd always been kind. "Just move the truck," she said wearily.

"Why do you have to be so stubborn?" Still gentle, but not quite as patient.

"Whose truck is this?"

"Yours." Definitely not patient anymore.

"And who has an extra set of keys in her pocket and can park it anywhere she chooses once you get out?"

"You."

"Then would you—" she put a heavy emphasis on the *you* "—quit being stubborn and move this damn truck like I told you to?"

With nothing either gentle or patient in his actions, he put the car in gear and, tires squealing, drove it to an open spot in the middle of the lot.

"How's this?" he asked.

"Wonderful."

He turned off the ignition and got out of the truck, while she opened her door and climbed awkwardly out. He'd better not even think about—

"Here." He was around at her side and ducking down to pick her up. "Let me—"

She whacked him with her crutch.

"What did you do that for?" he asked, rubbing his shoulder. "Man, I can see why you didn't get the part of Tiny Tim when we put on *A Christmas Carol* in fifth grade."

She just glared at him and made her way slowly across the lot. It was bad enough that she'd had to trick him into being with her. She wasn't going to let him wait on her, too.

"My goodness, Penny." An elderly man came hurrying over as they neared the door to the building. "What happened?"

"Nothing serious, Mr. Mayberry. I just twisted my ankle."

"You poor dear." The man hurried around them and opened the door for Penny. "Here you are, struggling with those crutches, while a big, strapping, young man is walking along beside you, doing nothing."

Brad just grunted under his breath, doubling Penny's guilt. It wasn't enough that she had tricked him, now others were thinking poorly of him.

"It's okay," Penny assured the old man slowly. "Really it is. I'm fine."

"You're so lucky that this didn't happen before that television interview of yours," he added.

Penny didn't comment, not sure how a sprained ankle would affect her speaking ability and not sure she wanted to know. They went down the hall and into the meeting room, passing a table of refreshments near the door.

"Want some iced tea?" Brad asked.

"Yes, thank you," she said. "That would be great."

She hobbled around the table to her regular place at the head. These crutches were awful. She wasn't sure she was going to last a couple of hours on them, let alone a couple of days. Sinking gratefully into her chair, she slipped her crutches under the table.

"Pen, what happened?"

Penny looked up and her heart sank into her toes. Dorothy.

"What are you doing here?" Penny asked. Her voice was as weak and wobbly as her ankle was supposed to be. All this to keep Brad safely with her, and they had to run into Dorothy anyway!

"Cross committee reports," Dorothy said. Her frown said something had been amiss in Penny's tone. "I've got the report from the parade committee to give you guys."

"Oh." Penny tried to make her voice all bubbly. "Great. I forgot we were due for the other reports tonight."

Dorothy looked up, sending a bright smile over Penny's shoulder. "Hi, Brad," she said. "I didn't know you were coming tonight."

"I hadn't planned on it." He put a glass of tea down in front of Penny, then put an arm briefly around Dorothy's waist. "But when I heard you were going to be here tonight I decided wild horses couldn't keep me away."

Dorothy laughed.

"Can I get you some tea, too?" he asked as he stepped away from her.

Dorothy took his arm with an intimate smile. "Yes, you may, but only if I can come with you. I want to ask you something."

Penny could do nothing but just stare as Dorothy and Brad walked toward the front of the room, arm in arm. Damn and double damn. Stuck with this stupid masquerade, she couldn't even go down and make it a threesome.

"Isn't that sweet?"

Penny turned. Nancy Abbott, the receptionist in Dorothy's office, had sat down next to her, a sappy smile on her face as she watched Brad and Dorothy at the refreshment table.

"I thought something was going on when I saw them this afternoon," she said. "I'm so happy for Dorothy."

Penny just watched the happy couple, a sinking feeling in the pit of her stomach. "I always thought Dorothy would end up with Toto."

"Not like Toto hasn't had his chances," Nancy remarked. "And Brad is just so perfect for her."

Was he? Or was Dorothy going to be hurt? Brad had told Penny that he was a loner, that he wasn't looking for a relationship. Maybe it was even more important to protect Dorothy.

But just how could she do that?

As Brad drove home he listened to the sound of the tires on the county road and breathed in the cool night air. It was relaxing, refreshing. All around them it was still, with just the occasional house light to remind him they weren't totally alone. About as far from Los Angeles as one could get and still be on this planet.

Penny was quiet, too. Almost too quiet. He turned onto a

smaller road, the headlights sweeping the cornfields for a moment before returning to bathe the blacktop. Two racoons scurried across the road up ahead, but he felt no answering smile from Penny. He felt the need to help her find it.

"I was glad somebody brought a copy of your TV interview to the meeting so I could see it myself," he said, drenching his voice in enthusiasm. "You did great."

"Thanks."

She sounded quiet, tired. Brad tightened his hold on the steering wheel. He should have made her skip that meeting tonight. Her ankle was probably aching and she needed distraction from the pain.

"And to have the clip included in a nationally syndicated show on festivals was really great," he added. "You're getting good coverage for the festival."

"Yeah," she said staring blankly out the window.

Well, that sure cheered her up. Maybe she was worried about all the work she had to do cleaning up the storm damage. Not that she needed to. He would take care of that, too.

"And I'll bet that coverage will bring in the donations. Heck, I wouldn't be surprised if someone wasn't writing a check for the Boys and Girls Club float right this very minute."

"I hope so," Penny said. "I can't believe that their sponsor backed out at this late date. The kids must be so heartbroken. They've always had a Munchkin float."

"And they will this year, too. I'll bet my last dollar on it."

She just sighed and stared out the window. Her obvious worry concerned him. He needed to hear her laughter, to feel her smile in the air.

"So, what do you say?" he continued. "Want to place a bet?"

"I don't think so."

"Ah, you're either chicken," he challenged, "or just bowing to my superior psychic skills."

"Neither," she said. A little of her normal spirit had come back into her voice. "I just don't bet on things that are out of our control."

But this wasn't. Did he tell her that or just send in the donation? He had wanted her to notice how he'd changed, but she hadn't yet. And maybe wouldn't. But still, telling her he would give the money seemed too much like bragging.

"What do you bet on?" he asked. "Sure things? That's not really betting, you know."

He could feel her bristle with annoyance and feel her glaring at him, but he just kept his eyes on the road.

"Have you ever been tempted by a long-term relationship?" she asked.

He glanced her way, startled by the sudden change of topic, but he was unable to read anything in the air around her. What had brought this up? Her voice had a quiet serious note in it that said this was not an idle question.

"Not really," he said slowly. He hated these questions that popped up literally out of the darkness. If he knew what she was upset about, he'd know how to answer. "I just don't want to share the things you have to share in a long-term relationship."

"You mean, you haven't ever told your feelings to anyone?" she asked. "You've never once found somebody you wanted to open yourself up to?"

"Nope."

"But you date," she said.

"Yeah." He wasn't sure where this was heading.

"So, you always know going in that it's only temporary?"

He slowed down to turn into her driveway. "Yeah. I know. But it's not like I keep it a secret," he said. He eased the truck over the gravelly bumps. "I never pretend otherwise."

"But people still could get hurt," she said.

"I guess." Damn, he wished he knew where this was heading. "But I don't normally stay around long, just so that won't happen."

"It's not always a question of time," she noted.

"True. So I'm careful. You'd be surprised how many women aren't interested in long-term, either."

"Maybe they've been hurt before."

"Or seen others who've been hurt."

"Or just like the solitude."

"Or have things they want to do before they settle down."

For some reason, the conversation died at that point. Maybe it was because he was pulling up to the house, or maybe it was just weariness catching up with her. He turned off the motor.

"I'll come around and help you," he said.

"I'm fine, really," she said and was halfway out the door by the time he got around. "My ankle really doesn't hurt much at all."

"Okay."

He let her go, just watching as she walked across the yard and up the steps. Something about her said he should give her space and he was not going to violate that, even though being pushed aside hurt. She went into the house and after the screen door banged shut, he heard muffled voices.

Turning away, he walked into the shadows of the oak tree by the old barn. The yard was dark where the lights from the porch and the house couldn't reach, and he felt himself relax. It had been a long few days. In some unexplainable way, he'd felt under siege and welcomed the chance to catch his breath.

It was so strange to be back in Chesterton. Sometimes it felt as if he'd never left. Other times, he felt like a stranger. Sometimes he wanted to try to push back time and remember the friendships they used to have. Other times, the past was stifling and today was freedom. The world was at his feet.

He sank down onto the old concrete bench and breathed in the cool night air. In it were all the smells of the growing earth, the rain in days past and the promise of warmth of tomorrow. If he looked up between the branches of the tree, he could see a sprinkling of stars across the night sky.

"You see that star over there?" Penny said. *She'd been sitting on the fence between the daylilies and the irises, her feet on the lower rail as her eyes gazed up at the night sky. "The really bright one? That's the wishing star. Anything you wish on it, you'll get."*

"Oh yeah?" He didn't bother to look at it, but went on

reeling in the hose. He was well acquainted with that star; he wished on it nightly from his bedroom window, and so far it hadn't produced a thing for him.

"Don't you believe in wishes?" she asked.

What could he say? That he'd wished for weeks, months, years even that she'd like him? That he'd wished for aeons to find clever words to win a smile from her? Yet she still saw him only as the kid who helped her dad and he still had no witty words to change that.

"I don't think wishing's going to get my chores done," was all he said.

She jumped down from the fence. "You're such an old grouch," she accused. "Someday you're going to want to make a really big wish and you're not going to know how." She stomped off into the barn and the night had gotten that much darker.

Brad got to his feet and walked slowly back to the house. He was too old to make wishes now, and too smart. Wishes wouldn't keep—

His foot struck something near the bushes along the drive and he bent down to see what it was. By the light from the porch, he pulled the old birdhouse from under the shrubs. It must have fallen from the oak tree during the storm the other night. Its roof was loose and the base was cracked.

As he touched it, the roof came off in his hand and on the inside, on the sheltered part of the wood, he could see writing. His heart faltered. It was the poem he'd written for Penny before he'd moved away. He'd used the most romantic thing he could find—a waterproof marker that would keep the words there forever.

He'd lied a few minutes ago to Penny. He had opened his heart to someone. And now if he didn't get out of town soon, everyone might be reminding him of that fact.

Carrying the birdhouse with him, he ducked into the barn and tucked it back behind some old tools on a shelf near the door. The tools looked like they had been there for centuries, and with luck, would be there another several before anyone found the birdhouse.

Brad awoke with the birds and stared for a moment at the clock, all bleary-eyed. Damn, but he was having a hard time sleeping in Chesterton. Maybe he needed smog and traffic noises around the clock to sleep.

He swung his feet out of bed and grabbed a pair of shorts from the chair, then slipped his feet into shoes. If Penny and Aunty Em had been considerate enough to go to bed at a decent hour last night, he wouldn't have to be sneaking outside this morning.

He grabbed his cell phone, then opened the bedroom door. The house was still. Moving quietly, he went down the stairs, and through the kitchen. Einstein met him at the door with a meow that seemed to echo through the house.

"Jeez, will you be quiet?" Brad whispered and let the cat out.

Einstein followed Brad across the yard and into the tree lot. Far enough from the house that there was no danger of being overheard in case Penny or Aunty Em had woken up. He dialed a number, then waited as it rang and rang and rang. Finally a sleepy voice answered.

"Hey, George," Brad said. "Rise and shine, big guy."

Brad knew that it was just a little past 2:00 a.m. in California, but this was the best time for a private talk with his attorney.

"Brad? Where the hell are you?" George Escarta asked. "In some damn zoo?"

"I'm in the middle of a field in Indiana."

"Sounds like a zoo to me."

"Did you get the report on Alex Waterstone for me?" Brad asked.

"Nothing there," George said. "Hardly any assets, but measly debts, no criminal history, not even a traffic ticket."

"Married or divorced?"

"Neither unless it was in a foreign country."

"Damn. I was hoping he'd been featured in some *Worldwide News* exposé or something."

"We can always plant something, if you'd like," George offered. "All it takes is money and you've got too much of that as it is."

Brad was tempted, but then sighed. "No. I've got to play this straight. If he's a saint, he's a saint. I have something else for you to do."

"Your word is my command."

"I want you to drop, oh—something like five thousand dollars—to the Chesterton *Wizard of Oz* festival committee—"

"I presume that's in the continental United States?"

"Shut up and listen," Brad said.

"You know it's two in the morning out here?"

"Yeah, and I'm sure you're charging me time and a half for the off-hours service. Wire five thou to this festival committee. And indicate the funds are to be used for a float for the Boys and Girls Club. Anything left over is to be used by the club for general program expenses."

"I'll get on it first thing. Uh, they do have banks out in the zoo, don't they?"

Brad closed his eyes with a sigh. "Yeah, but I bet they're closed until next week. Well, get it in the works and it'll be here Monday morning."

"You get your uncle's stuff taken care of?"

Brad opened his eyes and frowned at the brightening sky. "Not quite."

"Well, I've got Mainline America crying for you to fix their network—and offering enough to make your mother faint— and Technology Unlimited doubled their contract offer and added a bonus that would make my mother faint. And she's a tougher sell than yours."

"Tell them I'm busy."

"For how long? And ISCPP wants to know if you're coming to the conference or not. I would guess you won that award and they want you there in person."

"I don't know yet."

''You don't know? What the hell is going on there? This is your life you're putting on hold.''

''I'll get back to you,'' he said and broke the connection just as Einstein rubbed himself against Brad's legs. He bent down and picked the cat up. ''You ready to go back inside, little fella?''

''Okay, now this side.'' Dorothy moved to the far wall of the living room.

Penny limped with her end of the tape measure to the corner by the fireplace, her crutches abandoned at home. She hadn't been on them more than five minutes this morning and she'd discovered about ten million blisters and that the muscles under her arms felt as if they were on fire. The only thing that hadn't hurt was her supposedly injured ankle. If that wasn't poetic justice she didn't know what was.

''I shouldn't be here,'' she said. ''I'm not a real estate agent.''

''Brad won't care. And I can't measure these rooms by myself.''

Penny held the tape measure in place, then let go as Dorothy wrote the measurement down in her notebook. They were in Hal Corrigan's old house, measuring and making notes for Dorothy's real estate listing, but Penny was feeling out of sorts. She should have been working, even though it was Saturday. They still had storm damage to clean up, but it was raining again so the jobs had been rescheduled for Monday.

When Dorothy had called and suggested they join Heather for lunch, Penny jumped at the chance. Maybe this was the way to keep Dorothy safe—stay with Dorothy, not Brad. She did feel a little funny about stopping at Brad's uncle's house first, though. It felt almost like prying.

''This is such a great old place,'' Dorothy observed as she walked back into the foyer. ''It's a little run-down but not bad.''

Penny looked around. Obviously a service had been called to pack up the house after Hal's death. The furniture had been covered and the personal items packed into boxes and labeled. Even with the disarray the place had appeal. High ceilings. Carved woodwork. Brass light fixtures.

"Remember how we thought this was the perfect staircase," Dorothy said, her hand on the carved oak banister as she looked up the sweeping stairs. "I think we all dreamed of coming down it in our wedding dresses and making a grand entrance."

Penny remembered those days of hoping and wishing so hard that her stomach hurt. Of riding her bike blocks out of her way so she could pass by the house, hoping for a glimpse of Brad and yet terrified that he might see her and somehow know the truth. She had never progressed to dreams about the staircase, though.

"I never did," she replied. "Didn't seem much point since none of us lived in the house."

"Dreams shouldn't be tied into reality," Dorothy said. "That's always been your problem, Penny. You're too realistic."

The dumbest kid in class falling for the smartest one was realistic? More like proof of how dumb she really was. But she didn't want to go there. It was time to put those thoughts aside.

"Maybe we should buy the house and rent it out for weddings," Penny said lightly. "The rooms upstairs could be used by the bride to get ready. The wedding could be held in the living room and the reception in the gardens outside."

"What fun that would be!" Dorothy agreed and stepped back from the stairs with a dreamy look in her eyes. "I bet it would get booked up in a hurry and then the house would be a happy place again."

Penny's eyes widened. "Are you serious?"

Dorothy stepped back, the dreamy look gone from her face. "Me? Heavens, no. I think it's a great idea but I couldn't do it. I'm not even going to be here."

"You're not? Where are you going?"

"Paris, remember?" She took a last look around and then headed for the front door. "Ready?"

"Sure." Penny waited while Dorothy locked up the front

door, then they walked down the brick walkway to her car. Paris was no real threat. Dorothy had been talking about Paris for years now and the closest she'd ever gotten was using French dressing on her salad.

"So, where are we meeting Heather?" Penny asked.

"The Landing."

"Ooh, I'm leaving room for strawberry shortcake."

It was only a few minutes' drive to the restaurant. Heather was waiting at a table in the porch dining room, overlooking Lake Palomara. Penny felt her heart lighten as they approached her. This was just like old times.

"What happened to your ankle?" Heather asked as Penny sat down.

Her good spirits dimmed just a little. "Oh, I sprained it slightly yesterday. It's almost healed."

Heather frowned. "Sprains take a couple of weeks to heal up."

Penny just picked up the menu and began to scan the familiar items. "I don't have a couple of weeks to spare."

"Maybe you shouldn't have sprained it, then," Dorothy remarked.

Penny glanced her way. Dorothy couldn't know it was all a fake, could she? But Dorothy was just reading her own menu, nothing but indecision on her face. Penny was just overly sensitive.

"I'll remember that the next time I'm thinking of spraining something," she said lightly.

After they placed their orders, they settled back for a cozy chat. Penny'd thought she needed to warn Dorothy not to take Brad seriously but maybe she didn't need to. In the hour she and Dorothy had been together, Dorothy hadn't mentioned him.

"Is Brad still at your house?" Heather asked.

Penny glanced Dorothy's way but saw nothing to worry her. "For a few more days. He seems anxious to go. Guess he's got a life elsewhere." Still no real reaction.

"I would hope so," Heather said. "It would be pretty sad if he didn't."

Penny took a quick peek at Dorothy as she went on. "He might even have a true love waiting for him."

Dorothy wrinkled her nose. "I doubt that." She leaned forward with a smug kind of smile. "I think that he really cared about somebody back here when we were growing up and still might."

Penny felt her stomach clutch. "Heavens, we all had crushes back then but we've outgrown them."

"Have we?" Dorothy asked with that same little smile. "I know I have, but I'm not so sure about some others."

Penny was torn between worry and relief. Dorothy wasn't pining for Brad. That was good news. But that Brad might still be pining for Dorothy wasn't. Would Dorothy be able to remain unaffected by his attention? Penny thought of his gentle smile, his fiery touch, the way he was there to lean on. How could Dorothy not fall in love with him? How could any woman resist?

"Ladies, hello."

Penny looked up to find Toto at their table. "Hi," she said quickly, mixing her greeting in with the others. "Want to join us?"

He shook his head and turned to Dorothy. "Just saw your car in the lot and thought I'd stop in and say hi."

Penny bit at her lip to keep from smiling. Finally, he was going to pursue Dorothy. Dorothy, however, showed no emotion.

"Hi, Toto," was all she said. "How are you?"

He let his gaze take in them all. "You ladies going to the concert in the park tonight? It's supposed to stop raining by then."

"Not me," Heather replied. "The bugs will be terrible."

"I might," Penny said. "Gran was talking about wanting to go. What about you, Dorothy?"

She shrugged. "I don't know. I got some new tapes in the mail today and I was planning to listen to them."

"Oh, come on," Penny coaxed. "You can listen to tapes

any day. This will be fun.'' She turned to Toto. ''Can you get there early and save us a spot?''

''I'll be glad to,'' he said, his eyes going back to Dorothy. ''Should I save one for you, too?''

Penny held her breath. It seemed as if Dorothy hesitated forever.

''Sure, why not?'' she finally agreed. ''If the bugs are really bad, I can always leave early.''

Hardly an enthusiastic reply, but Toto didn't look upset. ''See you tonight, then,'' he said before taking off.

Their lunches arrived, giving Penny the chance to think undisturbed for a few minutes. It shouldn't be too hard to maneuver to give Dorothy and Toto some time alone. Of course if Brad was around, she'd have to work at keeping him occupied.

The main thing was to let Dorothy and Toto have time to discover their love. So she would make sure Brad was kept busy, even if she had to lock her lips to his.

She smiled down at her chicken salad. That might just be a perfect idea.

''More wine?'' Junior whined in answer and Toto frowned at his dog, who was lying on the blanket with him and Dorothy. ''No, not you. I was talking to Dorothy.''

But Dorothy shook her head. ''Gracious, no. I'm not done with what you poured for me already.'' She looked around with an audible sigh. ''I wonder where Penny and Brad are.''

Was it Penny she was looking for or Brad? Toto didn't dare look at her, but put the wine bottle back in the basket of food he'd brought, securely closing both against Junior. Maybe it had been a mistake to suggest this evening at the park, but he'd gotten a book from the library about women and it had said women liked concerts. It didn't cover what to do when the woman kept looking for some other guy, though.

He looked up at the sound of Dorothy smacking a mosquito that had landed on her arm. Junior dove for the wine that had splashed out of her glass and onto her leg.

"Junior," he snapped and the dog pulled back with a pout. No, this definitely wasn't turning out as the book had predicted.

"I've got some bug spray in my car." Toto got to his feet. "I'll go get it."

"Would you? What a sweetie you are." But her voice was distracted and her eyes were back to searching the crowd.

Toto just trudged around the groups spread out on blankets on the grass and in lawn chairs waiting for the concert to start. If he thought for a minute that Dorothy really considered him a sweetie, he'd be in heaven, but he knew better. Dorothy barely even saw him anymore.

"Hey, Toto!" a friend from the police force called.

"Hey," he called back and waved.

"Junior here?" someone else called. "Maybe we'd better lock up the beer."

Toto just smiled and waved and kept on walking to the car. He had lots of friends, there was no doubt about that, but he spent most of his evenings feeling lonely.

Still, he was not going to stand in the way of Dorothy's dreams. If moving to Paris was going to make her happy, then he'd drive her to airport.

He stopped walking suddenly. And what if marrying Brad Corrigan was going to make her happy?

He forced himself to start walking again, though it felt like a death march. Nothing had changed. Right was right. And if marrying Brad Corrigan would make Dorothy happy, then Toto would give her away at the altar.

Toto reached his car on that grim note and opened the trunk to get the insect repellant from a bag in the back. The sound of laughter made him turn. There in the corner of the parking lot, walking from her parked truck, were Penny and Brad. And Penny was draped all over Brad as if she couldn't walk on her own.

Toto just watched for a long long moment, then closed his trunk quietly. Thank goodness he'd found out how things really stood.

Brad was about as trustworthy as Junior with an open can

of beer. He'd make a play for whatever woman was handy, never mind who might get hurt.

Toto took a deep breath. He would talk to Penny and warn her, but his real concern was for Dorothy. Poor innocent naive Dorothy who wouldn't have an idea how to handle such a snake. He was going to have to protect her.

Chapter Seven

"Are you sure you can walk all right on this grass?" Brad asked. "I don't want you twisting your ankle again."

"I'm fine."

Penny held his arm tightly as they walked between the people milling about in Centennial Park. Well, Brad walked, she limped. But the last thing she needed was for Brad to decide to carry her. Throwing herself at him was one thing, having him sweep her off her feet was another. She was going to stay in control.

"You probably shouldn't have given up your crutches so soon," he advised.

"I'm fine, really," she replied a bit sharply. "Though another remark like that and I'll wish I had them to hit you with."

"Guess you must be feeling better," he said. "You would never have given up a weapon unless you felt strong enough to take me on without one."

Jeez, she had to watch her tongue. No more smart-aleck remarks. She leaned in a little closer and gave him a seductive smile. "Maybe I'm not in the mood for weapons tonight."

His dark eyes got a bit darker and he looked a little...odd. She wasn't sure if he was uncomfortable or puzzled or what. Damn. She wished she could read him better. It was probably surprise, that was all. She hadn't been falling all over him for the past few days so it was going to take him a little time to get used to the idea.

"Is that Dorothy up ahead?" he asked.

Penny looked up and saw her friend waving from under the trees ahead. She waved back, taking a deep breath. This evening could be tricky, depending on Dorothy's reaction. Hopefully, she wouldn't get upset.

"She looks like she's by herself," Brad observed. "I thought you said Toto was going to be here."

Oh, no, if Dorothy was alone, Brad would pay attention to both of them. How would she ever keep him distracted then?

"Oh, wait. I see Junior," she said. What a relief. "Toto must be here somewhere."

They wove around a family in lawn chairs and joined Dorothy and Junior. A picnic basket lay on the blanket along with two glasses, so Toto had to be around. Penny could have danced with joy, though that probably would call her injured ankle into question.

"Hi," Dorothy said and took the cooler from Brad's hand. "Didn't Aunty Em come?"

"Turned out Sam Spade was on cable tonight. Hi, Junior." Penny let Brad help her down onto the blanket, then smiled at him as she settled, giving his hand a squeeze. "Thanks. I'm afraid I'm such a burden. I should have stayed home with Gran."

"Don't be silly," Brad scolded as he sat down next to Penny—on the side away from Dorothy. Yes! "We don't mind, do we, Dorothy?"

Dorothy was watching Penny with a strange look in her eyes, her smile sly and speculative. "Not at all," she assured Penny. "We're happy your sprained ankle isn't keeping you home."

Penny had the feeling that Dorothy knew exactly what Penny was doing, but Penny didn't let that stop her. She gave her friend a bright smile. "This is a great spot. Where's Toto?"

"Right here." Toto sat down between Dorothy and Junior, handing Dorothy a tube of insect repellant. "Glad you both could make it."

Toto's voice was a touch cool, probably from worry over Brad being here at the same time as Dorothy, but Penny would show him he had no reason to fret. She took Brad's hand in hers.

"Remember how we used to laugh about these free concerts when we were kids?" she asked Brad. "We couldn't imagine anything more boring than sitting around on the grass listening to old music."

"Guess we've grown up," he said.

"In lots of ways." She let her voice be soft and ripe with meaning.

"Want some wine?"

Toto sounded rather sharp and she turned to him in surprise. "Sure. We brought some snacks, too. Gran sent some brownies and we picked up some chicken wings."

"Oh, I love Aunty Em's brownies," Dorothy said.

While Toto poured glasses of wine, Dorothy reached over to open the cooler and take out the dish of brownies. She offered one to Toto who took it grudgingly and then to Penny and Brad. She started to put it down in front of her, then frowned at Junior.

"Chocolate's bad for you, Junior. You're supposed to have dog cookies." She looked over at Toto. "Didn't you bring any cookies for him?"

Toto looked about as impatient as Penny had ever seen him look, which wasn't all that bad considering Toto normally had the patience of a saint.

"I have some in the car," he told her.

"Good." Dorothy got to her feet and pulled Toto up to his. "Let's go get them."

Toto's impatience vanished in the blink of an eye. "Okay."

He looked astonished, mesmerized. Like a man who'd just been granted his fondest wish. "Come on, Junior."

Penny watched them leave with a smile, but then turned to find Brad watching her. Her smile sagged. Some time alone with him was just what she wanted, just what she needed to further her plan. Yet the look in his eyes made her nervous. Made her stomach tie up in knots and her mouth go dry.

"Sure is nice weather," she said, then wanted to groan. That was hardly seductive conversation. "But even a storm can be nice with the right company."

"Speaking of the right company," he said. "I'm surprised you weren't coming here with Alex."

Alex? Why had Brad brought him up? Penny inched a little closer to Brad and sipped at her wine. "Alex doesn't come to these things."

"Not intellectual enough for him?"

She shrugged. "He just doesn't." She reached over and traced a soft line along his jaw. "Why do you want to talk about Alex?"

"I don't," he said and with a muffled groan, pulled her hand away, but kept a tight hold of it.

The band was starting to warm up and she was grateful for the slight distraction to catch her breath. She was doing great. Better than she had dreamed, though her heart was racing and her cheeks felt warm. Brad probably thought her blush was due to his nearness or the touch of his hand. But it was from the thrill of her success and the warm summer air. She was immune to Brad Corrigan's charm.

Toto and Dorothy and Junior came back just as the concert was starting. They settled themselves on the blanket, but off to one side. Penny relaxed and let the music swell around her, concentrating on just enjoying the old show tunes that the band was playing.

Except that she kept losing track of them. First it was Brad's hand on hers that kept distracting her. Then it was the touch of his thigh against hers when he shifted position slightly. She should have worn jeans instead of shorts. He should have worn jeans, too. And a sweatshirt so his arm wouldn't jolt her with electricity each time it brushed against her.

A brownie and some chicken wings brought her sanity back, but then it left again, blown away by his breath on her neck when he leaned close to ask her if she wanted more wine. Wine was the last thing she needed when her wits seemed to be scattered, but she agreed to some anyway, then sat sipping it and counting the number of times Brad accidentally touched her. Ten. Twenty. Fifty. She forgot how to count, too.

Suddenly the concert was over, much to Penny's relief, though she wasn't sure how it got to be almost eleven. Her confusion had to be because of the night air. Or too many saxophones in the band. Or Junior's flea soap. Once she got away from here, she would be fine.

"Gee, this was fun," Penny said brightly as she got to her feet. "We'll have to do it again. When's the next concert?"

"In two weeks, I think," Toto said. He and Dorothy folded up the blanket.

"What a shame," Penny said. "Brad'll be gone by then."

"Who knows where any of us will be?" Dorothy's voice was offhanded.

"True," Brad agreed. "Maybe I'll come back for it."

"Wouldn't that be great?" Penny packed up their cooler, her heart smiling while her brain froze in horror. This was a short-term plan. One to distract him for the few days he had left here.

"Sure," Toto said. "Just like you've come back for all our reunions and festivals."

They all laughed with him, though Penny's did have more relief than humor in it. She was worrying for nothing. Brad wouldn't come back. He was here for a few days and then they would never see him again.

The idea was suddenly depressing.

They walked back to their cars, Brad carrying the cooler and letting Penny lean on his arm. Toto and Junior walked ahead, with Dorothy lingering behind to talk to both groups. She hadn't seemed enamored with Brad though, Penny had to admit. Maybe she was pretending. Or maybe she had seen the light and knew Toto was perfect for her. But why then was she laughing with Brad like that?

"Want to come on over to my place?" Dorothy asked as they all stopped at Penny's truck. "We can play some Scrabble or Trivial Pursuit or something."

And remind Brad how dumb she was while giving him a chance to be awed by how smart Dorothy was? No way. "I'm pretty tired," Penny said.

"Oh, I'm sorry, Pen," Dorothy said, all apologies. "I wasn't thinking. Yeah, Brad'd better just take you on home. We'll do it some other time."

Penny just smiled and leaned a little more on Brad. "But you and Toto can still do something. I'd hate to think I broke up everybody's evening early."

"I think I'll call it a night, too," Toto said. "I've got the early shift tomorrow."

Rats. Penny let Brad help her up into the truck, then leaned out the open window while he went around to the driver's side. "What a shame. Now I feel so bad."

Dorothy just laughed and stepped away from the truck. "Take her home, Brad, before she really gets guilty and feeling maudlin."

Brad did as he was told, and pulled the truck from the parking spot. As they drove from the lot, Penny couldn't help turning to watch Dorothy and Toto walk back toward their cars. They didn't walk like lovers or even close friends. Darn. Hadn't this night accomplished anything?

"Your ankle bothering you?" Brad asked.

Her ankle? Oh, she'd almost forgotten. "A little," she said. "Not too bad."

He just looked at her, his lips in a straight forbidding line, then he turned onto Calumet Road. "I remember that time you fell from the ladder in the barn and broke your arm."

She remembered it, too. She had been watching him work on the tractor with his shirt off, his back all tanned and muscled, and her foot had slipped. "Yeah, so what?"

"You insisted you were fine, that nothing was wrong, and it turned out your arm was broken in two places. The doctor said it had to hurt like hell."

His memory was too damn good. "It was a little sore," she admitted.

"So, if your ankle is bothering you a 'little,'" he continued, "it must hurt like hell, too."

There was a big difference between that time and this one. Not that she could point that out to him. She just leaned back in her seat and watched the lights of town diminish in her side rearview mirror as they drove farther out into the country. Little by little her tensions drained away.

It was so peaceful here. She had no desire to live anywhere else. And she couldn't imagine not having a place to call home, either.

She turned to look at Brad. She couldn't really see him, except in quick flashes when another car passed them, but her heart could see him. See the loneliness that rested in his eyes in unguarded moments. That boy she had loved years back was still there, and still alone.

Brad turned the truck into the drive and Penny sighed. She wasn't sure she had accomplished anything with her ploy. Dorothy and Toto didn't look any closer and Brad was still a mystery to her.

Brad stopped the car and she slowly got out. Strangely enough she did feel tired. Almost exhausted. As if—

"Hey," she cried as Brad scooped her up into his arms. "What are you doing?"

"Taking you inside," he said though he didn't move.

"Oh, are you?"

But her arm had gone around his neck and she held him tight enough to feel that the racing of his heart matched hers. She looked up at him, so tall and strong and safe, and their eyes danced a strange and wonderful dance she'd never known before.

She had no idea how long he stood there holding her. Long enough for the moon to pass from one end of the sky to the other. Long enough for the crickets to play a dozen symphonies. Long enough for her to grow light-headed from lack of oxygen.

Then suddenly she realized they were in her room and he was gently setting her on her bed. How could he have carried her upstairs and she not have noticed?

"You okay now?" he asked.

Okay? She wanted to laugh but she didn't have the strength or the air. All she could do was nod yes.

He leaned forward then, drawn almost it seemed against his will, and lightly touched her lips with his. The heavens rocked and the earth moved. And her heart opened up to him, blossoming like a flower touched by the sun. This was what she had dreamed of in the dark lonely hours of the night—of a need so strong that reason was forgotten. Of a fire so hot it scorched all thought.

She sensed an uncertainty in him, a drawing back of his soul. Afraid his lips would follow, she slipped her arms around his neck, pulling him closer to her heart. He hesitated for a second, then slowly, almost reluctantly, his arms slid around her. For a long perfect moment, their lips whispered magic into the other's soul, their hearts soared as one and their dreams were close enough to touch. Then just as suddenly, words were forgotten and they both pulled apart. Shaken. Unsettled. Uncertain.

Brad didn't speak as he straightened up and left the room, shutting the door softly behind him. A relief, since she couldn't have answered him to save her life.

Damn. She tried to catch her breath and slow her heart. Okay, so she couldn't breathe. Or move. Or think. Or even talk. But at least, Brad hadn't mentioned Dorothy the whole ride home.

Brad slowly sat up on the edge of the bed the next morning and rubbed his eyes. What a night it had been, tossing and turning and reliving that kiss. Wanting Penny with a desperateness that defied reason.

It couldn't be just that she was beautiful—he'd been around beautiful women before and had never lost his head as he almost had last night. It wasn't just that she was nice—the world was filled with nice women whose touch never set him afire. And it couldn't be because he used to have a crush on her— he used to like marshmallow and banana sandwiches and now the thought turned his stomach.

So, what had it been? The moonlight? The music? A bug bite?

Sometime after the birds had started their predawn chorus, he'd fallen asleep but he hadn't really slept; it was more like he'd fallen into a coma for a couple of hours. Thoughts of Penny had still haunted him, but in his stupor he seemed unable to flee. Brad shook his head and pushed himself up.

Enough was enough. He had to get out of here—out of this house and out of Chesterton. He'd been back only a few days and things were getting out of hand. He was feeling like he had in high school, but with the reactions of an adult this time. Or perhaps the overreactions would be more accurate.

A chipmunk jumped onto the outside window sill and chattered at him. "Shut up before I call the cat," Brad growled, throwing a pillow toward the window.

The little rodent went squeaking off somewhere but continued its scolding. Probably Penny's guard these days. Took over when Brad had left and now wanted him gone. And rightly so. Brad had proven he wasn't to be trusted. He claimed he only wanted the best for Penny and then hadn't been able to control himself when she was near. Brad ambled over to the window and stared outside.

The rose fields were to the north of the house. Another few hours and they'd be a sea of color, light yellows to brilliant reds. Like his life felt since he'd come back here. Over to the east were the peony fields, a deep dull green. Like his life back in Los Angeles. Damn. Since when had he gotten so poetic?

He wiped his hand over his face and sighed. What was happening to him? He couldn't seem to be near Penny without his heart wanting to explode. Without his hands wanting to touch her and his lips needing to taste her. He seemed to lose all sense when she smiled at him. He had no willpower, no strength around her at all.

He should leave, but he couldn't. Not until he knew what was going on with Alex. Once he knew she wasn't being taken advantage of or about to make some big mistake, he'd go. Hopefully that would be in a day or two. Not that long of a time to be stoic. Not that long at all.

And in the meantime, he would change. He would take himself in hand and control all those urges. And he could. Maybe it wouldn't be easy, but it was possible. And necessary.

Both his attitude and steps were purposeful when he walked into the kitchen a little while later. Aunty Em was at the table, eating a bowl of chili. Einstein was in the window, giving himself a bath.

"How are you this morning?" Aunty Em asked.

"Just fine. Super."

Aunty Em raised an eyebrow at him and even Einstein turned to give him a look, but Brad ignored them both as he went to the cabinet for a bowl and some cereal. He wasn't about to let two people—or one person and one cat—derail him from his positive attitude.

"And how are you this morning?" he asked Aunty Em.

The old woman shrugged. "Tolerable. Tolerable."

Brad remembered enough of his Indianaese to know that meant as good as could be expected. He filled his bowl with cereal, poured some milk over it, then sat down.

"Looks like another hot one today," Aunty Em said, looking outside over the backyard and toward the equipment yard.

"That's summer in Indiana for you."

It didn't matter how hot it was going to be outside. He was going to stay cool. Cool enough to be unaffected around Penny and cool enough to get the goods on Alex.

"You have a nice time last night?" Aunty Em asked.

He thought of the wonder of Penny's kiss, of the heaven of holding her in his arms, of the hell his sleepless night had been. "It was okay."

The old woman snickered. "Just okay? Then why were you pacing all night?"

How could she know that? "It was rather warm," he said.

She laughed outright. "I guess. And not just for you. Penny must have been hot and bothered, too."

Brad frowned. She was getting the wrong idea. "Her ankle was probably bothering her."

Aunty Em nodded. "I'm sure that was it. Why else would she be walking around all night except that it hurt to be walking?"

Brad concentrated on eating for a long moment. His logic had been faulty, but he was sure something had been bothering her. If Penny had been pacing most of the night in spite of her sore ankle, she was fretting over something.

"Penny told me the business doesn't work on Sundays," Brad said when he finished up his breakfast. "So I thought I would take the Jeep and do a little investigating on Alex." Maybe he would just go talk to him and see what was going on. Anything to get to the bottom of this and get out of town while he could.

Aunty Em looked all too interested. "You want to bug his house?"

"Bug?" Good night. She was really into this investigating stuff. "Wouldn't that be illegal?"

She gave him a disgusted look. "For a big strong guy, you sure are a wimp. Isn't Penny more important than some legal technicalities?"

"I can hardly help her if I'm in jail," Brad drawled.

Aunty Em snorted rudely. "In jail? You only get tossed in jail if you get caught. Though on second thought, you haven't exactly proved your capability yet, have you?"

"Hey, that's not fair."

"A good PI doesn't get made on a tail."

"I never said I was a good PI," he argued. "I'm not a PI at all. I'm just all you've got."

She got slowly to her feet. "Sad how you're willing to settle for being mediocre, boy," she said and picked up her dish.

"Maybe if you were a bit better at this, Penny wouldn't've gone out to the trailer this morning to call Alex."

"She went out to the—" He stopped and scowled at the old woman. "How'd you know she called Alex? You have the phone bugged, too?" Thank goodness, he'd used his cell phone for his own calls.

"No. Penny found the ones I planted." She sighed, then she rinsed out her dish, not looking his way again until she'd put the dish in the dishwasher. "I went out to the trailer while she was showering and checked the phone. We've got a redial feature that shows the number you called last."

"And it was Alex's?"

She nodded, closed up the dishwasher and walked slowly over to the back hallway. "Maybe Penny did just have an 'okay' time last night. Maybe you're mediocre at more things than just being a PI," she said wearily. "You gonna be able to drive us to church this morning?"

For an old lady, she sure knew how to hit below the belt. "Aren't you afraid my driving will be mediocre, too?"

But she just laughed and waved over her shoulder. "Service starts at ten," she called back to him. "We need to leave by nine-forty-five."

"I'll be ready." But she was already going into her room and gave no sign she'd heard him.

Brad got to his feet and took care of his own dishes.

Mediocre? That was a laugh. If he was so mediocre, how'd he get so much money in his bank account? And why were people all over the world calling him with jobs?

But if he was so good, why had Penny rushed out to call Alex?

Penny had never sat through a church service that was so long. The pastor must have gotten his notes mixed up and was somehow preaching the sermon over and over and over again.

And it was all about love! You'd think he could have found a more original topic than that.

It didn't help that Brad was sitting right next to her in those narrow rock-hard pews. She couldn't move without brushing his thigh with hers. This stupid cotton dress was about as much protection as a breeze. And she couldn't take a breath without inhaling the scent of Brad's aftershave which would remind her of the concert last night. Which would remind her of him carrying her up to her room. Which would remind her of him kissing her. Which was not something she needed to be thinking about in church!

Thank goodness Matt Harris was coming back tomorrow and Brad would be gone by tomorrow night. Her heart didn't quite agree, but her heart was not in charge.

The service finally ended and she was free to breathe again—though only for a few moments since they'd soon be packing into the truck to go home. Why had she thought this sprained ankle was such a great idea?

"Wonderful sermon, pastor," Brad said as they walked out into the warm summer air.

"Inspirational," Penny added. She took a church bulletin and limped ahead to give Gran room.

"Beautiful day for a beautiful service," Gran told the man.

"How would you know the sermon was inspirational?" Brad leaned close and whispered to Penny. "You weren't paying attention."

"I was, too." She fanned herself with the bulletin as she waited for Gran at the top of the church steps.

"No, you weren't."

"How would you know?"

He smiled at her. "I could tell. I know you."

"Not all that well." She smiled at her grandmother and took her arm to help her down the steps. "Shouldn't be too much longer before you're through with that cane."

Gran didn't looked fooled by Penny's bright tone. "You two bickering again?"

"We weren't bickering," Penny said.

"Discussing," Brad added.

"Sure." Gran looked in front of her. "Hello there, Thomas. How are you these days?"

Penny found Toto standing at the foot of the stairs. He was in uniform, and from the serious look on his face, probably on duty.

"Morning, all," he said, then turned to Gran. "You're looking fine this bright sunny morning, ma'am. Would you mind if I steal Penny away for a minute?"

"I wouldn't, but Brad might," Gran said with a laugh. "Best not keep her too long."

Penny tried not to roll her eyes. Toto gave a weak smile, then took Penny's arm. They walked along the white clapboard building, through the iron gate and into the old churchyard. It was cool here in the shade of the massive oaks, and quiet, too. Her skirt danced lightly about her legs in the gentle breeze.

"You go back to Dorothy's last night?" Penny asked, rolling up the church bulletin. "It wasn't really that late."

Toto shook his head. The radio on his belt cackled something and he flicked a switch to stop the static. "Look, Pen, I'm not sure how to say this, but I think you need to be careful."

She frowned at him. "Of what?"

"Of Brad." He sighed, looking uncomfortable, then glanced away from her to run his fingers over the top of a weather-worn gravestone. "I'm not sure you can trust him."

Toto looked so serious, so worried, that Penny's heart sank right into her stomach. "Trust him how?"

"Oh, you know." Toto picked at the moss growing on the stone.

"Leave Ebeneezer alone," Penny said and whacked his hand with the bulletin. "Did you run some kind of check on Brad?"

He still didn't look at her, but she could tell by the sudden redness of his cheeks that he had.

"Toto, how could you!" She took a deep breath and her glance somehow fell on Brad and Gran up near the church. Dorothy had joined them and was talking animatedly. Too animatedly for Dorothy before noon. They always joked that she never woke up until after lunch. Penny turned back to Toto. "What did you find?"

"Nothing," he said. "No debts. No traffic tickets. No outstanding warrants."

Penny was relieved. "So, why shouldn't I trust him?"

Toto looked her square in the face, his mouth a tight serious line. "Because I don't think his intentions are honorable."

Penny just stared at him, trying hard not to laugh. Dear sweet Toto who lived and breathed honor and assumed everyone else did, too. She took his hand and squeezed it.

"It's okay, Toto. I have no illusions about Brad Corrigan. My heart is not involved." Oh no? Then why did it race whenever he was near? She ignored that troublesome little voice and went on. "In fact, he's probably leaving town tomorrow. Matt Harris will be back from vacation and Brad'll get the probate papers taken care of."

"Oh, yeah?" Toto looked measurably relieved. "I guess then it's all right."

"And I think you're a dear to be worried," Penny said and took his arm. They started back toward the others. "How are things going with you and Dorothy?"

"Real good," he said. "I got a book from the library."

Penny didn't quite make the connection. "A book about what?"

"About the differences between men and women."

Toto! she wanted to cry. But they were getting too close to Brad and Dorothy and Gran. "Just don't spend so much time studying that you forget to take the test," she said under her breath. "Hi, Dorothy. Didn't see you inside."

"I snuck in late," she said. "You know me and mornings. Hey, Toto, want to walk me to my car? I need to ask you something." Dorothy took his arm, then waved to the others. "See you later."

Penny watched Dorothy and Toto leave, feeling as if the sun had come out after a storm. Maybe she had accomplished something last night. Maybe Dorothy was finally seeing Toto's worth. Until she overheard Dorothy say something about not being able to take care of Junior this afternoon. This wasn't the kind of conversation Penny had wanted between them!

Maybe Dorothy wasn't in danger from Brad, but she sure wouldn't be falling for Toto, either, not unless he found a spark.

"Ready to go?" Brad asked.

Penny just nodded and walked along with him and Gran across the gravel parking lot toward the truck. The sun was suddenly oppressive instead of warming and nurturing. Darn it, anyway. Toto needed to do something besides get a book out of the library.

"We've got tomorrow all worked out," Gran was saying.

Penny woke from her thoughts as they reached her truck. "Tomorrow?" What was there to work out?

Gran nodded. "Brad's going to drive me to physical therapy and then come back and work the office for you."

"Work the office?" Penny said. "But you're—"

"Unless you want me to drive you to your jobs," he said and opened the passenger side door for her.

"I don't need you to drive," she snapped. She wanted to whack him but the church bulletin was too flimsy. "I could have driven today just fine."

"Mustn't push it, dear," Gran said.

"I'm not pushing anything," Penny assured her. "But tomorrow's Monday."

"Yes?" Both Brad and Gran were staring at her.

"Matt Harris is back in town," she stated.

Brad just shrugged. "No rush with that," he said. "When I get to it, I get to it."

"Speaking of getting," Gran said, poking Penny with her cane. "Would you get in the truck?"

Penny was too stunned to do otherwise.

The Silhouette Reader Service™ —Here's How it Works:

Accepting your 2 free books and mystery gift places you under no obligation to buy anything. You may keep the books and gift and return the shipping statement marked "cancel." If you do not cancel, about a month later we'll send you 6 additional novels and bill you just $3.57 each in the U.S., or $3.96 each in Canada, plus 25¢ delivery per book and applicable taxes if any.* That's the complete price and — compared to the cover price of $4.25 in the U.S. and $4.75 in Canada — it's quite a bargain! You may cancel at any time, but if you choose to continue, every month we'll send you 6 more books, which you may either purchase at the discount price or return to us and cancel your subscription.

*Terms and prices subject to change without notice. Sales tax applicable in N.Y. Canadian residents will be charged applicable provincial taxes and GST.

If offer card is missing write to: Silhouette Reader Service, 3010 Walden Ave., P.O. Box 1867, Buffalo, NY 14240-1867

BUSINESS REPLY MAIL
FIRST-CLASS MAIL   PERMIT NO. 717   BUFFALO, NY

POSTAGE WILL BE PAID BY ADDRESSEE

SILHOUETTE READER SERVICE
3010 WALDEN AVE
PO BOX 1867
BUFFALO NY 14240-9952

NO POSTAGE
NECESSARY
IF MAILED
IN THE
UNITED STATES

Chapter Eight

Penny just leaned back in the chair and stared at the computer screen. Sundays were about the only time she had to work on her own things, but today was certainly turning out to be a bust. This paper was going nowhere fast. Alex's suggestions had been good, and his pep talk on the phone this morning before church had been even better, but she just couldn't seem to get it together.

She leaned forward and deleted the chunk she'd just written. This computer was fast all of a sudden. Since Brad had gotten his hands on it, to be exact.

Brad. Couldn't she do anything without her thoughts turning to him? Well, she could if he would leave like he was supposed to. Everywhere she turned, she ran into him either literally or figuratively. He was supposed to see Matt Harris tomorrow and then be on his way. She would drive Gran to physical therapy around her work schedule like she had for the past month. And the answering machine would pick up the calls while Gran was out of the office like always. They didn't need him here. She didn't need him here.

And she certainly didn't need his kisses. Which was why she was going to be very careful around him until he finally did decide to leave. Protecting Dorothy was one thing, but getting burned herself was another.

On that note, she flipped through her folder and pulled out the notes Alex had made on her last draft of the paper. This time they would make sense, because this time she was not going to let her heart go off on some dumb tangent about Brad.

The trailer door swung open. "Thought this had to be where you were hiding," Brad said as he stepped inside.

Damn. What was he doing here? Had her crazy heart conjured him up because her brain had banished all thought of him? No, he was real, not some figment of her imagination. Her heart had come alive, suddenly beating double time, and her cheeks had turned hot. He was definitely real.

"I'm not hiding." She sounded all too breathless, as if she'd been running a marathon or something and that annoyed her. She shoved her folder under some papers, while bringing up a different document—a safe one—onto the screen. "I'm just catching up on some paperwork."

"Just show me what needs to be done and I'll do it tomorrow." Brad pulled a chair up next to her and sat down. "Might as well keep me busy. Or are you going to want me to drive you around after all?"

Heavens, no. She needed to stay clear of him, not have him at her side all day. "No, the ankle's good as new." She swung her leg out from under the desk and rotated her foot. "See. Nothing wrong with it."

He bent over so that she couldn't see his face. "I'm not so sure. I think I need a closer look, just to be certain." His voice was teasing, but she pulled her foot away just to be on the safe side.

"I don't think so."

He straightened up. "You always were a spoilsport."

"How would you know?" she said. "You never even knew I existed when we were kids."

"Oh, you are very wrong there," he said, his voice suddenly a whisper and his gaze intense. "I most certainly knew you existed."

Her cheeks flamed under his regard and she quickly turned away before her dumb heart tried to read something in his words or her silly brain decided it saw a flame in his eyes.

"You're right. You had to know I existed," she agreed with a laugh and turned back to the computer screen. What was this file she had hidden her paper behind? Oh, last month's billing. "After all, doing my homework kept you coming to my house day after day."

"Interesting way to put it."

He had pulled back in some indefinable way and she felt herself relax slightly.

"I'm going over to my uncle's house to sort through some family papers and stuff," he said. "I thought you might like to come with."

And be alone in that big old house with him? She wasn't that dumb. "I think I'd better get this finished up," she told him. "That storm last week really put us behind."

"Okay."

He got to his feet. She couldn't tell from his voice or his manner if he was disappointed. But then, why would he be? He'd probably asked her along to be polite. Or to have an extra pair of hands.

A little shadow fell across her soul. He'd been so great about helping them out and when he asked her to do one little thing, she was scared to do it. She felt awful. Petty. Wimpy. Ungrateful.

"Toto might be able to help you," she said quickly. "He should be off duty by now. Give him a call."

"He's probably got plans."

She shook her head. "I doubt it. Dorothy's got an open house at one of her listings all afternoon so he's probably looking for something to do."

But Brad just shrugged as he moved the chair back to where it had been. "I'll think about it. See you later."

It was quiet in the trailer after he'd gone. No pounding of her heart. No raspy breathing. Good. Maybe she could get some work done now.

She brought her file back to the front of the screen, then closed her eyes. She could still smell Brad's aftershave in the air. But then come to think of it, she could still feel his lips on hers from last night.

Damn. She was never going to be able to concentrate.

"Now, don't let Alex make you this time," Aunty Em said. "You're never going to find out anything if he makes you."

"I'm not doing surveillance." Brad climbed into the Jeep. "I'm going to Uncle Hal's house. I've got stacks of personal papers to go through."

"Sure." The old woman waved his words aside, then turned thoughtful. "I wish we had time to tap his phone. Then we'd really get the goods on him."

Afraid that Aunty Em was about to suggest Brad take along the truth serum she kept hidden with her knitting, he started the engine. "See you later," he called out from the departing Jeep.

He drove off quickly, but once he got out to the main road he slowed down. It was a beautiful day. Sunny. Warm. A day made for the beach.

If Penny had been free, they could have gone to the dunes and lain in the sun all afternoon. She could have brought the blanket and he would have sprung for the suntan lotion to spread all over her—

He jammed on the brakes as he almost missed the turn into town. No, no suntan lotion. No days at the beach. No Penny in a swimsuit.

From suntan lotion they'd move to kisses and then to caresses and then making love. Then she'd be spilling her heart out to him and expecting him to do the same.

Definitely no suntan lotion.

He drove past the library and turned down Second Street, but went right by his uncle's house. The papers could be shipped to Los Angeles and he could sort through them there; they weren't holding him in Chesterton. Penny was, her and her situation. Once that was resolved, he could go.

But it wasn't going to get resolved with him sitting in his uncle's study sorting through old receipts. Neither would it get resolved by following Alex. No, it needed action and that's just what Brad was best at.

He pulled the Jeep up in front of Alex's small frame house. White aluminum siding, neatly trimmed evergreens around the foundation and a finely manicured lawn. Everything neat and precise and ordinary. Not one blasted thing that reflected Alex's personality. Or maybe the whole thing did—maybe he had no personality.

Penny could do better.

Brad marched up onto the small porch. The inside door was closed, but that just could mean Alex had the air-conditioning on. Brad rang the bell and, sure enough, a moment later Alex opened the door. The inside door, that was.

"Hello." Cool air spilled out through the screen door, but Alex made no move to ask Brad in. "What can I do for you?"

"I want to talk to you," Brad said.

"Now?" He didn't seem impatient or annoyed. He didn't seem anything, in fact. How could Penny be attracted to someone who never showed emotion?

"You got something to hide?" Brad asked. Wouldn't that be perfect? He'd come over for a talk and stumbled onto Alex in the midst of an assignation. That would stop whatever nefarious plans he had.

"Not at all," Alex said and opened the screen door. "Come in."

The front room was depressingly tame. It held no lingering trace of cheap perfume or stashes of X-rated videos. No empty beer cans tossed under the end tables, no overflowing ashtrays. Okay, so there were no visible sins. That didn't mean that Alex didn't have any.

"Want to sit down?" Alex asked. "Can I get you anything?"

Ha, this was where he'd get caught. "Wouldn't mind a beer," Brad said slyly.

Alex shook his head. "Sorry, I should have been more specific. I've got some soda and iced tea."

"No beer?"

"I don't drink so I don't keep it in the house."

But Brad saw through that. He hated to use it, but Penny's happiness was at stake. "Recovering?"

"From what?"

Alex was a good actor, Brad had to give him that. "Alcoholism," Brad said. "I have a friend who never keeps alcohol in the house and that's why."

"Oh." Alex shook his head. "No, just don't care for the stuff."

"Ah." Brad just sank down onto the sofa. No rings from wet glasses on the low table in front of it. The guy probably didn't even eat in the living room and used coasters with his drinks. "An iced tea would be fine."

Alex went into the kitchen and Brad forced himself up. He couldn't get discouraged just because no vices had fallen into his lap. Alex was a college professor, for goodness' sake. He had to put on a good show.

Brad sped over to the bookshelves surrounding the television. The books were all leather-bound classics. Thoreau. Hemingway. Hawthorne. The videos were all specials that had been on the public broadcasting stations. The few small statues were copies of famous works...maybe.

With a furtive glance at the kitchen doorway, Brad picked up the statue of an embracing couple. That could be it. Under all this perfection, Alex was a secret collector of rare art objects. Stolen from museums and worth millions. He wanted to have them to satisfy his own ego, but that same ego forced him to put them on display.

The label on the bottom said Middlebury Mint. Number 8,445 out of ten thousand copies. Rare and priceless all right.

"Interested in artwork?" Alex asked.

Brad caught himself before he dropped the statue and put it carefully back. "Yeah. Can't afford even this kind of stuff but do admire it."

"Uh-huh." Alex's voice sounded almost mocking, but his gaze was bland as he handed Brad a glass—and a coaster. "Here's your drink."

"Thanks." Brad went back to the sofa. He took a short drink. It was real tea not a mix. Was the guy perfect, or what?

"Now what can I do for you?"

Brad carefully put his drink on the coaster, then looked up. "I want to talk about Penny," he said. "Specifically, your intentions toward her."

Alex didn't look intimidated. More amused. "My intentions? I can't see where they're any of your business."

"Penny's an old friend of mine and I don't want to see her hurt."

Alex raised his eyebrows. "I daresay Penny's an older friend of mine," he said. "Since I've known her consistently over the years. Not just in and out like some."

As if you could measure friendship in terms of years. Brad ignored Alex's argument. "So, are you serious about her?"

"Perhaps you should be asking her if she's serious about me," Alex said.

"Penny's feelings are her own business."

"And maybe mine are, too," Alex said. "I think it would be much more interesting to discuss why you want to know so badly."

Brad glared darkly at him, but it had no discernable effect. "I told you. She's a friend."

"Like she was a friend back in junior high and high school?"

"What's that supposed to mean?"

Alex snickered. "Oh, come now, Brad. You had it bad for Penny when you lived here before. It might not have been common knowledge, but it wasn't a secret, either."

Brad didn't know what to say. For a moment, he was a kid

again. A secret was out in the open and he was feeling exposed and vulnerable. Something inside him pulled up tight.

"I did not," he denied. "She was just a friend."

"A friend?" Alex grinned. "You wouldn't let another guy get within ten feet of her. You concocted the wildest stories to get rid of your rivals."

"No, I didn't."

Alex seemed not to hear him. "I always wondered why you never dated her. She wouldn't have cared that you didn't have much money to spend."

She might not have cared, but he would have. She deserved the best of everything, and that included a boyfriend who could take her places. Not one that worked every spare hour of the day and even then could rarely afford to go to the movies himself, let alone take someone.

But he hadn't come here to discuss his past. He'd come to protect Penny's future.

"We've gotten pretty far off track here," Brad stated. "I just want your guarantee that Penny's not going to be hurt."

Alex shook his head as he got to his feet. "I don't know what right you have to demand it, but I can guarantee I won't hurt her. I happen to be fond of her, too."

Brad wasn't sure that was real reassurance, but knew it was the best he was going to get at the moment. Was it enough to allow himself to leave Chesterton, though?

Penny bit her lip as she listened to the phone ring and ring and ring. Weren't doctors supposed to have an answering machine? She thought it was a law or something.

"There's no answer," she told Gran as she hung up the phone. Worry ate at her stomach. "We'll just go to the emergency room."

"I'm fine," the old woman snapped. "I just got a little dizzy from the heat, that's all."

"Better to be safe than sorry." Penny picked up her purse and grabbed the truck keys from the basket under the phone. "Come on."

But Gran didn't move from the kitchen chair. "What about Brad? We should leave him a note."

With a loud sigh of exasperation, Penny found a piece of paper and a pen and scribbled out a note to Brad, saying that Gran had had a dizzy spell and that Penny was taking her in to be checked. This was crazy. If it was nothing, then they'd probably be home before Brad. And if it was serious, then they really shouldn't be wasting the time with this note.

"Tell him not to worry," Gran insisted, looking over Penny's shoulder. "Gracious, that's messy. How's he ever going to read it?"

"He's used to my writing." Penny added Gran's admonition not to worry, but she was not going to rewrite the thing in neater penmanship! "Now, let's go."

"Oh, all right."

Gran took her own sweet time getting into the truck while Penny wanted to scream in worry and frustration. Finally she got the old woman in the passenger side and she hurried around to the driver's side.

"You know, you shouldn't be driving with that sprained ankle," Gran said. "Why don't we wait for Brad?"

Penny started the truck. "It's better. I can drive."

"You might get a relapse."

She put the truck in gear and started down the drive. The truck was stifling inside, even though it had been parked in the shade. The air moved now that they were driving, but the air-conditioning sure took forever to start working. She turned the dials on high.

"I mean it," Gran said. "You hurt your ankle some more and you'll have to be off work."

The air was finally starting to feel a little cool, and Penny relaxed. "I never did hurt my ankle," she admitted. "I did it so I could keep an eye on Brad."

Gran started to laugh. "You sly one," she said. "And here you were pretending not to like him."

Trust Gran to misinterpret things. "Not because I was attracted to him,'' she said and turned onto the main road. ''But because I didn't trust him.''

''Sure.'' Gran's smile was smug. She was certain she knew the real truth.

It wasn't worth arguing. Certainly not now, when Gran might not be well. Penny just held her tongue and sped over to the hospital. It only took a few minutes, and Gran didn't seem any worse.

Penny pulled into the emergency room drive and honked the horn. An orderly came out with a wheelchair and helped Penny get Gran into it.

''I'll park the truck and meet you inside,'' Penny said.

But by the time she got into the emergency room a few minutes later, Gran had already been taken into the back for tests. There was nothing for Penny to do but wait. She sank into a vinyl-covered chair that held the chill of the supercold air and gave free reign to her worries.

Nothing could happen to Gran, nothing. She was all Penny had left. Oh, sure, Will and Thad were still around, but not close by. Not really a part of Penny's life. Not somebody to come home to.

A little voice pointed out that Gran was in her seventies and wouldn't live forever. That maybe Penny should be looking elsewhere for someone to come home to. Like in Brad Corrigan's direction.

Penny jumped to her feet and hurried over to the desk. ''Can I wait with my grandmother?'' she asked the nurse.

The nurse shook her head. ''I'm sorry. She's been taken down for an EKG. You need to wait here.'' She smiled sympathetically. ''Are you all alone?''

Like it was a fatal disease. ''I'm fine, thank you.'' Penny went back over to the chair.

She liked being alone. There were things she wanted to accomplish and she wasn't ready to tie herself down yet. Her life was fine. Perfect. She didn't need anyone else in it.

An emergency code rang out over the public address system and Penny's heart stopped. She sprang to her feet again, gazing at the double doors leading to the examining area. What if it was Gran?

Penny vaguely heard the whoosh of the outside door opening and felt the heated summer air wash over her briefly. But all she could do was stare at those examining room doors.

"Penny?"

Brad was there and she went into his arms. She must have, for she suddenly found herself in his embrace. And it was perfect. For a wonderful minute, she let him be strong. Then she pulled away.

"How is she?" he asked.

"I don't know. They're doing tests. She said it was just the heat."

"It is awfully hot out," he agreed. "And you know she would tell you that she's always right."

Penny smiled slightly. "Always. But there was just some code blue they were announcing—"

"In surgical preop. I doubt they rushed Aunty Em off for surgery and didn't tell you."

She nodded. "I guess you're right. They were giving her an EKG."

He took her hand and led her back over to the chairs. "You need to be patient. Want to hear about the time I broke my arm in diving class?"

"Diving class?" She shook her head at the rapid change of subject. He was just trying to distract her, but it was working. She leaned back in her chair. "I can't imagine you as a diver." She looked at his broad shoulders and solid build. "Football player, yes. And you're tall enough for basketball. But diving?"

He nodded with a sheepish grin. "When we got to California, my mother decided I needed California skills. She really felt awful about uprooting me and so once she got a decent-paying job—which was pretty fast—she enrolled me in a swimming and diving class."

"And how were you?"

"After about three weeks of sinking like a stone, I finally

got the hang of swimming. I did okay in diving because it was just a matter of making my body follow orders.''

''Just?'' she ached with a laugh. ''What if your body is too smart to do a back flip no matter how much you order it to?''

''Mine wasn't,'' he replied. ''Besides, the reputation of Indiana was riding on my shoulders. I had to prove to those California kids that us Hoosiers were every bit as good as they were.''

She heard a darker undertone in his voice that said he'd carried his pride with him—and the demons that went with it—when he'd moved. But she knew better than to let on. ''And did you?'' she asked lightly.

''Damn right I did. Completed every single dive for my final exam.''

''So, how'd you break your arm?''

He grinned. ''Tripped when I went into the locker room. Fell right on my face and broke my arm in two places.''

She laughed. ''At least it was after you proved yourself,'' she said, then let her laughter dwindle to just a smile. ''So, was the move good for you?''

He leaned back in his chair with a twisted grin on his face. ''You sound like my mother,'' he said. ''Every night she'd ask me if I was happy. Was it working out for me? Did I miss my friends?''

''And what did you answer?''

''That it was great. Best decision she ever made. Never gave Chesterton another thought.''

''I'm glad. It can be hard starting over at that age.''

''Or easy,'' he said. ''No one knows about all the dumb mistakes you made. You get a clean slate.''

''But no friends.''

He shrugged. ''You make new ones. Real ones.''

That kind of hurt, that they hadn't been real friends. But who was she kidding? She had been madly in love with him and he had thought she was a way to earn some extra money. That wasn't friendship, not even in the twisted world of junior high school. She looked away and saw Doc Pierce approaching.

She jumped nervously to her feet. Brad rose also, slipping an arm around her. She leaned into him and found strength there.

"How is she?" Penny asked the doctor.

"Just fine." He smiled. "A little too much sun and not enough liquids. She was just overheated. We gave her some fluids and she can go home anytime." After patting Penny's shoulder, he hurried down the hall.

Penny felt herself go limp with relief for just a quick second. Brad's arm tightened and then she was fine. She turned to smile at him.

"Guess I'll never hear the end of this," she said. "Gran said it was just the heat."

"But you can point out she needs to watch her fluids, too," he suggested. "Don't let her get off scot-free."

By that time a nurse was wheeling Gran out. "Am I interrupting something?" Gran said. Her glance was most definitely on Brad's arm around Penny's waist. Her smile was smug. "I can feel faint again, if you two want some more time alone."

"Gran." Penny hurried over to take the wheelchair. "Would you stop kidding around? You had us worried."

She just reached over her shoulder to pat Penny's hand on the wheelchair's handle. "I know, honey. I'm sorry." With her other hand, she reached for Brad. "I'm so glad you were here for Penny. This is a horrible place to be by yourself."

Actually, there were lots of places that were horrible to be by yourself, Penny thought as she wheeled her grandmother outside. But she was not going to dwell on those. "Brad kept me quite entertained," she said. "I heard all about how he broke his arm during his diving lessons."

"Broke your arm?" Gran sounded surprised. "Hal told me how you were a diving champ in your high school for a couple years running, but he never mentioned breaking your arm."

"Prechampionship days," Brad said. They stopped outside under the covered entrance to the emergency room. "Why don't I drive the truck up here? Save you all some steps."

He took Penny's keys and hurried off across the parking lot

while Penny watched. A diving champ, huh? Looked like the move really was great for him. California must have been just what he needed. No wonder he never looked back here with regret.

Unaccountably, the idea made her sad.

Dorothy hurried into the Yellow Brick Road Bar and Grill, her stomach growling at the wonderful smell of food. She was starving. Lunch had been too small and too long ago.

"Dorothy, over here."

She looked around at the sound of her name and saw Toto and Junior at a small table near the back. She waved back and then wove her way over.

"Sorry, I'm late," she apologized. "It's been some day."

"No, problem," Toto said. "We didn't mind waiting." Junior grumbled a little as Toto held a chair out for her.

"Not sure your buddy here agrees," she noted and she sat down.

"He'll get over it. How was your day?"

"Just great." She couldn't help but laugh. "Fabulous, actually. I sold the Kramer estate. A couple came by the open house, made an offer on the spot, and the Kramers accepted."

"Wow, calls for a real celebration. Sure you want to stay here?"

"And break a long tradition of Yellow Brick Road Sunday dinners? No way. Years of bar food has probably brought me my good luck."

Toto waved the waitress over and they both ordered dinner, then he ordered a near beer for Junior as well as a bottle of champagne.

"We have to celebrate right," he told her. "This will be your third year as the agency's top seller."

"In terms of units sold, I'm not the leader this year, but in terms of dollars I am."

The waitress brought over Junior's nonalcoholic beer, then the champagne and glasses. Junior was too busy with his drink, but all around them, people turned to watch the waitress open the champagne. Their eyes said they were putting their own interpretation on the champagne. Toto didn't seem to notice, but it made Dorothy wistful.

Toto held up his glass. "Here's to staying the leader," he said.

She clicked her glass with his and took a sip, keeping her eyes from him and from their audience. What was she moping about? This sale was huge. Which meant her commission was fantastic. Which meant her bank account was almost big enough for her move to Paris. But somehow it didn't feel as exciting as it should have.

"Did I tell you Brad gave me the listing for his uncle's house?" she said, then wished she hadn't.

Selling that house would put her over her goal. Was that something Toto would celebrate? Probably. After all, they were friends. That was all he had wanted to be for years now.

"Really?" Toto topped off her glass. "That would be a great place to raise a family. Even the carriage house where Brad and his mom lived is nice."

Dorothy didn't know what to say. For some reason, the whole subject left her feeling down and depressed. Maybe it was the champagne on an empty stomach. Maybe it was the normal letdown after a big sale.

The place was just a house. Not the magical setting for a wedding that she used to think it was. Not the variations of home that Toto saw it as. Just an old building that would bring in some good money when it sold.

"It's kind of run-down now," she said. "The whole place will need some work."

Toto just shook his head. "I have a feeling it will sell well and sell soon." He raised up his glass again. "Here's to becoming the home it was meant to be."

Dorothy clinked her glass against his but never felt less like celebrating.

Chapter Nine

Brad picked up the ringing phone. "Donnelly Tree Service."

"Brad? It's Penny."

He knew that. He'd known it as soon as the phone had rung, centuries before he had picked it up. His heart had beat faster, his breath had been caught in his throat.

"You okay?" he asked. "Your ankle's not bothering you, is it?"

"I'm fine," she said, her impatience with the question quite obvious. "Hey, we're running behind and we aren't going to make all the scheduled jobs today. I need you to call the Sharpes and the Miluskis and see if tomorrow's okay. Give them our apologies and all that. This tree at the Braxtons' is just giving us fits."

"Don't try to do it all yourself," he said quickly. He could just see her and her chain saw up in a tree.

"Just make the calls, Brad." The second ice age had started. "The telephone numbers are on the work orders."

"I mean it, Penny. That's what you have crews for."

"And make sure Gran takes it easy when she gets back home, will you? I don't want a repeat of yesterday." Then she hung up the phone.

A repeat of yesterday? Aunty Em getting sick, or Penny leaning on him? He had the sinking suspicion it was the latter, but he shouldn't be surprised. She was so damn independent that she couldn't lean on anybody more than a minute or two. And after she did, she had to run out and be doubly independent.

He frowned at the computer screen in front of him, but not really seeing it. He had the awful feeling that was what she was doing now—something stupid to prove she was still just as strong as before.

He looked at the notes in his hand about the calls he had to make and then at the clock. He had another hour until he had to pick up Aunty Em from physical therapy. These calls shouldn't take more than a few minutes, and then he could drive over to the Braxtons' and see just what was going on.

Great plan. He flipped through the work orders on the desk but didn't find what he was looking for. He glanced at the top of the pile. No wonder, these were completed jobs. So, where were the scheduled ones?

He began to dig through another pile of papers. Nope, not in this one. Maybe—

"Oh, damn it." He'd knocked a folder of papers off the desk, scattering them over the trailer floor. "Nuts."

He got down on his knees and began to scoop them up, then stopped. This was the folder Penny had had in the Pizza Prince when she had met Alex last week. And these papers were all school papers. Notes. Assignments. First drafts of papers.

Brad tried not to look, really he did, but it was hard not to see the notes scribbled in red across the papers, or the grades— C's and C pluses mostly, an occasional B minus—on the tops. Aunty Em had told him that Penny was majoring in English literature, but looking at the papers and then the office of a successful business, he couldn't figure out why. She had a knack for business. Why wasn't she majoring in that? She'd probably be getting A's and B's if she did.

A sound at the door sent him scrambling to his feet, but he still had the folder in his hand when Aunty Em came in the door.

"What are you doing here?" he asked. "I was supposed to pick you up." He glanced at the clock with a frown. No, it was just past three. "Did I get the time wrong?"

She came in all the way and closed the door behind her. "No, all I had left were some little exercises I can do here and Marilyn was going so she gave me a ride."

"I would have come."

"I know you would have." She sat down in the spare chair. "What's that in your hand? Looks like Penny's folder."

He looked down at it as if seeing it there for the first time. "I knocked it down. It was in one of the piles on the desk."

"Oh, yeah? Penny must have left it in here. Not like her. She's usually so careful with her stuff. Guess that's why she's getting such good grades." She pushed herself to her feet. "Well, just wanted to let you know I was back. I'm going over to the house to do my exercises."

"Why is Penny majoring in English literature?" Brad asked.

"Why not?" Aunty Em just shrugged. "I guess she likes it."

"I would have thought business would be more in her line," Brad said. "She's doing so well here that she must be a natural at it."

Aunty Em laughed. "Well, if grades are any indication, she's a natural at English literature, too. Getting all sorts of honors."

Brad looked down at the folder in his hand, then back up at the old woman. "Oh?" He tightened his hold on the folder though Aunty Em didn't look like she was going to make a flying tackle to take it away.

"Not that she shows me her work or nothing. She's never liked to brag. But I saw one of her papers last spring. It was an A, and I just know her others are, as well. She's as smart as they come and I keep telling her how proud I am."

"You should be," he said and stuck the folder back on the desk, under some papers. "But not just about her schoolwork. She's doing so well with the business—I imagine you're proud of her for that."

"But you know Penny. Some things don't count in her mind. And some do." Aunty Em just waved her hand as she walked slowly over to the door. "I'll be back to take over here after I do my exercises. This is no place for a man to be working."

"A man works wherever he's needed," Brad said. "You stay in the house and take it easy. I've got everything under control here."

What did he do now? He could go check on Penny and let Aunty Em man the office or he could stay here and keep the older woman from overdoing it. Either way, someone would be mad at him and someone would be on their own. How did he ever get mixed up with two such stubborn, know-it-all, independent women?

Brad never did make it out to check on Penny. By the time he finished his assigned calls, tomorrow's schedule needed redoing. Then he decided he'd better move the boxes of old files into the storage shed before Penny or Aunty Em decided they would move them. And since he was going that way anyway, he might as well pull the other outdated files that ought to go into storage next.

When he got back to the trailer, Aunty Em was at the computer. "You aren't supposed to be here," he told her.

"We've been taking advantage of you for too long," she said, keeping her eyes on the computer screen. "Weren't you supposed to see Matt Harris today?"

"No," he said. "He was getting back from vacation today. I didn't have an appointment to see him."

"So, call Nancy and make one."

Brad wheeled the chair back slightly and turned it so she faced him. "How about if you go back to the house and let me finish what I was doing?" He took her arm and gently raised her to her feet.

She allowed him to walk with her toward the door. "You're doing too much for us. Penny better be paying you."

"Don't you dare talk to her about that," Brad said. "Or I'll have to start paying you room and board."

She stopped. "No, you don't. Room and board was in exchange for helping me investigate Alex." She gave him a thoughtful look. "I'm thinking we can ease up on our investigation. She hasn't mentioned him for days."

"That's fine."

But when Brad opened the trailer door, he heard Penny's truck coming up the lane. He and Aunty Em waited on the trailer steps as she pulled into the yard and parked under the oak.

"You're home early," Aunty Em said.

"You okay?" Brad asked.

Penny gave Aunty Em a smile and him a glare, then closed her truck door. "I just thought I'd quit a little early and get cleaned up. I'm going out tonight."

Brad and Aunty Em followed her across the yard. "Out where?" Aunty Em asked the question on Brad's lips.

"With Alex," Penny replied and hurried up the steps into the kitchen. "If you haven't started dinner yet, don't make any for me."

She was already halfway to her room by the time Brad and Aunty Em got into the kitchen. Aunty Em grew visibly more annoyed.

"I thought she was done with him," Aunty Em said and threw her cane up against the counter. "Why can't she see he's no good for her?"

"Maybe they planned it ages ago."

"Hmph. She could've canceled."

"She's too polite."

But he wasn't feeling any better than Aunty Em. His talk with Alex hadn't reassured him at all. And obviously his own support at the emergency room yesterday meant nothing, not in the long run.

"Maybe you need to work him over," Aunty Em said. "Rough him up a bit until he promises to leave her alone."

"I don't think violence is the answer. I'd just get arrested and then where would we be?"

"You sure are scared of getting arrested."

"Aunty Em," Brad said with a sigh. "Maybe he's what Penny wants."

"But he isn't right for her."

Brad felt weary all of a sudden. "That's not for us to decide."

"Even if we know he can't make her happy?"

This was a no-win conversation and the more they talked, the heavier his heart felt. Not that it had any business being that way. Penny was free to do what she wanted, when she wanted and with whom she wanted. It was nothing to him. Nothing at all.

"How about some dinner?" he said to Aunty Em. "You sit and I'm going to make you my world-famous noodle omelet."

Aunty Em looked less than excited, but she put on a good show, insisting on helping him chop the onions and green peppers while he cooked the noodles and beat the eggs. After he'd made the omelet, she slowly ate her share. But then he wasn't all that hungry, either. The thought of Penny and that jerk Alex gnawed at him. The idea of Penny in his arms twisted in his gut. The image of Alex kissing her was enough to make him want to throw his plate of food against the wall. What was she thinking of?

Penny came down as they were finishing eating. Her blond hair was still damp from her shower and her skin was aglow. She looked fresh and lovely and alive. And it was all for Alex.

Brad pushed his plate away, no longer able to eat. He needed to get out of town. He didn't belong here anymore. Probably never did.

"What's the matter, hon?" Aunty Em asked Penny.

Brad turned. Penny was flipping through some papers lying on top of the phone book. She wore a definite frown on her face.

"I can't find my folder," Penny muttered. "I usually keep it in my room but it wasn't there."

Much as he'd like to keep her from her date with Alex, Brad couldn't stand to see that worried look in her eyes. "I think it's in the office," he said.

She looked startled, and even more worried if that was possible. "How could—" She stopped and her face seemed to fall. "I must have left it there after working yesterday."

Grabbing up her purse, she hurried out the door. Through the screen, they could see her dash across the yard and into the trailer.

"What kind of date is it that she has to bring her schoolwork?" Aunty Em grumbled. "Does he give her a test to see if she's smart enough to spend an evening with him?"

But Brad was watching the closed trailer door. It didn't take that long to walk across and pick up the folder.

"I'd better see if she's having trouble finding it." In a few broad strides he was at the screen door.

"Steal her truck keys," Aunty Em said, getting to her feet. "Let the air out of her tires. Kiss her until she comes to her senses."

Brad gave the old woman a look, then went outside. Well, they were interesting ideas, he had to admit. Though Penny was liable to slug him if he tried to take her keys. And he doubted he had time to let the air out of her tires. But now, kissing her until she changed her mind did sound doable. Or at least, tryable.

Penny knew the minute that she pulled the folder out from under the papers that it had been opened. Her papers were sticking out slightly and her current essay wasn't on top anymore. Her heart sank into her toes. Brad knew. It had to be him. And what if he told Gran? This whole thing would become common knowledge.

She blinked back a stinging in her eyes. Damn him, anyway. Why did he have to come back?

Hearing a noise at the door, she spun around. It was Brad,

those darn broad shoulders of his filling up the doorway, his soft smile wreaking havoc in her heart.

"I just wanted to make sure you found it." His voice was as gentle as it had been years ago when she didn't know her verb forms. His eyes held that same shadow of pity.

For some wild reason, she wanted to burst into tears. How could he spoil everything like this? He had thought she was smart and he had treated her like an equal. Now he would feel sorry for her again. And she just couldn't bear that. A fire flared up and she let anger have the upper hand. She'd rather have him hate her, than pity her.

"I found it all right," she snapped. "And you had no right to look in it."

"I didn't mean to." He came in and let the door close behind him.

The room suddenly got way too small. Penny gulped down her pain and tears. "Yeah, right. You didn't mean to. Like you didn't have any choice."

Clutching the stupid folder to her chest, she marched toward him. He stepped aside and she gave the door a mighty shove.

"Penny, wait," he said, putting his hand on her arm. "It fell when I was looking through the work orders and I picked it up. I wasn't trying to snoop or anything."

She pulled away so that his hand fell. "But you still looked at the papers," she said, wanting and praying that he would deny it and they could pretend it hadn't happened.

But he couldn't. His eyes said it before his words even tried.

"So what if I saw your papers?" he said, his voice losing some of its softness. "I don't give a damn about them. I'm more interested in why you're going out with Alex again."

"Why? You think I'm not smart enough for him?"

"I never said that." His eyes narrowed in irritation; his lips were a tight angry line. "I think he's a jerk and you're too good for him."

"Yeah, right." She pushed past him and practically ran to her truck.

In the space of half a second, she had climbed in and had

the motor running, but she needn't have worried. He was still at the trailer door, watching her but doing nothing to stop her.

She turned away and backed the truck up, then sped down the lane. Damn. Damn. Damn. Everything was ruined now. No matter if she was invited to speak at that conference, she'd seen that look of pity in Brad's eyes and that was all that counted. It had taken her eighteen years to forget it, and then it was back in a split second.

She turned the truck onto the county road but slowed down. It was a warm sunny evening, the birds were singing their hearts out, and the scent of millions of flowers seemed to ride on the air. And she was miserable.

The closer she got to town, the slower she went. Good thing there wasn't much traffic. She came to the road to Alex's house but turned around instead, then pulled off to the side of the road and picked up her cellular phone. Alex answered on the first ring.

"I can't make it tonight," she told him. "Something's come up."

"Okay. No problem. Want to make it tomorrow night instead?"

"Let me call you tomorrow," she said. "I don't know."

"Are you all right?" he asked suddenly and she could hear his frown.

"Just tired," she said. "It's been a hellish day."

She hung up and then pulled back on the road, but she didn't drive home. She just drove. South past the acres and acres of corn that grew here each summer. East into Valparaiso and past the old quaint homes in the center of town that had lasted a century or more. Then back up north on backroads that wandered up and down hills and around curves and past stands of oaks that had been huge since before the Civil War. Finally as it was getting dark, she pulled into the nursery driveway and parked the truck in the yard.

For a long moment, she just sat there, staring at the house. She wasn't angry anymore so much as tired. Lights were on in the kitchen and living room and she could see the flickering bluish glow from the television set. Gran and Brad were probably watching TV. She ought to join them and—

There was another sound from back of the barn. A dull thud. Then another and another. She got out of the truck and walked slowly past the storage shed. Brad had found the old basketball and was shooting baskets in the dim glow from one of the yard lights. He either heard her or sensed her, for he turned as soon as she stepped from the shadows.

"Hi," he said.

"Hi." She nodded toward the ball in his hand. "I wouldn't have thought that had much air in it."

"It doesn't, but it's got enough for my skill level." He tossed the ball up again and it bounced off the backboard and away from the basket. He ran it down.

"Gives you an excuse, is what you mean."

He held the ball out. "Want to shoot a few?"

She shook her head and sat down on the overturned wheelbarrow. "I would hate to show you up."

He just grimaced, but let it pass, and came over to stretch out on the grass next to her. "I'm sorry about the folder."

She nodded and looked away into the growing shadows. "That's okay. I shouldn't have left it lying around."

They went silent again, waiting for the world to take a couple of spins. He rolled the ball slightly on the grass, then looked up.

"What do you see in Alex?"

She sighed. The wheelbarrow wasn't a very comfortable chair and she moved to the grass instead. It was cool and tickled her bare legs. Almost enough to make her smile. "He's a nice guy," she finally said.

"What do you have in common?"

"Enough."

"Enough for what?" He was getting upset again and sat up. "Don't you have anything to talk about unless you bring your notebook with you on dates?"

Penny didn't say anything for a long moment. She watched

the shadows grow darker and listened to the crickets grow louder. Who was she really fooling?

"Alex and I aren't dating," she said. "I'm paying him to tutor me."

"Tutor you?" His voice sounded stunned, as if the concept were totally foreign.

"You know," she snapped. "Like my father paid you when we were kids."

"But why?"

"You saw my papers."

He frowned at her. "Well, maybe then you're majoring in the wrong thing. Why English literature?"

"You think it's a strange major for a dummy?"

"No, I think it's a strange major for someone running a business. You've got yourself a good-size operation here. And from what I can see, highly successful. A business major would be a snap for you."

"I don't want something easy," she said.

"Why not?"

She didn't know how to tell him. But then, didn't know how not to tell him. His hand was near her, too near, and the temptation to stroke it with a blade of grass was too much. She ran one lightly over the back of his hand until he grabbed her hand in his. Was that what she wanted all along?

She held on to him, but looked up at the moths flying around the yard light. "You remember when we put on *The Wizard of Oz* play in seventh grade?"

"You played the Scarecrow."

"I wanted to play Dorothy."

"What for? All she did was run around and whine about her dog."

Penny turned from the light and the moths, to picking at the blades of grass. It was a long time since she'd opened her heart up.

"I had done really poorly on one of my English tests," she said. "Mrs. Hartman was going to let me take it over, but the only time available was during the Dorothy tryouts."

He shrugged. "You made a great Scarecrow."

"Yeah, right." Penny snorted. She looked at him then, but his face was turned so that his eyes were shadowed. "They wanted somebody tall and skinny. And you and Joe Wenzel were the only ones taller than me. Joe wasn't anywhere near skinny and you never went out for the plays."

"The Scarecrow was always my favorite."

"Dorothy was the star."

"The Scarecrow was the one who figured out how to get them all out of danger."

She knew he wouldn't understand, but she was laughing in spite of herself. "You've always been a stubborn cuss."

"Hey, when I'm right, I'm right."

She looked up at the sprinkling of stars newly appearing in the nighttime sky. Diamonds twinkling just for her. Somewhere up there was the wishing star, but she'd lost track of it over the years.

"I guess, just once, I'd like to be the star," she said.

"You were a model."

"That was nothing. People figured you were a statue that could walk around."

"And talk," he added.

"Nobody listened if you did." She brought her gaze back down and looked at him. "That's why I hired Alex."

"To make you a star?"

"Kind of. You see, there's this big conference in Washington D.C. next year to celebrate the one hundredth anniversary of the publication of *The Wizard of Oz*. The Smithsonian is sponsoring it and all kinds of educated people are presenting papers about the Oz stories and their significance on society."

"How does Alex fit in?"

"I want to present a paper and he's coaching me."

"But why all the secrecy?"

It was getting too hard to look at him. Even though his eyes were shadowed, she could still feel the intensity of his gaze. She stretched out on her stomach and picked at the grass in front of her.

"It's Gran," she told him, then looked up. "She didn't see the·papers, did she?"

He shook his head, and she went back to her grass with a sigh. "Thank goodness. She thinks I'm some A student and I couldn't bear for her to know the truth."

"She wouldn't care," Brad said. "She doesn't love you more or less depending on your grades."

Penny rolled onto her side, propping her head up with her hand. "But she's proud of me now and I like that. She saw the one paper I got an A on and jumped to the conclusion I got A's on all my papers. At first, I tried to tell her the truth, but I liked having her proud of me. When I mentioned the conference, she took it for granted that I would present my paper. Now she's told the whole town that I'm an honor student and a famous scholar."

"And so you hired Alex."

"Yes. His job is to help me write such a good paper that I'll make part of Gran's story be true."

He sighed and lay down next to her, reaching out his hand to brush some curls back from her face. "Penny, you can't make yourself into something you're not and you shouldn't even try. People love you for who you are—a warm, generous, interesting person. Anyone who thinks you should be something else doesn't count."

"It's not that easy," she said, though she was having a little trouble concentrating. His touch was soft and gentle, but sent tremors all along her skin. "I know people care about me, but I want to be respected. I want to do something no one else has."

His fingers were running lightly over her cheek, then touched her lips with the merest of caresses. "Lots of people respect you. And every day you do things no one else has."

There was a tremble building down deep inside her and with his every touch, it was growing stronger. "Name one thing," she said. She tried for a laugh but it came out shaky.

"You're running the business better than your father did."

"That doesn't count."

"Why not?" He half growled the words as his hand came down on her shoulder. "You know you are the most aggravating, impossible—"

But his words died off as his gaze locked with hers. She forgot what they were talking about. Forgot why she was so impossible. And knew only a desperate longing to taste his lips. To feel that wild ride of wonder deep in her soul.

She leaned forward a bit and he leaned over just a fraction and then it was as if they were magnets, pulled together by some greater force. His mouth was on hers and she felt the magic inside her. His kiss was hungry and needful with all the force of a spring storm, raging over the land with its power and strength.

But as heavenly as his touch was, it wasn't enough. She rolled slowly onto her back as his hands slid under her and her arms held him close. His chest was pressed against her; her breasts radiated the pounding of his heart. It was splendor. It was wonder. It was everything her most private dreams ever wished for.

She kissed with a lifetime of longing. He kissed her with a lifetime of loneliness. And somehow those lifetimes met and exploded into the most wonderful fire. It consumed everything until there was nothing but them. Nothing but the flaming needs and the magic of each other.

And something damp and cold on her ear.

"What?" she cried against his lips and pulled away as best she could.

Brad raised himself up on his hands and they both turned. Einstein was standing there next to them. Once they were both looking at the cat, he meowed in satisfaction, then climbed onto Penny's chest for scratching. Penny started to laugh.

"This your chaperon?" Brad asked.

His voice was harsh and sounded strained, but he reached out to scratch the cat also so Penny knew he wasn't angry.

"My father figure," she joked. "That meow was asking you what your intentions are. And this purr is saying he likes you."

But Brad's scratching was short-lived and he sat up suddenly, moving away from her. He looked like he was trying to catch his breath as he gazed off into the darkness of the nursery fields. Putting her arms around Einstein so he wouldn't fall, Penny sat up also. Just as Brad finally turned her way again.

"Hey, I'm sorry about that," he said. "I never meant for this to happen."

She laughed though she wasn't sure why. Or was she not sure why he was apologizing? "We're both adults," she said. "And both free to enjoy ourselves. There's no need to apologize."

"I guess."

Einstein protested his confinement so she let him go, then watched as he bounded off toward the barn. It was better than watching Brad fight some demon inside him. She didn't know whether she should be flattered or insulted, and decided she was too tired to be either.

In too many ways she was still that girl who thought Brad Corrigan hung the moon. Except she was an adult now and she ought to know better. He was a wanderer, a loner, a man who wouldn't love. So, did she take what she could get and be satisfied, or did she say it was all or nothing? Luckily no one was asking her to make a choice.

She got to her feet and brushed the grass off her legs. "I'm going inside," she said.

He took a deep breath that seemed to echo in the yard. "I think I'll shoot a few more baskets."

Penny wasn't the most knowledgeable woman in the ways of men, but she knew he wanted to be alone. What a coincidence, since she thought alone might be good also. No, that was a lie. But she would be damned if she'd admit that to anyone but herself.

"Good night," she said.

"Good night."

She walked slowly across the yard but she still hadn't heard the dull thump of the ball hitting the backboard by the time she went into the kitchen.

* * *

Brad left the house in the early morning hour just before dawn again, with Einstein trailing along, and headed out to the tree lot. They passed behind the barn where the basketball net was and Brad felt a sudden burning in the center of his soul. Things had almost gotten out of hand last night, and he was glad they hadn't. Well, sort of glad. No, not glad at all. Just the thought of Penny lying on the grass there beneath him was enough to start him on fire. But he knew it was best that they had stopped when they had.

"Yes, I know, little busybody," he said to Einstein. "You were only doing what came natural. But you were right."

Taking advantage of Penny would have been wrong—even the small amount he had last night—but there was a way he could make it up to her. He could make it up to her for his suspicions of Alex and his snooping around. For looking at her papers—though he was sure glad he had. Otherwise, she never would have confided in him.

Once in the privacy of the young trees, Brad dialed George's number. He'd do this one last thing for Penny, this one big one, and then he would move on. It was fate, him coming back when he had. Fate that sent him into that bar the night of her poetry reading. And fate that he had it in his power to grant her fondest wish. His lawyer answered, as sleepily as last time.

"George, it's Brad."

"I figured," the man grumped. "Who else calls me from a zoo at this time of the night?"

"It's morning and I'm on a tree farm."

"Whatever. You calling to tell me that you're leaving for the conference or that you're ready to talk contract with Technology Unlimited?"

Brad ignored his question. "You know that Ray Bolger hat we bought in auction? The one he wore in *The Wizard of Oz*? Has the paperwork gone through for its donation to the Smithsonian?"

"Not yet."

"Great," Brad said. "I want you to finagle a deal with the

Smithsonian people. They get the hat and we get to choose a speaker at their *Wizard of Oz* seminar next year.''

George groaned. ''And do we have a speaker in mind?''

''Of course.''

''Somehow I knew that was going to be the answer. And is this speaker female?''

Brad frowned. ''I don't usually trade favors just to please some woman.''

''No, and you don't ignore business to camp out in some zoo, either,'' the lawyer groused. ''But you seem to be doing both now.''

''She's an old friend.''

''Uh-huh.''

''That's all she is,'' Brad snapped, his hand tightening around the phone. George was lucky he was thousands of miles, and two time zones away. ''I want to keep on top of this one so I'll be calling you in a couple of days.''

''What if I have to get ahold of you?''

Brad hesitated, then gave George the office number for Donnelly's Tree Service. ''Just tell whoever answers the phone that you're with Techno-Personnel.''

''Techno-Personnel?''

''Yeah, people around here think I'm a freelance programmer between jobs.''

''That's not too far from the truth.''

But it wasn't the truth. None of what he was pretending to be was the truth and Brad suddenly felt uncomfortable. He broke off the connection and slipped the cellular phone in his pocket. Then he stared down the tree line of red maples stretching down to the far horizon. The birds were still singing and the air still smelled musky and alive. But he didn't feel as great as he had several minutes ago.

It wasn't that he was doing anything wrong. He was just helping out an old friend.

Penny had always been sensitive about this kind of thing, saying that the only reason Brad was helping her was because he thought she was incapable of doing things herself, but this was different. He wasn't doing anything for her. He was just making sure that she'd have a chance.

Though it was definitely best done in secret.

Chapter Ten

Staying up half the night didn't bring Penny any great insight. And neither did waking up groggy Tuesday morning. She had no idea how she felt about Brad or how he felt about her. Or whether she should be enjoying what they had. Or even if they had anything right now. Maybe the embraces of the past few days were nothing more than hormones run amok. Or the moon in the wrong house or something.

If only she had more experience in relationships, Penny thought as she showered and dressed for work. She'd dated and had relationships but never anything very lasting. Never anything that she'd wanted to last.

But then she'd never felt in anyone else's arms what she had felt with Brad last night. But what was it? What did it mean? He was a loner, he'd said, but maybe she was, too. Maybe all this worrying was crazy. She should relax and see what happens.

By the time she went out into the yard, Penny had a bounce in her step and a smile on her lips. She wasn't going to fre and worry and stew. Whatever came, came. Her crews were checking their equipment, getting their work schedules from Carl, and complaining about the heat. It wasn't even seven in the morning and already the temperature was over eighty degrees. A beast of a day to be working outside, but she didn't mind. The less she fussed over this, the better it would be.

"I'm going to be doing estimates in town all morning," she told Carl. "I'll catch up with you after lunch."

"If we haven't melted," he said.

She just laughed. "You've all got a ways to go until you melt into a little puddle." With a half skip, she hurried over to the trailer to get her own schedule. She had a full morning of appointments, if she—

Brad was coming down the porch steps. He didn't look particularly lighthearted and her good spirits took a slight hit. Was he still fretting over last night? But when his eyes met hers, he smiled and his mood seemed to brighten.

"Good morning," she said, stopping to wait for him. The light breeze still carried a hint of the night's dampness and memories of being close.

"Hi."

His blue eyes spoke volumes even though his words were clipped and short. His eyes warmed and remembered last night also, showing a flicker of the fire that had almost consumed them. Inviting her to linger in his arms again.

"Aunty Em insisted that she would work the office today."

His words held no invitation, though that was just his way and it didn't bother her. She knew what was in his soul. His eyes told her.

"She said she was going to," Penny said.

"You need me for anything else, then?"

How about to kiss me? she thought. Or to tell my troubles to? Or just to laugh with me over some small silly thing?

"No, I don't think so." She would play his little game.

"I thought I'd go on over to Uncle Hal's and work some more on his personal stuff."

"Sure. That's what you came for, after all."

"Yeah." He looked like there was something else he wanted to say, or something else he wanted to do. She could read the indecision in his eyes, along with a craving for something more. But after a moment, he turned and went back into the house.

With a sad smile, Penny hurried into the trailer. And he claimed that he never opened his heart to anyone! Obviously he didn't know about those eyes of his. She got her own list and hurried off to the first stop.

The library needed the trees trimmed around the parking lot and she counted the number of trees and made some notes. Then they wanted to discuss some new plantings around the front door. And what would grow and bloom there on the shady east side of the building?

Maybe she had been planted on the shady side of a building. She hadn't really bloomed until Brad had come along and brought the sun.

Then she had to hurry off to a church on First Street. This stop was fast. An evergreen ravaged by pine borers needed removing. Measure, count, check access, make notes and promise an estimate within a few days.

Funny how something so small as a pine borer could take down a huge old tree. Or how something so small as a touch of Brad's hand could erase years of keeping her heart safe.

Next she drove over to Lincoln Avenue where several blocks of new sidewalks were going to be put in. She wanted to bid on the tree work involved, but it was a big job and she had to make sure she covered the costs. More measuring, counting and note taking.

The old overgrown trees and bushes would have to be taken out, roots and all, so that a good, smooth, lasting sidewalk could be put down. Just as Brad's old habits and wariness would have to be torn aside if a new relationship was going to bind them.

And was one? By the time noon rolled around, Penny was pretty sure she wanted to try. All she needed was a plan. A workable plan. She drove over to Barbeque Bill's to pick up some lunch before she headed back to the nursery. But as she was about to pull into the drive-through lane, she saw Dorothy at the restaurant door, waving at her. With a little fast maneuvering, Penny pulled into a parking space.

Dorothy came rushing over, her eyes sparkling with excitement. "I've been trying to find a minute to call you," she said. "You'll never guess what happened?"

Penny felt her heart leap with hope as she got out of the truck. Were things falling into place for all of them? "Toto proposed?"

Dorothy gave her an odd look. "No, the Boys and Girls Club float got funded. And we're going to need some press releases on it."

"Sure." That was great, really it was, but a different kind of great. They walked toward the restaurant. "What happened?"

"I have no idea. I got a call from the bank yesterday afternoon that a donation had been sent in."

"From whom?"

Dorothy shook her head and pulled open the door. "Mr. Anony Mous."

"Wow." She couldn't help but laugh and give Dorothy a hug. This was an answer to their prayers. "Any clue as to who it is?"

"Five thousand dollars was wired in from some bank in Colorado so I don't think it's somebody local. Maybe somebody sent it because of you being on that TV show."

"Five thousand!" Penny cried. "Good golly!" This was so exciting, especially if she had a hand in it. "I suppose it's possible it was because of the TV show." They got into line to order their lunches and reality caught up with her. "Unless it was specifically sent for the float. That came up after I was on TV."

"Oh, yeah." Dorothy frowned. "And nobody knew about it except a few people."

"So, it's got to be somebody local."

"But who?"

"Good question." They moved up a few feet. "I thought we had tapped all the local sources of funding ages ago. Hard to believe there's somebody out there we didn't know about."

Dorothy's eyes narrowed with thought. "What about Brad? He's sort of local and sort of not."

"Brad?" Penny laughed. "Brad doesn't have five thousand dollars to give anyone. You saw his car."

"But maybe—"

The soft ringing of Penny's cell phone interrupted them and Penny unclipped her phone from her belt while the other people in line turned to look at her.

"They calling you for dates while you're getting lunch, Penny?" someone farther back in line called out.

"Maybe it's Hollywood asking her to star in some Mel Gibson movie," someone else said.

Penny just laughed. "It's probably Carl. Or Gran reminding me to have some lunch." She opened the connection. "Penny here."

"Ms. Donnelly?" It was a stranger's voice. "This is Jane Danvers of the Smithsonian—"

Penny stopped breathing as the woman rattled on about *The Wizard of Oz* in Retrospect conference, then about the prestigious nature of the event and the eminent scholars that would be there. Fear clutched at Penny's stomach. They were telling her she wasn't good enough to even have applied. That she should just withdraw her abstract quietly or they would make a laughingstock of her.

Penny felt her heart drop to her feet as Dorothy dragged her a little farther up the food line.

"—and we'd like you to lead that workshop."

"I beg your pardon?" Penny must have missed something. Her ears must not work when her feet were moving. For a minute it sounded like they wanted her to speak at the conference. "I'm sorry I didn't quite hear what…"

The woman was going on. "We were really impressed by the way you were able to relate the whole Oz theme to today's culture."

"Oh?"

"And so we were hoping you would be able to present at the conference."

"I see." She was feeling light-headed, like she had when she'd been under the klieg lights too long when modeling. Maybe this was all a hallucination.

"I can understand if you want to think about it," the woman said. "But—"

"No," Penny said quickly.

"No?" The woman's voice was regretful. "I'm so sorry—"

Oh, heavens, what had she done? "No, I mean I don't have to think about it," Penny said. "I'd be happy to."

"Wonderful," the woman replied. "We'll have the specifics out in the mail to you sometime after Labor Day."

The connection was broken, but Penny just stood there, holding her phone. She had done it! She had been asked to be part of the conference.

"Penny?" Dorothy touched her arm. "You okay?"

Penny took a deep breath and turned her phone off, then carefully clipped it back on her belt. Okay? She was better than okay, she was great! But how did she play this?

Gran had already told everyone she was speaking at the conference, like it was a done deal, so to start screaming and jumping up and down would make people ask questions.

"Yeah. Sure. I'm fine," she said, lightly, offhandedly. "That was just a call inviting me to speak at that Oz conference I told you about ages ago."

"Really? How cool!"

But Penny just looked ahead of them at the line as if the call had been nothing. "Oh, terrific, it's almost our turn. I'm starving."

It was one thing to pretend nonchalance for a few minutes, but something in her needed to celebrate. She had to share this with someone—someone who knew the true situation.

Brad.

Dorothy pulled out first, taking a left out of the parking lot. Penny gave her a honk for good luck, then she took a right onto Calumet and headed for Brad's uncle's house. The truck smelled of barbeque chicken but it wasn't her stomach that was hungry.

She parked the truck in the alley behind the old redbrick house, then grabbed up the lunch and got out. The yard was weedy and overgrown, and the paint trim on the house was flaking, but the place looked like a palace. And she was Cinderella arriving for the ball.

She cut across the yard, skipped up the front porch and through the wide-open front door. "Hello," she called out. "Anybody home?"

There was a moment of silence, then Brad appeared at the top of the grand old staircase. Looking pretty darn grand himself.

"Penny?"

"You look disappointed. What's the matter? Did you order a redhead?"

He gave her a questioning look as he came down the stairs, then stared pointedly at the covered paper cups in her hand. "What's in the glasses?" he asked. "Or would it be more appropriate to ask what used to be in them? You look like you've been sampling the happy juice."

"Don't be a fuddy-duddy," she said and brought the lunch into the living room where she put it down on a sheet-draped end table. "Here I come, ready to celebrate and you're trying to put a damper on things."

He had closed the front door and come into the living room doorway, leaning against the door frame. "What are we celebrating?"

She just grinned at him and spread her arms wide. "I'm in. I'm in."

His expression was so befuddled that Penny burst into laughter and danced across the floor to throw her arms around him.

"Oh, I am so happy, I can't stand it," she said.

His arms came around her, maybe to steady her, maybe to hold her, but she didn't care the reasons. This was the right place to celebrate her triumph and this was the right person to celebrate it with. She leaned forward and brushed his mouth with hers.

It was supposed to be a celebratory kiss. A kiss between friends. A kiss that was like the clinking of champagne glasses. But the soft sweetness of his lips caught her by surprise and something moved in her soul. She felt a stirring that had little to do with her invitation to the conference and absolutely nothing to do with Oz.

She moved closer into his arms. A fire exploded inside her, engulfing all her senses into a hot, burning torrent of need, even as warning lights went on in her head. That fire wanted to consume her as she wanted to consume him, but she needed to think this through.

They pulled apart slowly, and a measure of sanity returned. But only a small measure. And even that was not too strong as she saw echoes of her own confusion in his eyes.

"Congratulations," he said. "I don't know what for, but I've always liked to see you happy."

Her joy came rushing back, almost sending her teetering out of control. What was she so worried about? This wasn't forever, it was just now. And wasn't that all she wanted?

She threw her arms back around him, needing him near, needing to hear his heart beating so close to hers. "I'm going to speak at *The Wizard of Oz* conference next year."

His arms came around her in a gentle enfolding. "That's great."

His voice was so soft, but the emotion in it was so strong. He knew how much she had wanted this, and he seemed as pleased as if he had done it himself. The honor was even more special because she could share it with him. Of all her friends and family, Brad was the person who best knew what a struggle this was. And what a victory. Not even Alex realized how long or how desperately she'd dreamed of this sort of recognition. How had fate sent Brad to her at this time?

"I almost can't believe it." She let go of him enough to

look up into his eyes, to revel in the joy there. "I never expected to hear this soon. All they have is my abstract."

"They just knew a good thing when they saw it."

She laughed and cuddled up close again. "Maybe they hardly got any and everyone who submitted got accepted."

"Hey!" He held her away from him, a frown on his face and anger in his eyes. "Don't put yourself down like that."

She'd only been joking, but laughed at the outrage in his voice. He was so cute. She pulled him back into her arms. "It's okay," she said. "'Cause I'm going to wow them with my paper. They won't know what hit them."

"I can relate to that," he murmured.

All of a sudden everything changed. They weren't talking about the conference anymore. She looked up at him, her smile fading slightly. Or maybe it went inward somehow so that it warmed her heart instead of her lips.

A bemused look rode on his face, but his eyes kept straying to her mouth. Kept flickering with a hint of the fire she felt in his hands. A burning that was flickering deep in her own heart. When had longing turned to need and wishing turned to necessity? When had his arms become her haven of happiness? When had childish dreams become an adult reality?

"I brought us lunch," she said. Her voice was a hoarse whisper.

"That might be a good idea."

But his arms did not release her, his gaze did not let her go. His eyes just searched hers for aeons of time, asking questions his lips dared not say.

"It might be," she agreed. "Though there's no need to rush it."

"It might spoil."

"Not for ages."

"Are you sure?"

The question wasn't about feeding their bodies but feeding their souls. It was about the touch of their hands, the hunger on their lips, the brief union of their souls. It was about a moment of passion and a moment of ecstasy.

"Yes, I'm sure," she said softly.

But neither moved. They stared into each other's eyes for what seemed forever. Long enough for the angels to gather a choir. Long enough for Penny to change her mind a hundred thousand times, if she had wanted to. Which she didn't.

"You sure you're hungry?" she asked.

"More than you can imagine."

She went ever so slowly back into his embrace. It was ever so sweet. A thousand times more perfect than she could have dreamed. His lips were water to her parched soul. His touch was the sun to her chilled heart. She felt as if she had been asleep and was now coming back to life.

The touch of his mouth on hers had been tender, gentle, and then grew harder and more demanding. She felt an answering hunger deep in her soul. A hunger that could not, would not, be contained.

She ran her hands over his back, pulling him close, delighting in the feel of him. Her fingers slid over the soft fabric of his shirt, but underneath she could feel the warmth of his skin and the steel of his muscles. She could feel, too, in some way, the racing of his heart. Maybe it was through her touch, or maybe through her lips still on his. Or maybe it was as an echo of the pounding of her own heart.

His hands were on her, awakening a passion she'd never known before, but his was a need less patient than hers. He pulled her shirt from her jeans and let his fingers feel her skin. Over her back in a slow and steady caress. Up toward her shoulders, and down below her waist. His hands were on fire, and spreading heat over her. The slightest touch, the merest whisper of his hand on her, left a fiery trail for her heart to follow.

They pulled slightly apart as if of one mind, but still lay in each other's arms. Hearts pounding. Breath a memory. But the blaze still consumed them.

"This isn't how I planned to spend the lunch hour," Brad whispered into her hair.

"We can still stop," she said.

He laughed. She could feel his body tremble though he barely made a sound. "You think so?" he asked. "I don't think there's enough cold water in all of Indiana."

She turned back to his lips, heady with the knowledge that she stirred him. And heavy with the hunger that his nearness arose in her.

Her touch was less patient and slow as her hands ran over his body. Under his shirt they slid, to feel the magic of his bare skin. His back, his chest, then down across his stomach, her splayed fingers felt a tremor deep within him. Or within her. An explosion building.

He undid her bra, then pulled it and her T-shirt off so that his lips could move from hers, to capture the tips of her breasts. First one, tugged and sucked at, licked and teased and tormented. Then the other, as her heart raced out of control. Her hands, somehow still able to move even as her body cried out for Brad's, tugged at the buttons of his shirt until she finally freed him of it.

But then Brad stopped and looked around them. "Are you game for this?" he asked. "We can go upstairs."

"Maybe you can," she said. "But I'm not in the mood for a walk." She took him over to the sofa and tossed back the sheet covering it, then pulled him down with her.

Lying on the old sofa, their bodies pressed together, seemed to shorten their fuses and added urgency to their every move. His kiss was hot and hungry, searing and searching as his tongue probed into her mouth. Her hands were demanding as they clutched at him, held him, pulled him closer than it was possible to be.

Then he was tugging off her jeans, she was pulling off his shorts until there was nothing between them. Flesh against flesh. Hot need against moist hungry heat. Entwined, heart to heart, their bodies spoke to the other. Racing pulse to racing pulse. Hungry lips to hungry lips. Burning soul to burning soul.

She'd never known such hunger, such elemental need. It was as if part of her had been missing and now was found. Her hands wondered at the feel of him, her lips marveled at his taste. She wanted to touch him all over, to caress every inch of him, and to know he came alive at her stroking.

But his hands cupped her breasts and he took the tender tips into his mouth, and she forgot everything else. She was all hunger and need. The fire she'd felt earlier was nothing compared to the desire shooting through her now. She melted under his touch, becoming one with him in spirit and in time.

Moving beneath him, she opened her heart and took him in, and they became one in body. As they lay together, their bodies pulsed to a timeless rhythm. A symphony fashioned in the stars. Locked in each other's arms, they let the heat engulf them and throw them into the heavens in a wild spray of shooting stars.

It was magic and more. It was the world coming to an end, or maybe beginning. It was wonderful.

Then afterward, as their hearts slowed to a mere mortal speed, they still lay on the old sofa. As if neither could break the spell.

"This wasn't how I had pictured this," he said after a long moment.

"Oh?" She was still trying to catch her breath, her mind was still fuzzy. She had thought it was perfect. Magic. Heaven here in Chesterton. "What do you mean?"

He smiled down at her, planting gentle little kisses along her neck. "I had thought maybe candlelight and soft music. A romantic setting."

"This isn't romantic?" she teased and let her fingers slide down his jaw.

He caught her hand and brought it to his lips. "Actually, it's perfect. Me and you."

"What more do we need?"

"Exactly," he said as he leaned down to take her lips with his once again.

Brad looked across the VFW hall at the couples forming up their squares for a dance. This had to be a nightmare. Or some diabolical form of punishment. He'd had his moment of ecstasy earlier that day in Penny's arms and now he was paying for it by having to go to a square dance.

"Are you all right?" she asked.

Her eyes were like two lakes, radiating pools of soft concern as they had back in the seventh grade when she'd ask him why he came to school so early. He used to worry back then that she knew Mrs. Hartman was secretly slipping extra food into his lunch and that, in gratitude for both the extra food and the fact she never said a word to him about it, he'd started coming early to help the teacher with classroom chores. After a time though, he realized Penny just wanted everyone to be happy. And she still did.

"I'm fine," he said, though his heart was heavy. Remorse was the only feeling he could put a finger on, not annoyance at being here. How could he be annoyed at anything when he was with Penny? "Ginger, peachy dandy fine."

"Are you sure?" She moved up to him and put her arms around his neck. "We don't have to stay if you don't want to."

A hint of the day's earlier fire threatened to overcome him and he had to fight it back. "No, no, this is great. I just haven't been to a square dance in a long time."

A frown settled on her beautiful lips and worry flickered in her eyes. "Probably because you hate them, right?"

"Stop fussing, will you?" He brushed a curl back from her forehead, knowing he should minimize his contact with her but unable to help himself. "New things are good for me."

"You look like you're at the doctor's office, waiting for a shot."

He brushed her lips with his, then moved gently from the circle of her arms. "Just worried about do-si-doing when I should be swinging my partner."

"Silly," she said with a laugh. She turned to watch the dancers from his side.

Silly didn't begin to describe the feelings churning around inside him. Wonder and awe at being in the light of Penny's smile for even a short time. Guilt for taking advantage of her sweetness for his own pleasure and agony at the thought of leaving her. Yet there was no way he could stay.

They had shared a moment of passion, but that wasn't a relationship. If he stayed, she would want one. Expect one. Deserve one. And there was no way he could give her one. There was no way that he could share the secrets that lay deep inside his soul. Hell, he didn't know what they were, so if he didn't share them with himself, how could he share them with someone else? No, the best he could do was make sure she enjoyed the last few days he would be here. No moping, no letting his guilt pull him away.

"Hi, Penny. Brad."

He turned to see Dorothy and Heather approaching, both in the same type of full-skirted cowgirl outfit Penny was wearing, and he smiled. The more people around them, the easier he could escape his thoughts.

Dorothy gave Brad the once-over and then frowned. "You're not exactly dressed for square-dancing."

He glanced down at himself. Casual Egyptian cotton shirt, linen pants and custom-made leather loafers. But Penny slipped her arm through his, bristling like a mother dog about to protect her pup.

"There's nothing wrong with what he's wearing."

"No boots," Dorothy said.

"No cowboy hat," Heather added.

"I actually do have a pair of cowboy boots back home." He jumped into the teasing with relief. "Just forgot what a world-class center of cowboyism Indiana is."

"How about the hat?" Heather asked.

He shook his head. "Nope. No cowboy hat."

"You could've worn a baseball cap," Dorothy suggested. "They're almost as good."

"Sorry, no baseball caps, either."

"Well, a knitted stocking hat wouldn't hack it," Heather said. "So don't even suggest it."

"Wasn't going to," he replied. "Don't have one of those, either."

"Jeez, don't you have any hats?" Penny sounded shocked.

"Hey, I live in the land of sunshine, remember?" he stated and glanced around. "Is that Toto over by the bar?"

"Probably." Dorothy wasn't even looking in that direction. "He sometimes works as a security guard at the dances."

"Must cut into his social life."

"Toto has no social life," Heather said.

Dorothy put her hand on Heather's arm. "Oh, look, Heather. The Kirby brothers are here. Let's see if they want to dance in the next set."

Suddenly Brad and Penny were alone again. Or as alone as they could be, surrounded by a hall full of people. Yet his awareness of her was growing as if they were alone, and so was his guilt. The first dance set had concluded and new squares were forming.

"Do you want to dance?" he asked her.

"Are you sure?"

"Hey, if your ankle's up to it, so are my feet. Just remember I'm a rookie and take pity on me."

He was rewarded with the sunshine of her smile and let her lead him over to the dance floor. Okay, so he was willing to walk barefoot over hot coals just to see her smile. And would even square-dance to hear her laughter. It didn't change who he was and what he wasn't. Or what he could not do.

"Hey there, Brad," someone called out as they took their place in a square.

"You a dancer?" someone else asked.

"Just watch out for your toes," he warned the other couples in the set.

"Oh, you'll be fine," Penny said. "Stop putting yourself down."

Her cheeks were a tantalizing rosy hue, and her eyes glittered with joy. He would dance like an angel if that's what she wanted. Just to see that smile.

Well, maybe an angel was a little bit of an exaggeration. But he tried. He allemanded left and allemanded thar. He chained down the line, courtesy turned, and scatter scooted. Not that he had any clue what he was doing, only tried to follow the others. Around and back. Up and down. In and out. Doing his best to keep Penny alive with laughter.

Actually square-dancing wasn't so bad. No, it was pretty good. That full skirt of Penny's swung and swayed and flipped as she danced and gave him enticing glimpses of her gorgeous long legs.

He wasn't allowed to hold her enough, though. She'd just get close and send his temperature soaring, then she'd be swinging off again on someone else's arm. It was downright annoying at first, but then he got used to it. Made himself get used to it. That was what was going to happen in a few days anyway. Only he'd be the one going away.

"Hey, what's wrong?" she asked him when they had an all too brief promenade left together.

"Just untangling my legs," he told her and forced a smile. "This is hard work, you know."

"You're doing great," she said and blew him a kiss as they parted again.

He steeled himself against the pain of seeing her dance away from him. Tomorrow he would go see Matt Harris and find out if Dorothy had the real estate contract ready for him. And then he'd make his plane reservations for that conference in Paris.

By the time Penny was back at his side, his plans were etched indelibly into his heart. He was safe from his weak resolve, and so was Penny. He had to stay strong so that she wouldn't get hurt. He could do it. He would do it for her sake.

"And kiss your lady goodbye," the caller sang out, wrapping up the dance.

The couples all clapped and laughed, and Brad allowed himself one more swing of his partner, just to see Penny's smile light up her face. The end was far too prophetic for him, cut a little too close to his heart. But Penny seemed not to notice. She laughed and fell back into his arms for a moment of pure rapture, then she stepped back.

"Now, wasn't that fun?" she said.

What—seeing her laugh? Holding her hands? Being caught

up in her delight? "Yeah, it was," he agreed. "But I'm dying of thirst. Want to get something to drink?"

"Sure." She wrapped her arm around his. "The caller's taking a break anyway."

They joined the throng moving toward the bar. He was ready to push his way through, but she was content to linger and chat, so he forced his feet to move slowly. Trouble was, slow-moving feet meant an active brain.

Did he need to tell her he was leaving soon? He thought he'd been pretty clear about his intentions when he'd first come, but did she remember?

"Bradley!" A middle-aged man slapped him on the back. "Good to see you. Are you back to stay?"

"Uh, not exactly," Brad said. He had no idea who this guy was, but was annoyed with him anyway. He hadn't wanted to tell Penny of his plans here like this.

But she was laughing. "Oh, Mickey. Can you imagine Brad living here? That would be like the Wizard moving to Kansas."

They both laughed. Brad tried to join them but found it hard going. Didn't she want him here?

Chapter Eleven

Penny had about three weeks' worth of work to do the next morning, but couldn't concentrate on any of it. Oh, she waded through it somehow, but used the excuse of a broken chain saw to come back to the nursery at lunchtime. Not that she knew why.

Brad was leaving. He hadn't said anything about it, but she had seen his face last night when Mickey Juarez had asked him if he was back to stay. Horrified was a polite way to describe it.

She had known he wouldn't move back here. At least her head had known. He'd been upfront about himself right from the start. There really was no reason to think he'd change his mind. Well, maybe a little reason. They had made love, after all. But that obviously wasn't enough.

Penny got her lunch from the truck and walked across the deserted yard to the trailer. It was empty except for Einstein sprawled out on the desk.

"Where's Aunty Em?" she asked the orange tabby. "Up at the house?"

Einstein flicked his eyes open for an instant, just long enough to give her an am-I-Aunty-Em's-keeper? look before quickly closing them again.

"Sorry to disturb you, your highness."

Penny sank down into the desk chair and pulled a sandwich out of the small cooler. At times, Brad had seemed to care about her. And he certainly seemed to feel at home in Chesterton. So, why wouldn't he stay? All that nonsense about not being able to open up was just that—nonsense. There had to be another reason.

"It's not like he's got a real home somewhere," she mused to Einstein as she ate. The cat had opened one eye and was watching her sandwich. "He says home is where he hangs his hat, but then he doesn't even have a hat. Doesn't even have a job as far as I can tell."

She stopped. Maybe that was it. Maybe he didn't want to be living off them, but if he had a job, he would stay.

So, all she had to do was find him a job. Simple. Sure.

Einstein got up slowly and walked over to sniff at the ham. She broke off a small piece for him. "Brad did a good job on the computer. I don't know what he did to it, but it is a lot faster now. And Gran can surf the Net." Penny wasn't exactly sure that was a good thing since Gran mentioned yesterday that she could order a cigarette lighter surveillance camera without leaving home now.

Obviously Brad knew computers. How hard could it be to find a job in computers these days? She put the remains of her sandwich back in the sandwich bag and pulled the Yellow Pages from the file cabinet. Turning to the personnel agencies, she found a whole list of them that specialized in computer personnel.

She closed her eyes and picked one. Compu-Staff. Looked good. They had a big ad and a 1-800 telephone number. She dialed it.

"Marty Simmons, how may I help you?"

"I'm looking for a job," she replied. "For a friend."

"What's your friend looking for?"

Penny hesitated. Good question. What did Brad do with computers? "Repair," she guessed.

"Mainframe? PC? Peripherals? Networks?"

"Uh…" There was a lot more to computers than she'd realized. "All of those." Heck, he'd always been the smartest kid in their class. "He's quite versatile."

"Wow. A guy like that can pretty much write his own ticket." Then the man quickly added. "Or gal. The computer field is very equal opportunity."

"It's a guy," Penny said. "His name is Bradley Corrigan."

"Brad Corrigan?" The man laughed. "Not *the* Brad Corrigan?"

"Huh?" Penny must have looked as confused as she felt. Gran had just come in and was giving her a quizzical look.

"I'm just joking," the man said. "It can't be *the* Brad Corrigan. He wouldn't be looking for a job repairing equipment. In fact, with all his money, he doesn't have to look for any kind of a job. People come to him and beg."

Penny closed her mouth. "Well, this Brad Corrigan definitely isn't rich. He's just an ordinary guy."

"Yeah," the man agreed. "It's not that uncommon a name, I guess."

Actually she was wrong. Brad was far from ordinary. He had the most piercing eyes, the softest smile, the—

She sat up straight and cleared her throat. "I'll give Brad your name and number and have him call you himself, okay? Thanks for your time." She hung up the phone.

"Who were you talking to?" Gran asked.

Penny got to her feet, feeling more alive than she had all morning. "Some guy from Compu-Staff. It's an employment agency."

"Looking for another job?"

"No," Penny replied, laughing as she gathered up her lunch. "I'm trying to find something for Brad."

"He ask you to?"

Penny shook her head. "A body doesn't always have to wait to be asked."

"How do you know he doesn't have a job?" Gran asked. "He's got some nice-looking clothes. Had to have some way to buy them."

"They have all sorts of clothes at resale shops these days," Penny told her. "Or he could have saved up to buy them just for this trip. He always was awfully proud."

"But wouldn't mind it if you found him a job, I take it?"

Penny felt a glow build up in her traitorous cheeks and quickly pulled a peach from her cooler. "I'm just looking around for him, Granny," Penny said and took a bite of the fruit.

Gran sat down at the computer. "You know, it's going to take more than a job to keep Brad in Chesterton. You want Brad to stay, you're going to have to give him a reason." Gran hesitated a moment. "A good reason. A personal reason."

"I'm not playing those kinds of games," Penny replied and finished her peach, then wrapped the pit in a paper napkin and tossed it into the trash. "I'm just trying to help him find a job."

"I can't see that doing anything but aggravating him."

Penny's head shot up and she glared at her grandmother. "Why?" she asked. "I'm just trying to help him."

"Didn't make you happy when he tried to help you."

"That was back in junior high. We aren't kids anymore."

"Kids don't change all that much when they grow up," her grandmother replied. "They're just more of what they used to be."

"Hmph." Penny went over to the door. "I'm going back to work."

Dorothy hurried back into her office. "Sorry about that, Brad." She closed the door and went around to her desk.

The scent of roses was strong in the room and she suddenly felt blue. It was so sweet of Toto to have sent her flowers to celebrate her sale last Sunday. He really was rooting for her. So, why then did she feel sad about it?

She sat down. "You'd think the festival was tomorrow, not in six weeks, the way everyone needs things now."

"No problem." He tossed a guidebook to Paris onto her desk. "You planning a trip?"

She glanced down at the book, feeling her cheeks blush slightly. Damn, she'd left that out. "Not exactly," she said and put the book into a drawer with what she hoped was indifference.

"Not exactly?"

Obviously she had fallen a little short. She sat down in her chair and took a deep breath. "I'm planning on moving there," she told him. "I've got my visa and everything."

"Wow." He looked surprised. "I had thought you were a dyed-in-the wool Chestertonian."

"Not me." She leaned forward, putting her arms on her desk. "It's always been my dream to move someplace exciting."

"And Paris is it?"

There was something in his voice that irked her, a hint of skepticism or cynicism or something. Whatever it was, it was annoying. "Yes, it is," she said. "It's a city of romance."

He shifted his position, as if to see her better. "Speaking of romance, I thought you and Toto were an item."

She sat back in her chair. "Not since high school." But the roses seemed to mock her and she looked away.

Back in high school, she'd loved everything about Toto, thought their future had been all sewn up together, but then he'd pulled away and decided they should just be friends. She'd resurrected her old junior high Paris idea to see if she could light a fire under him again. It hadn't worked, but the idea had hung around until it was the only dream she trusted now.

"He doesn't object to your moving?"

Dorothy frowned at Brad. "What right would he have to object? Not any more than Penny would have to object to something you do."

"Penny?" His color seemed to heighten. "What does she have to do with anything?"

Dorothy sighed. The man was dense. "Toto having a crush on me back in school is the same as Penny having a crush on you back then. Neither—"

"She didn't have a crush on me," Brad said. "She didn't know I was alive hardly."

"Oh, come on, Brad. You had to have known." But from the look on his face, he hadn't. "Well, it doesn't make any difference now. What you two are working on now, that's what's important. Not how one of you felt in the past."

He hardly seemed reassured. "We're not working on anything now," he said. "Well, we're friends, but I'm going to be leaving soon myself."

"You are?" Her heart fell. She had thought something was developing between him and Penny, but she must have been wrong. Or was this one-sided? She had seen how Penny's eyes glowed whenever she looked at Brad. Poor Penny!

He cleared his throat and leaned forward in his chair, but his eyes didn't quite meet hers. "You have a contract for me to sign so the house can be put on the market?"

Subject closed, that was clear. "Yeah, it's right here." She took some papers out of a folder lying on the desk. "Here's the data on the house, with the pluses I'll stress and a few of the problem areas we'll have to allow for in the pricing. There are some repairs that should be done now—the lock on the front door should be fixed, the bushes along the south side of the house need trimming and that broken windowpane in the dining room needs to be replaced—but I'll see to them and—"

He waved his hand at the papers. "I don't care about any of this. Repair what needs to be repaired. Don't repair what doesn't and sell it for whatever you think. Just give me what I have to sign."

"But don't you care about the details?"

"Not really."

"If it's priced too high, it could sit for months. But if it's too low, you might not get what you want out of it."

"I don't want to get anything out of it. I don't need this money."

She sank back in her chair, just staring at him. It all became very clear. She didn't know the whys and wherefores, but she sure did know the whos. "You donated the money for the float."

Restless and impatient, he got to his feet. "Where's the contract? I just want to be done with all this." His voice was strained.

She put the contract on top of the other papers and pointed to the line for his signature. He signed it in a quick scrawl, then tossed the pen back on the desk. It was done. He would be gone soon.

"So, when are you leaving?" he asked.

"For Paris?" She was weary all of a sudden. Nothing seemed to be as easy as it was supposed to be. "The commission on this house would do it."

He laughed, a bitter sound. "So if this sells fast, we could be traveling together then. I'm supposed to be in Paris next week for a conference."

"I don't think the house will go that fast. Though I could leave once an offer was accepted." The idea of traveling with someone was tempting. The idea of it being so soon was scary.

"Where are you going to live?"

She shrugged. "I don't know yet. I figured I'd find a place when I got there." She tore off the bottom copy of the contract and gave it to him.

"I have an apartment there. It's not much, but you're welcome to use it for as long as you like."

"You have an apartment there?" She was dumbfounded. Who just happened to have an apartment in Paris? No one else that she knew. "What for?"

"For when I'm in Paris," he replied. He folded up his copy of the contract and slipped it in his pocket. "I don't use it much since I finished up a job there, so it won't be any inconvenience."

"Thanks." There was no real reason to stay in Chesterton

any longer, then. She didn't really need that commission now to fund her until she found a place to stay and a job. So, why wasn't she more excited?

"No problem," Brad said and started for the door. "Nancy can witness my signature on the probate papers can't she?"

"Sure, or I can." There was something in his step that tugged at her. Not weariness, resignation maybe.

"Brad?"

He turned.

"How many languages do you know?"

"One," he said sharply. "So don't even think about it."

The Jeep was parked right next to Dorothy's office but Brad wasn't ready to drive someplace. He needed to work off some energy. He started down the block in a solid stride, fast enough to get his heart pumping and quicken his breath.

But not fast enough to escape thoughts of Penny.

She couldn't have had a crush on him back in junior high, could she have? He would have known. And heaven knows, he watched her constantly for any sign.

No, he was more worried about her feelings now. She seemed to be assuming he was not going to stay, but the longer he did, the more she would be questioning that. So he ought to just get off his duff and go.

By some strange coincidence, he was across the street from the Flying Monkeys' Travel. A sign, surely. He crossed over and walked to the door. There was a display in the window for fares to Europe with a cardboard Eiffel Tower in the middle. Another sign.

But try as he might, he could not open the door. Oh, it was openable for other people, since a couple went in while he stood there and some people came out. But he could not get his feet to cross that threshold.

Which was only right. He couldn't buy tickets for Paris and risk Penny finding out from someone else. He had to tell her himself, then get the tickets. It was the right way to do things. The way a gentleman should.

He drove back to the nursery, trying to formulate a plan. That should be easy for him; he was good at plans. So, why wasn't one coming?

He drove slowly, he drove fast, but nothing seemed to jog his brain into working. By the time he pulled the Jeep into the yard, he was still at a loss.

It was this place, he decided. His plan had to go into action somewhere else, not here. Not on Penny and Aunty Em's turf. He'd take them out for dinner, someplace nice to show them how much he appreciated their kindness. And they'd see how successful he'd become so when he casually dropped in that he'd be leaving, they wouldn't be surprised. Simply perfect.

Except it proved to be neither. Aunty Em couldn't see wasting good money on dinner out.

"I can make us a dinner much cheaper here at home," she said.

"I want to save you the work."

"Restaurant food is full of chemicals and preservatives."

"Not necessarily."

Penny was no better. "Dress up?" she said. "Can't we just go to the Pizza Prince?"

"You go there all the time." He was starting to get annoyed. "I want to take you someplace different."

"How about the pancake house, then? We've never been there."

The pancake house? Why didn't she just offer to run to the grocery store for some microwave dinners? The discussion was over.

"We're going to the Prime Table," Brad announced. "I am making reservations for six-thirty. That gives us all an hour to get ready."

There was a lot of grumbling, but both women went off to their respective rooms. Or they did once Brad parked himself in the kitchen to make sure Aunty Em didn't sneak in and cook something anyway. The grumbling changed to sharply closed doors and something that sounded suspiciously like boots being thrown across a room. He didn't care; he was taking them out for a good time tonight.

An hour later, they were ready to go. They didn't look all that thrilled, but at least they had stopped grumbling. They piled into the truck and he drove them there in silence. Luckily the restaurant wasn't too far.

"Either of you ever been here before?" he asked as he parked. It was time to start having fun.

"No." They answered in surly unison.

"Great, then it'll be a new adventure for us all."

The restaurant went in heavily for atmosphere. Massive dark wood, trimmed with brass and very dim lighting. Not exactly his taste, but the food smelled delicious. They were shown to a secluded table in a small dining room and given menus that dwarfed them.

"Heavens to Betsy!" Aunty Em cried. "Look at these prices! We can't eat here."

For goodness' sake. Maybe they didn't recognize a Rolex, but didn't they realize the shirt he was wearing was silk? Or that his linen pants were handmade? Did they still really think he was penniless?

"Of course, we can," Brad said quietly.

"No, she's right," Penny said in a harsh whisper. She leaned closer to him. "We can go to the Pizza Prince. Or we'll stop at the grocery store and get some microwave—"

"We are staying," he informed them.

"Is there a problem, sir?" The waiter had obviously been hovering nearby.

"Not at all," Brad said. "Shall we order some drinks first?"

Penny closed her menu with a bright smile. "I'm ready to order. I'll have a salad. A small salad."

"And I'll have soup," Aunty Em said. "A cup, not a bowl."

"Very good." The waiter was trying to hide a frown. "And to drink?"

"Water," they both said.

Brad leaned back and glared at them both. They really were determined to not have a good time. He looked at the waiter.

"With their soup and salad, we'll each have an order of prime rib, medium rare. Duchess potatoes and the vegetable of the day. And—" he opened the wine list "—a bottle of Château Lafite Rothschild."

The waiter's note taking faltered. "Uh, are you…"

Brad slipped him his American Express card. "Yes, I'm certain. A 1985, if you have it."

The waiter collected the card, the menus, and slunk away. No doubt to make sure Brad could afford several hundred dollars for a bottle of wine. Which is exactly what Brad would do in his case.

Aunty Em rapped his knuckles. "For a man who claims he's got no job, boy, you spend money like a drunken sailor."

He should tell them. There was no reason to keep it a secret, except that the words just would not come. He'd waited for them to see the new him for so long, he didn't know how to point it out to them.

And if these words wouldn't come, these easy words of no consequence, certainly the deeper, harder words of sharing would never come. It was just as well he'd be gone in a few days. For Penny's sake.

"I'm good at washing dishes," he said.

They both glared at him, but the wine steward was carrying the wine over as if it were the Crown Jewels. Good thing Penny and her grandmother didn't know wine or he'd be in real trouble. After the bottle was opened, tasted and approved, they settled back with their wine.

"Well, here's to Penny's speech at the Oz conference," he said, raising his glass.

"Bet they'll want her back all the time," Aunty Em responded.

"It's a one-time thing, so I don't need to worry." Penny sipped at her wine. "This is good. I hope it's not very expensive."

Aunty Em frowned at her glass. "It sounded expensive."

"Yeah, kind of fools you, doesn't it?" Brad said.

"It is pretty good," Aunty Em admitted.

The soup and salads came and Brad got a few minutes' respite to plan his next moves. He would ease into a discussion that would end in the natural assumption of his departure. Jeez, he was starting to sound like Alex.

"I signed a contract with Dorothy to put Uncle Hal's house on the market," he told them as he dug into his salad.

"Such a nice house," Aunty Em said. "Needs a family living in it."

"Holds a lot of memories," Penny agreed. "I would think it would be hard for you to sell it."

"Not really." He slowed his salad eating a bit. "It always felt like Uncle Hal's house, not ours."

"Hal was a fool," Aunty Em snapped. "He should've married your mom and been done with it, instead of being afraid to speak his heart."

Brad felt his fork slip from his hand. "He should have what?" A waiter rushed over to retrieve the fallen utensil and give Brad a clean one. "Uh, thanks."

"He should have married your mom," Aunty Em repeated as she ate her soup. "He was in love with her for years. In fact, he had dated her before your dad did. After your dad died, we all thought Hal would propose but he never did."

"I never knew any of that," Brad murmured, feeling slightly stunned. Had he been blind or had his uncle hidden his feelings well? "He never acted like he was in love with her."

"That was Hal. Gave you a place to live, worked like a dog to pay off your dad's medical bills and never said a word."

"He paid off Dad's bills?" Brad said. He felt lost for a bit, like he had wandered into the middle of someone else's dream. "I always wondered where his money went. He never seemed to have any more than we did."

"Took him years, but he paid them all off."

"And then you and your mom left," Penny said. "That's so sad."

Aunty Em snorted rudely, but waited until the waiter had cleared their plates before speaking. "It wasn't sad, it was stupid. He lived a miserable sad life because he didn't have the guts to speak up.''

Brad picked up his wineglass and stared into the dark red liquid. Sad or stupid? Maybe his uncle's life had been a little of both. But then, wasn't everybody's? So his uncle had been no good at opening up, either. Of course, that didn't mean he'd had to wait around for his heart to be broken. He could have left, or sent Brad and his mother away. That's where he and Brad were different. Brad wouldn't just hang around. He'd find a life that fit him and live it.

''Guess it's best that house and its sad memories have a new start. One away from the Corrigan family.'' Brad took a long sip of wine and then put the glass down. ''Maybe Corrigans just don't do well in Chesterton.''

''Actually, we always thought the house was haunted,'' Penny stated.

Brad sighed. Derailed again. ''The Civil War widow?''

''I heard it was a poet,'' Aunty Em said.

''Oh, speaking of poets,'' Penny added, leaning forward, ''I almost forgot to tell you. Alex has rescheduled the poetry reading. Next Monday at Sam's.''

''Really, honey?'' Aunty Em was grinning. ''I can hardly wait. There's gonna be no keeping me away this time.''

Penny just smiled, then looked at him with eyes so full of hope and excitement and worry. It was like a burning arrow straight to his heart and there was nothing he could do.

''Hey, no keeping me away either,'' he assured them. ''That goes without saying.''

Okay, so he'd stay another few days. No big deal.

Something was wrong, Penny could tell. The dinner had been delicious and probably far more than Brad could afford, but she didn't think he was concerned about that. No, his worry was deeper than money. He talked all through dinner, telling stories about people he knew in California, but there was a shadow in his eyes the whole time. They all were silent on the drive home, but it was a good silence. A restful one. Except for Brad.

What was wrong? It nagged at her as she tried to work on some festival business, but folding and stuffing press releases into envelopes was hardly engrossing work. Maybe Brad's job situation was bothering him and she should talk to him about the call she made. Though she hadn't quite found the way to broach the subject yet.

"I'm going to bed, honey." Gran stopped at the kitchen table where Penny was working. "Brad still sitting on the porch?"

Penny nodded. "Unless he's been carried off by the mosquitoes."

"How about if I make you a partner in my PI firm and send you out to investigate?"

She smiled at her grandmother. "Might be a good idea."

Penny had thought he had wanted to be alone, but that was hours ago. Enough was enough. Once Gran's bedroom door closed, Penny slipped her sandals on and went out onto the back porch.

The porch lights were off, but she could see Brad sitting on the swing. There was a square of light near him—a laptop computer. The quiet click of the keys stopped as the screen door swung shut. He hadn't just been sitting there in the dark.

"Am I disturbing you?" she asked.

"Constantly, but I'm learning to live with it."

His voice was laughing so she assumed he didn't mind her coming out. She went closer, then leaned against the porch rail. Now that she was out here, she didn't know what to say.

"Want to take a walk?"

"Sure." He shut off the computer and got to his feet, leaving the machine on the swing.

Side by side, they walked down the porch steps and across the yard. Neither said anything, but somehow their hands found each other. The silence was sweet then, a sharing of their souls.

"Where we going?" he asked as she led him around the barn.

"The moon garden."

"Moon garden? You grow moons there?"

"Very funny. It's a garden that's viewed best by moonlight."

"Vampires, huh?"

"I should send you back to the porch and your computer."

But she held tight to his hand as she led him behind the barn and down a path through the daylilies. The night was cool and the smell of rain was in the air, even though the sky overhead was clear.

She could spend forever like this, she thought suddenly, walking hand in hand with Brad. Was this what love felt like? The thought made her feet stumble.

"You okay?" Brad asked.

"Just fine."

She was not in love. She might not be the smartest person in the world, but she wasn't that dumb. Falling in love with Brad Corrigan was the craziest idea ever. Totally ridiculous. Bizarre, even.

She liked him. Enjoyed his company. Had fun when she was with him. But her heart wouldn't break if he left town. Except that the organ in question almost stopped at the very idea of it. Time to change the subject.

"I really enjoyed dinner," she told him. "Though it wasn't necessary for you to take us out."

"Yes, it was," he said. "You and Aunty Em have been wonderful during my visit. It was just a small way to repay you."

Her heart turned cold. She didn't like the finality in his words. "You've more than earned your keep. You've helped in the office. Drove me around. Kept Gran company."

"All things you could have hired some local teen to do."

"I doubt it. They couldn't have fixed the computer." Now was her chance to ease into the subject of those jobs in the area. "You know, you seem really good with computers."

He just laughed. "I've been told that."

"So, why don't you do something with that skill?" she

asked. This was going better than she had hoped and she slowed her pace so they wouldn't reach the garden too soon. "I bet there are lots of jobs for computer people."

She felt something change in him, something grow still and quiet. "Actually…" he began, then stopped. She felt as if he were wrestling with some problem, some weighty dilemma, then he sighed. "Actually, I might just do that."

They had reached a break in the bushes and turned to enter a small clearing. The beds of white flowers all glowed in the moonlight, looking even more intense as the shadows drifted away into darkness under the trees and bushes. She felt peace wash over her.

"Wow," Brad said in a hushed voice. "This is really something."

"Kind of spooky, isn't it? Besides being beautiful."

She drew him over to the concrete bench off to one side and they sat down. Crickets chirped in the distance and an owl hooted, but the world was almost still.

"What kind of flowers are these?" he asked. "Are they some special variety?"

"Not really. Mostly just white flowers. Geraniums. Sea Foam roses. Petunias. That vine on the arbor is a moonflower. It opens at dusk and closes at dawn."

They sat for a long moment, drinking in the peace and serenity. August and September were the best time for the garden and she was glad she was able to share it with him.

"Your dad didn't have this here when we were kids, did he?"

"No, I put it in. It was one of the first things I did when I came back from New York."

She took a slow breath, then rushed ahead into things that she'd never said aloud before. "It's hard to explain, but I hated so much of what I did in New York. Everything was focused on some superficial idea of beauty, and everyone was chasing it. Or sure they possessed it. Or sure they knew what the next idea of beauty would be. I needed some way to cleanse my soul when I got home."

"Yet it sounds like you did well in New York," he said.

She shrugged and looked off at the moonflower, its large trumpet-shaped flowers swaying gently in the breeze. "I earned enough money to come back and get the nursery out of hock," she said. "The reason I went there in the first place."

She could feel his surprise. "I didn't know the place had been having financial troubles. When did they start?"

She laughed, the sound coming out soft and gentle, but then her anger over the nursery affairs had been long gone. "When wasn't it in the red? I can remember Dad talking about second mortgages and installment plans way before you worked here."

"I had no idea." His voice was regretful, as if he had been to blame somehow.

"How would you?"

Sitting here in her magical garden with him, sharing her secrets, suddenly seemed too intimate. It was a crazy feeling, considering that they had made love, but she couldn't explain it. Making love had been sharing their souls, but this seemed to be giving up the last hidden piece of herself. And even as it made her feel wonderful, it scared her.

She got up and walked slowly down the path among the flowers, stopping to finger the soft petals or pull off a spent blossom. He followed her, but his eyes and attention seemed to stay on her.

It made her more nervous. No, more aware maybe. Aware of him in oh, so many ways.

"You were a great worker," she told him. "You really gave us our money's worth and more. I don't think Dad noticed but you worked longer hours than you ever marked down on your time card." She bit her lip to keep from saying that she used to correct it for him.

"I liked working here."

And she had liked having him here. She still liked having him here. But that was a road she had vowed not to go down. She stepped off the path to straighten the rusted metal frog statue.

"Isn't this a fun statue?" she asked. "This catalog has all

sorts of them—frogs and lizards and even a gargoyle. I'd like to get more to mix into the various gardens.''

Brad seemed to ignore her attempt to change the subject. ''So, you went off to New York to model in order to save the nursery. How did your dad feel about it?''

''To be honest, I'm not sure.'' Well, she was the one who brought this all up; she might as well finish the discussion. She bent down to nip the buds off the chrysanthemum. ''I think he was amazed at how well I did, but then I don't think he ever realized just how shaky the situation was here.''

''And did he live to see you come back?''

She shook her head and stood up. The night seemed darker all of a sudden, and cooler. ''No. I had just a few commitments to finish up. A month's worth of assignments, then I was coming home. He went to a national daylily association meeting in Florida and was killed in an automobile accident down there.''

''So, he never knew you had saved the place.''

''But I don't think he ever thought it needed saving, so it's not like he died worrying about it.''

She walked farther down the path, feeling the soft moss beneath her feet, and then ended up back by the bushes and the way to the house. She wasn't sure why she had brought him out here, and she wasn't sure if she'd accomplished anything. Her job discussion certainly hadn't gone anywhere.

They started back to the house, his arm around her waist as if it were the most natural thing in the world.

''You know what I find ironic?'' he said. ''Your father had a wall full of degrees in botany and agriculture and almost lost the nursery. His daughter, who has never thought she was ever half-smart, comes in and saves it.''

''It wasn't that hard,'' she protested, but couldn't deny the warmth his words gave her.

''Then why didn't your father do it?''

''He would have when he had realized there was a problem.''

Brad stopped walking and pulled her to a halt with him. With soft hands on her shoulders, he turned her to face him. ''Bu that's just it,'' he argued. ''By the time he realized it, it would have been too late. He wasn't smart enough to see that. Only you were.''

''It wasn't intelligence, it was common sense,'' she said.

''But that's a form of intelligence and one you are blessed with in abundance. You have nothing to be ashamed of, nothing to apologize for. Nothing to feel you come second in.''

He stopped talking just in time to take her lips with his. It was a hard kiss, an almost angry one, but it melted into something much sweeter before she could even get her arms around his neck. It was the magic of the moon garden, but all hot and fiery. It was the mystery of the shadows, but filled with promise and wonder.

They pulled apart slowly, still tasting the magic and splendor. Then, hand in hand, they walked back toward the house.

''Want to hear something funny?'' she said. ''I was really worried when you came back.''

''Why?''

She shrugged and laid her head on his shoulder. ''Remember when you left? You promised you'd come back someday and make us all sorry.''

''Did I?'' he asked with a laugh and pulled her closer to his side. ''Kids sure say some dumb things, don't they?''

Chapter Twelve

"That should just about do it." Penny turned the chain saw off and stepped back from the bush.

"Looks much better," Brad agreed. "Now make sure you send a bill for this."

She pushed her safety goggles up onto her forehead. "Oh, come on. It only took an hour."

"I mean it. The estate will pay for it."

She could see the mulish look in his eyes and the stubborn tensing of his jaw. She was dancing too close to the man's pride, so she nodded. "Sure. I'll send a bill."

"I'll be watching for it."

She just made a face at him as she carried the chain saw over to the porch and sat down on the top step. Brad followed. It was another doozy of a day, hot and humid with storms hovering on the horizon. The kind of storms that never cooled things off, but only made them worse. She just hoped they wouldn't leave a lot of damage in their wake. The extra income it brought her was never worth the heartache of others.

"Dorothy called just before you came," Brad said. "Somebody's coming to look at the house tonight."

"Already?" Her heart sank. "That's fast."

"She doesn't know who it is, but he sounded serious when he made the appointment with Nancy."

"Great." She hoped her voice sounded more excited than she felt and thought it was time to send her feelings on vacation. "Oh, I think I've finally convinced Gran to let me get her some office help. I'm going to look for somebody part-time, and then hopefully have them take over completely. Let her work some if she wants, but only if she wants."

"She should enjoy that," Brad said. "It'll give her time to work full-time on her private investigating."

Penny lay back on her elbows with a groan. "That's all that I need."

"It's a harmless hobby," he said.

"That could land her in jail one of these days."

"I doubt it. She's not going to do something dumb."

But how did one define *dumb?* Maybe letting her heart wander into wherever it wanted this past week was dumb.

As if to defy her own troubling thoughts, she reached over to lightly caress Brad's hand. Their eyes met, his darkened, then he leaned forward to brush her lips with his.

It was just a light touch, a teasing caress, but the fires seemed to take hold of them both and burn them with a scorching flame. Supporting herself with one elbow, she wrapped her other arm around him to hold him close. But it was not nearly close enough. Even as his lips took hers, devouring them with his hunger, the yearning within her grew and grew until she was all too conscious of that big empty house behind them. That—

He pulled away from her with a frown. "What's that?"

She heard it then. Her cell phone was ringing. One part of her wanted to just let it ring, the other part knew she had to answer. What if it was Gran?

She pulled completely away from Brad and walked over to

get the phone from her tool pack. "Penny Donnelly," she said into it.

"Ms. Donnelly?" A vaguely familiar voice was at the other end. "This is Jane Danvers, calling from the Smithsonian. I spoke to you earlier in the week about the Oz seminar."

"Yes?" Penny felt her stomach turn to lead. Something in the woman's voice scared her.

"I'm afraid that there's been a mistake," she said. "We are going to have to withdraw our invitation to speak at the seminar."

Penny's stomach fell, all hollow and empty, and her heart ached. Somehow she had known it was too good to be true. Somehow she had known they would realize she wasn't what they thought or wanted.

"I see," Penny said slowly. Brad frowned in concern, and Penny reached for his hand. This felt worse than she could have possibly imagined—to have her dream snatched away like this! "Can you tell me what happened?"

"I'm afraid I'm not at liberty to say more," the woman said. "I really am sorry if this caused you any inconvenience."

Inconvenience? This wasn't about inconvenience, it was about a broken heart. "Was it my abstract?" she asked. "I can redo it."

"Really, I am not at liberty—" The woman sighed. "I shouldn't be saying anything more, but it had nothing to do with any abstract."

"Then why?"

There was a long pause, then the woman spoke again. "Look, someone tried to buy you an invitation to speak at the conference. The committee is working very hard to make this a respected academic event and even that attempt at impropriety was enough to make them back off."

The more the woman spoke, the more confused Penny was getting. "But who did that?" she asked.

"I've said more than I should have," the woman told her. "I'm sorry about it. I really am. But I cannot say more." The connection was broken.

Penny slowly brought her arm down, feeling stunned. She couldn't believe this had happened. To go from her ecstasy at being asked to the reality of rejection.

"Penny?"

She looked at Brad, his blue eyes so concerned and caring. For ever so short a time, they had radiated pride, but that was turning out to be a distant dream.

"They withdrew the invitation to speak at the conference," she told him.

"What!"

His shock matched her own. No, maybe it was greater. Deep down, she had always marveled that she had been asked, had never quite believed it could be happening. Somehow he had never doubted.

She squeezed his hand. "Looks like Gran's not going to be able to brag about me," she told him. "They don't want me after all."

"What happened?"

She shrugged, fighting back the tears of shame. It would have been better not to have been asked, than to have them take it back. "I don't know. Somebody tried to buy me my spot."

"But they had already asked you," he said.

"I don't know." She sank back down to the porch step, letting the tears slowly trickle down her cheeks. "It doesn't make any sense to me. Who would try to buy me a spot, anyway?"

"They didn't say?"

Shaking her head, she stared off down the street. "It can only have been one person," she said slowly.

"Oh?" He sounded hesitant, as if he couldn't think of anybody.

"Alex," she stated. "Who else? We had this deal. He was going to help me and I would cut down his elm tree."

"He did this to get you to cut down a tree?"

It did sound fantastic. "No. It probably was just because he knew how important this was to me. He must have known I couldn't do it on my own and tried to use his influence to get me in."

"You think he has that kind of influence?"

She got to her feet with a bitter laugh. "Apparently not, since they got mad at his attempt." She picked up the chain saw. "I'm going to go down and have a talk with him."

"Maybe you should leave the chain saw here."

She looked at it in her hand, and then over at him. She laughed, a real laugh this time. "I'm not going to use it on him," she said. "It was a stupid dream. One I should have known I had no chance of reaching. I just wish he hadn't interfered."

"Don't talk that way, Penny. It was a good dream."

She said nothing, just carried her chain saw to the truck while he brought her tool pack. She tossed the chain saw into the back, then her tools.

"I'll see you later," she said.

He grabbed her hand as she turned. "Pen, I'm so sorry."

His voice tore at something inside her, his regret was so real. All she could do was nod or she'd start crying again. She got in the truck and turned toward Alex's house.

Damn. Damn. Damn. What in the world had happened?

Brad went into the house, slamming the door behind him. All he could think about was Penny's words last night. How she'd been afraid he had come back to make them all sorry. That hadn't been his intent, but it sure had been the result.

He got the cell phone and dialed his lawyer in L.A. George must have screwed up. Normally he handled Brad's negotiations just fine, but maybe these had been more delicate. Maybe he'd bullied when he should have groveled. No matter now, Brad would find out what happened and then fix it. He was not going to spoil things for her.

His lawyer came on the line in about a half second. "Hey, Brad."

Brad found the cheery tone more than a little aggravating,

but swallowed his annoyance. "I want to talk about this *Wizard of Oz* conference. What the hell did you do?"

"What do you mean, what did I do? I did what you told me to. I contacted some people and offered the deal. The last I heard, they had tentatively agreed."

"Yeah? Well, whoever agreed got overruled. Penny got asked a few days ago and then just got a call that they dumped her."

"How can they do that? Somebody's jerking us around."

Brad sighed. "Just tell me what you did and who you talked to."

"Well, you called early Tuesday morning and I had Edna track down the program committee. Late Tuesday morning, I called the chair and when I couldn't reach him, I called the next in line. And got a tentative okay."

"Well, I guess the chair disagreed because—" Brad stopped. Damn. "Late Tuesday morning, Pacific time?"

"Yeah, Pacific time."

"Penny got the call Tuesday around noon. Indiana time. That would have been about an hour before you talked to anybody."

"So?"

"So she had gotten in on her own and I blew it for her."

"Hell."

Brad would have put it a bit stronger, but it wasn't worth arguing right now.

"Let me make some calls," George said. "I'll blame it on moonbeams. Or a bad batch of tofu. You know, some California nut thing."

As tempting as that was, Brad knew he couldn't do it. "No. It's my fault and I need to make the call. I need to apologize. Just give me the names of the people on the committee."

George offered a few more words of argument, but in the end, he just gave Brad the name of the committee chair—a retired professor of English at an elite university out East. Brad dialed the man.

He answered on the second ring. "Hello." The tone was old

and formal. Even though his name was Michael, Brad would've bet he was never called Mike.

"Dr. Bennett? My name is Brad Corrigan. I'm calling about the Oz seminar and a Ms. Penny Donnelly."

There was a long, tense silence on the line. "I know who you are, Mr. Corrigan." Brad could hear the icicles crackle on the line. "And about your attempt to corrupt this committee. The situation is closed."

"Wait a minute. I'm the one that screwed up, not Penny. It's not fair to punish her."

"I will not have coercion attached to this seminar, Mr. Corrigan. Not the slightest hint of it."

He wanted to call the guy names, to tell him he was acting like an idiot. No one had treated Brad this way since he was a kid, not with his money and power. Yet for Penny's sake, he held his temper. "Look, I really am sorry. I was completely wrong and—"

"The matter is closed. Please do not call me again." The dial tone filled the silence.

Brad slowly hung up. He had screwed up royally. All he'd wanted was to make Penny's dreams come true, and he'd spoiled everything for her.

No, he had made her dream come true. Her dream that he'd come and they'd all be sorry. Damn.

It was time to face the music. Time to take the blame.

"Why are you denying it?" Penny cried as she paced Alex's living room.

She ached all over—her eyes stung from fighting back the tears, her throat was so tight it hurt to breathe and her stomach was a solid rock of nerves. She just wanted to know why Alex had interfered, but all she'd gotten out of him was denials.

"Because I didn't do it," Alex said, his voice so reasonable and calm that she wanted to throw something at him. "I don't have the connections to try something like that."

"Oh, come on. Who else knew how much I wanted it?" She stopped pacing, and glared at him, arms crossed over her chest.

This was worse than her worst nightmare—that would have been just not to get invited. She'd never considered the horror of getting asked and then unasked.

Alex leaned against his bookcases. "Somebody else obviously knew and thought they had the connections to pull it off."

"Yeah, like who? Gran?" Penny waved her hand in a sweeping gesture. "Oh, wait. I know. It was Junior."

"No, it was me."

Startled, Penny spun toward the open door. Brad stood there. With a nod toward Alex, Brad took a step inside, his blue eyes dark and serious as he faced Penny.

"I was the one that messed up," he said. "You'd gotten in on your own and my meddling ruined it."

"What?" Penny couldn't believe this, didn't know what to think. It felt like the bottom had just dropped out of her world. "Why in the world did you butt in?"

He shrugged, but didn't flinch from her gaze. "You wanted it so badly." His voice was ragged with remorse. "I had no idea your invitation was in the works already when I tried to help."

That was his reason? She wanted it so he had to run out and get it for her? Some of her hurt began to harden into anger, numbing her and making her strong.

"You figured I couldn't get it on my own so you would do it for me?" she snapped. An old familiar hurt was growing. That the one person she wanted to prove herself to, just didn't believe in her. But she wouldn't give in to the hurt now. Not here. She let anger have the upper hand.

"I can't believe this," she said loudly.

"Why don't we all sit down?" Alex said. His voice had grown calmer if anything. "Nothing's going to be solved by shouting."

Ha! Maybe shouting just made her feel better. Hands on her hips, Penny advanced slowly toward Brad. "Jeez, if this isn't just like old times! The dummy can't do it, so do it for her."

"It wasn't like that at all," Brad protested.

She stopped a few feet from him, hoping—praying—that she was going to see something in his eyes that would prove her wrong. But she was afraid to look and turned away at the last moment.

"Oh, no?" she said. "You didn't do all my homework for me back in eighth and ninth grade?"

"Well, yes."

"But I know." She glanced back at him, her voice ripe with sarcasm. "It was because I was so smart and you thought it would give me an unfair advantage over everyone else."

"Actually…" It was his turn to look away.

She had him. He was going to have to admit the truth, but the victory felt very empty. Like dreams that had been smashed to pieces on the shore.

"Actually, you hardly even talked to me," she said.

"Now, that's not one you can blame him for," Alex interjected.

She turned. "You're on his side now?" she asked. She might have known men would stick together, yet it seemed almost too hurtful.

Alex just shook his head. His arms were crossed on his chest as he sat on the arm of a chair. He looked relaxed. Uninvolved. "I'm not on anybody's side," he stated. "But you do have that effect on males."

"Can't you speak in plain English for once?" she snapped. "What are you talking about?"

"Striking men dumb," Alex explained. "Even back then, there was something about you that made adolescent males lose the power of speech around you."

What nonsense! She just rolled her eyes; it was better than rolling heads. "You expect me to believe that Brad—" Her laugh was a short bitter laugh. "Yeah, right. And even today, he's—"

Something suddenly struck her and she slowly turned back to Brad, her eyes narrowing. "Wait a minute," she said. "How did you have the clout to even try this?"

Brad shrugged and looked away for a split second, then back

at her. But he didn't quite meet her gaze square on. Couldn't meet it?

"I knew some people," he said.

"You knew some people?" The light dawned and she felt doubly a fool. Triply. A hundred times. "My God, you are the Brad Corrigan the computer guy talked about, aren't you?"

"What computer guy?" Brad asked.

Alex whistled softly. "So I was right." He sounded pleased with himself. "Designer of the IDD-4 network router. *Technology Today's* Man of the Moment a few years back."

"You knew?" Penny frowned at Alex—whom she had thought was her friend. "You knew and didn't tell me?"

"I wasn't sure," Alex said with a small shrug.

"What computer guy?" Brad repeated, a little louder.

She turned, angry at them both. Angry at herself for being so stupid and trusting. "Some guy at Compu-Staff."

"That's an employment agency," Brad said.

"So? I called them to see about a job for you."

"You what?" he cried. "I don't need a job."

"You said you didn't have one." She wasn't letting him turn this all around. She hadn't done anything wrong. She hadn't butted in and spoiled his dreams.

"I never said any such thing," he argued.

"You drove a junky car," she returned. "You don't have a home. And you've got a cheap watch."

"Uh, Penny—"

She ignored Alex, pressing her defense with Brad. "What was I supposed to think?"

Brad looked annoyed. "I drove a junky car because, among other things, I'm majority owner of Rented Dented and that's what we rent. I don't have a home because I travel all the time and this is not a cheap watch. It's a limited edition, custom-made Rolex."

She felt a small flush in her cheeks, but raised her chin just a fraction in defiance. Okay, so he'd proven her dumb again. She didn't have to let him know it. "Why didn't you just say so?"

"I didn't think I needed to," he snapped. "How was I supposed to know you were going to think the worst? That you were going to butt in and take care of me?"

Alex held up a hand. "Hey, let's take it easy. It's a habit for her, too. Not all that different from—"

Penny just knew what he was going to say. "Alex!"

But it didn't stop him. "—back in high school when she put extra sandwiches in your lunch."

Brad went deathly pale and turned slowly back to face her. Horror. Dread. Loathing. They all crossed his face. "That was you?" His voice was almost a whisper.

She was not going to be cowed by his reaction. It wasn't as if she'd done something to be ashamed of. Looking him straight in the eye, she nodded. "Yes, it was."

But he just looked over at Alex. "And you knew?"

Alex shrugged. "Everybody knew," he said. "I can't believe that no one ever told you."

But Brad was not ready to marvel over everyone's silence. The horror in his face increased and he sank into the chair next to him. "My God," he muttered. "The whole town must have been laughing at me!"

This was getting a little much. It was just a few sandwiches. And he had to have known someone was putting them there! "No one was laughing at you," Penny snapped. "I was trying to help. At least I didn't take over instead of letting you do something for yourself."

"Oh no?"

"Actually I think you both were meddling," Alex stated.

Brad got to his feet. "Well, no more," he snapped and looked her in the eye. "I have a few more things to finish up in town and then I'll be gone. You won't have to worry about me meddling anymore."

"And you won't have to worry about hanging around with somebody too dumb to recognize a Rolex," she said.

That seemed to make him even angrier. Too close to the truth perhaps? She ought to be too numb to hurt anymore but the pain kept finding ways to sneak through.

"You always were a stubborn—" He stopped, locking his lips shut.

"Fool?" she finished for him. "That is what you thought, isn't it?"

He just turned on his heel and left. The room seemed deathly still, unnaturally still. Penny couldn't even hear her heart pounding. Maybe it had stopped. Maybe she had just broken it in two.

"Are you going to let him leave like that?" Alex asked.

She just looked at him. She'd almost forgotten he was there. "He wrecked my dream."

"And you stole his pride. Sounds like you're even."

"Shut up, Alex." She walked slowly, wearily, to the door. She was exhausted and strangely detached. As if it took too much energy to feel. "You didn't help in all this."

"I thought it was time for a little honesty," he said. "You know, you're both doing these things because you love each other. You have for years, maybe it's time to stop running from it."

She stopped at his door, turning to frown at him. "If you aren't careful, I'm going to dump that tree on your house."

He got to his feet. "No, you won't. You're too honorable. You'll forgive me and you'll forgive Brad. The question is whether or not you forgive him in time."

Toto sat down on the Corrigan house porch steps and looked across at the big yard. Overgrown and weedy, it still held a hint of the beauty it must have once had. And would have again, one day soon, he hoped. That old birdhouse in the maple there was nice. Maybe he'd put in a birdbath at the base of the tree. And a few bushes with berries on them for the birds to eat.

With a contented sigh, he patted Junior's head. "You're gonna like living here," Toto said. "Lots of room to run around in. Nice for kids, too." He felt his stomach quiver a little. "You'd like that, wouldn't you?"

Junior wagged his tail and Toto smiled. The big dog would

be great with kids. If Toto and Dorothy were lucky, they'd have—

Junior jumped to his feet and wagged his tail as he looked around the side of the house. Dorothy came around the corner.

She gave Toto a sharp look. "What are you doing here?"

His own smile died, fell right down into the pit of his stomach. It was now or never. "Waiting for you."

He waited for Dorothy to smile, even saw her do it in his mind, but it never showed on her face. Instead, she glanced at her watch with a frown. "Can we talk later?" she asked. "I'm supposed to meet a potential buyer here."

Toto had gone over the scene hundreds of times in his mind. It was why he'd had a friend call and make this appointment. Dorothy would squeal with surprise, then grin with curiosity. He'd pop the question and she'd jump into his arms. Then they'd go out for dinner to celebrate. But the scene had never included this block of cold fear settling in his stomach.

"That's me," he replied.

"I don't know how long I'll—" Her frown disappeared, replaced by bewilderment. "You want to buy this house?"

"I've got the money. I've been saving for years, looking for the right place to invest in." Not for financial return, but for his dream to come true.

"You want the house as an investment?" she asked slowly. "I just never..." She let her voice die out.

It was suddenly important to prove that he meant this. That this wasn't some whim. "I know it's run-down," he said. "But that's what makes it special."

"As an investment?"

He nodded. "And I already talked to the bank and got preapproved for the mortgage."

She smiled then, a slow smile that spread over her face like the sun coming out after a storm. "You really are serious," she said, though her voice lacked some of the excitement he'd hoped for. "That's great."

He grinned back at her. It was working out, just like he'd

planned. He started to take her hand, but she had turned and was walking up onto the porch.

"This is just such a surprise," she said. Her voice grew brighter, riper with expectations, as she ran her hand over the porch railing like it was an old friend. "I never dreamed that the buyer would be you. I never had any idea you were interested in buying a house."

He laughed a little and went up to stand next to her. She was staring out at the yard as if she were taking in every detail. Dreaming of tomorrow like he was? He reached again for her hand, but she had turned to face him.

"Do you know what this means?" she asked.

Did he? His grin just deepened. Someday he'd tell her how he'd been dreaming of this moment for years, that it had started back in high school. And had kept growing even during those dark days after he'd offered her her freedom, and she'd taken it. Hell, yes, he knew what this meant.

It meant he and Dorothy together for the rest of their lives. It meant a home of their own. Children. It meant—

"It means I can finally go to Paris."

"Paris?" His world came to a screeching halt.

"Bet you thought it was all talk, didn't you?" she asked with a laugh. "But now, thanks to you, it's going to be real. With the commission from this house, I can do it."

And then she kissed him lightly.

Toto just stood there, a lifetime of dreams turning to ashes. He wanted to cry. To beg her to stay. To tell her how much he needed her. But he'd never done that before and he wasn't going to start now.

They'd been chosen Most Romantic Couple their senior year of high school and had their picture taken for the school paper at Glinda's Flowers, surrounded by bouquets of roses. He had known then he would love Dorothy forever and thought she felt the same.

But just a few months later, at their graduation, she'd given a speech about reaching for the stars and following your dreams, and he began to have doubts about her feelings. What did her speech really mean? Doubts began to grow and he started to notice her making more and more references to leaving and adventure. Finally when she began to talk about Paris, he suggested they break up. She had agreed. At first his heart had broken, but lately he'd begun to think maybe it was just talk and not really a dream. Now he knew her true intentions.

"That's great," Toto murmured and stepped back out of her embrace. "Not too many people get to realize their life's dream."

She reached for his hand, squeezing it. "I'm going to miss you."

Don't go, then. But he just put a smile on his face. "But you'll have Paris."

"Yeah." She let go of him and looked around at the house. "What are you going to do with a big place like this?"

Toto stared for a long moment at the yard. The yard that had been filled with their kids a few minutes earlier.

What was he going to do with this big house? Burn it down? Blow it up? Turn it into a museum for broken hearts?

A cold nose poked him in the hand and he petted Junior gently. "Oh, the usual," he said. "I'll fix it up and sell it for twice what I paid. Not like me and Junior here need a big place."

Chapter Thirteen

"What's going on, Penny?" Gran asked as soon as Penny walked in the kitchen door. "Brad was here about an hour ago. Took all his things and said goodbye. Wouldn't even stay for supper."

Penny just looked at Gran for a moment. She knew she was going to have to tell Gran the truth, but she had been hoping she could stall a little. Wait until the hurt wasn't quite as fresh. But an afternoon spent tossing logs into the wood chipper hadn't helped ease the ache, so why did she think time would?

"We had an argument. I'm not surprised he left." Penny started up the back stairs.

Gran wiped her hands on her apron and followed her. "Land sakes, girl," she snapped. "And you let him? You get out there and tell him you're sorry."

"That I'm sorry?" Penny spun to stare down at her grandmother. "What makes you so sure I was in the wrong?"

"I never said you were in the wrong," Gran stated. "I said to tell him you were sorry. Two different things entirely. Get him back here and sort it all out. Being right ain't no consolation when you're alone.''

"You don't understand," Penny said, suddenly too exhausted to feel anything. No, that wasn't true. She felt something all right; she was just too tired to figure out what. "I'm not going to be able to speak at the Oz conference. He meddled and they got mad and withdrew their invitation."

"That's it?" Gran cried and with a grunt, turned back to making dinner.

"What do you mean, that's it?" Penny came back down the stairs. "Isn't that enough? I've been wanting for years to do that."

"Wanting ain't the same as needing." She took two taco salads out of the refrigerator. "What else happened?"

"He's rich," Penny said.

Gran nodded as she put the salsa sauce on the table. "There's an unforgivable crime."

Gran just wasn't getting it. "He pretended he wasn't," Penny added.

The old lady twisted her lips as she shook her head. "Oh, I don't know about that. He didn't say he was or he wasn't."

"Same thing." Penny took two glasses from the cabinet and banged them down on the table.

Gran raised one eyebrow. "Maybe we should use the plastic glasses until you're not quite so moody."

"I intend to be moody the rest of my life," Penny informed her. "That's what happens when you're denied your dreams."

"Hogwash," Gran said. "It wasn't that big of a deal."

That hurt! "I thought you were proud of me."

"Of course, I'm proud of you," Gran said. "For how hard you've been working. And that's not going to change if you speak at that conference or don't."

"Brad's not proud of me," Penny said. "He only meddled because he thought I was too dumb to get an invitation to the conference on my own."

"Gracious, we are full of ideas today," Gran said. She put out a bag of tortilla chips and sat down. "Did he tell you that?"

Penny glared at her and sat down. "Not exactly."

"Didn't think so." Gran spooned salsa sauce onto her salad, then dug in. "He said he was moving into his uncle's place. You can go on over there after dinner and have a little talk with him."

"I have a festival meeting tonight."

"So, go afterward."

Penny stared at her grandmother eating like there was no tomorrow, and then looked down at her own salad. She was not in the least bit hungry. She pulled a handful of chips from the bag and munched on one.

Why did life have to be so complicated? She was furious with Brad. He'd really hurt her with his meddling and lying. But she missed him, too. Not that any of that mattered. Even if she decided to forgive him—a mighty big *if*—she had no idea if he could forgive her. And she hadn't even done anything that warranted forgiveness.

She didn't know why he had made such a fuss. That sandwich thing was years ago. Who cared about it anymore? And so what if she called about a job? She just got some information for him, that was all. No big deal. Maybe making it possible for him to stay—

That was it.

"I don't think he wants to work it out," Penny muttered. "I think he was looking for reasons to break it off."

"That doesn't sound like him," Gran said. She put her fork down and reached over to squeeze Penny's hand. "He's probably just hurt bad over the disappointment he caused you. A man doesn't like to hurt someone he cares about. When it all boils down to nothing, honey, a man's nothing but pride."

Penny's heart sank even lower, though she hadn't thought that was possible. Gran was right, and it meant she had lost Brad forever.

Dorothy waited for Penny out in the library lobby, pretending to look through the used paperbacks for sale. She could have gone into the meeting, but she just wasn't feeling all that social this evening. Must be that microwave popcorn she had for dinner.

"Hi, Dorothy."

Dorothy turned. "Hi, Nancy. Mr. Mayberry." The meeting must have ended. She put down the book she'd been staring at and watched for Penny, nodding at other committee members as they left.

"Heard you sold the Kramer place," someone said. "What're the new people like?

"Seem nice."

Maybe she just should have called Penny, or gone out to the nursery. This smile was getting more and more painful to hold. Must be all the excitement getting to her. It wasn't every day that a person got to escape her boring town and her boring life for romance and adventure. Her stomach churned. Damn popcorn.

"Dorothy?" Penny was there, looking as tired and worn as Dorothy felt. "What are you doing here?"

But even at her most exhausted, Penny knew how to read Dorothy. She had to be careful. "Waiting for you," Dorothy said, careful to sound as cheerful as possible. "Do you know where Brad is? I've been trying to reach him for hours."

"Brad?" Penny's eyes were shadowed with darkness, her voice echoed with pain. "I thought he was at his uncle's."

"I didn't see the Jeep there."

Penny started out the door. "He's not using it anymore. He moved into his uncle's place this afternoon and left the Jeep back out at the nursery. Maybe he rented a car from the gas station."

Dorothy rushed out after her into the sultry night, trying to look into her friend's face, but Penny was too darn tall and it was too darn dark outside. "Wait a minute," Dorothy said. "What happened?"

Penny stopped and turned. Her face was still in shadow. "Nothing happened. He's just about done here and thought it would be easier to finish up if he was actually in the house."

"Don't give me that," Dorothy said. "You two had something going."

"Friendship, that's all," Penny said. "What did you want him for?"

Dorothy started walking toward the cars, slowly though, as if each step hurt. "I sold his uncle's house."

"Really? That was fast."

"Toto bought it."

"Toto?" Penny's step seemed to falter, even as a little quiver of excitement came into her voice. "Does this mean you're—"

"Going to Paris soon?" Dorothy jumped ahead to finish the sentence, unable to bear any other idea Penny might have had. She put every ounce of perky she possessed into her voice. "Yep. Isn't that exciting?"

"Sure," Penny agreed, though her voice seemed to express the opposite. "That's wonderful."

"What I've always wanted."

They had reached Dorothy's car so they stopped, but just long enough for Dorothy to get inside. Her perky level was about to take a dive and she needed to be gone.

"Can't believe I'm actually going to pull it off," she told Penny through the open window as she started the car. "Seems like I've been dreaming it forever."

Penny stepped back, clutching her folder to her chest. "I'm really happy for you," Penny said. "I'll miss you, of course, but it's so great that your dreams are coming true."

"Yep." With a wobbly wave, Dorothy backed out of the spot. In spite of the fact that the world got a little blurry from a sudden rush of tears, she made it to the street and down toward her apartment.

This was what she wanted. That stupid little hope that had sprung up when she'd found out Toto was the buyer meant nothing. A habit somehow left over from their long-dead relationship. A reflex.

All he wanted the house for was an investment. Well, maybe someday it would get the family it deserved.

Except she would be in Paris and would never know.

* * *

Brad carried the last box out to the alley and stacked it with the others awaiting the trash pickup. He'd gotten more done this morning than he had in the whole week or so since he'd arrived. He should have done this sooner. It had been a huge mistake to stay at Penny's.

Not that he'd actually stayed at Uncle Hal's last night. After Brad had come back with his things, he'd realized it was too late to get the power and water turned on, so he'd gone to a motel. A nice, impersonal motel south of the tollway with a nice impersonal coffee shop. Nobody knew him, nobody cared to know him. The way he liked things to be.

Best of all, he didn't have to wonder the whole time he was eating dinner if that woman at the counter knew Penny had made him lunches years back. And then that thought didn't remind him of how he'd hurt Penny and shattered her dreams.

He hurried his steps and went in the back door. He would be gone in another day and at least he couldn't ruin things anymore for Penny. And maybe one day he'd figure out a way—

There was a thumping noise from the front of the house. He went down the hall. Someone was at the door. He pulled it open to find Aunty Em standing there.

"Aunty Em. What are you doing here?" He looked around outside, but she was alone. "You didn't drive here, did you?"

"Land sakes, boy, Penny dropped me off for physical therapy and I walked all of two blocks." She stomped into the house, using her cane a bit more noisily than he remembered. "I don't need a keeper, you know. Not like some I could name."

She was here to scold him, and rightly so. "I know I shouldn't have interfered with that seminar stuff," he said. "I just thought I could help."

"Doing for ain't helping." She frowned at him. "Is this where you entertain your guests? Here in the entryway? Or don't I rate an invite to sit down?"

He ran his fingers through his hair. Jeez, where were his manners? "I'm sorry," he said and showed her into the shadowed living room. "Come in and sit down."

She stopped in the doorway. "On sheets and in the dark? Let's go into the kitchen and you can get me something cool to drink."

At least, he did have a cooler of pop. He led her down the hall and into the sunny kitchen. A soft cooling breeze came in through the open windows. Even old and worn as the kitchen was, it was still a welcoming room. A family room. Not that he had any need or use for such a place.

"Cola all right?" he asked.

"No beer?"

He pulled a can of cola from the cooler and popped the top, then poured it into a paper cup. She was roaming over the kitchen, running her hands over the worn surfaces as if feeling the years of living that had been done here. And would be again. Just because he didn't want the place, it didn't mean that it would be torn down.

Aunty Em finally came around to the kitchen table and sat down. "You staying here now?" she asked.

"Depends on how soon the power company comes out," he said. "I went to the Road Star Inn last night."

"Heard it was a decent place," she said.

"Not bad."

She sipped at her soda, then looked back up at him. "Always thought that Alex was no good, and I was right."

Brad felt a moment's panic. "What's he done now?"

Aunty Em looked up with a frown. "He told things he had no business telling. Things that were better left in the past."

Brad sat back in his chair with a sigh. "I was glad he told me. I shouldn't have been the only one in town who didn't know."

"Oh, now don't get all mopey on me," she snapped. "Men sure do love to mope. My first husband was a champion moper. Never figured he'd stay dead. Thought Saint Peter would get tired of his moping and send him back."

"I didn't know you had been married more than once."

"There's a lot of things you don't know. Like how to let yourself be loved."

He wasn't sure what she was talking about, but knew enough not to ask. "I never claimed I was an expert on love."

"Nobody is, but some seem to want to learn the hard way."

"And some don't want to learn at all."

"There's worse things than disappointment," she said.

"I imagine." He just got up and got himself a soda. Not because he was thirsty but because it was something to do. A way to avoid her cryptic conversation.

"Pride, for one."

"I was thinking along the lines of famine and pestilence."

She finished her cola and put the glass down with a thud. "You two are a matched pair. No use talking to either of you."

He felt bad then. She was only here because she cared; she just didn't realize yet how much better off they all would be without him here. He came back to the table. "You will take care of her, won't you?"

"I'm an old woman. Seems that's a job for a young man."

"Hello?" someone called from the front of the house.

For a moment, a split second, his heart danced. The sun came out and it was forever spring.

Then Aunty Em called out, "In the kitchen, Dorothy. Come on back." The old woman got to her feet and picked up her cane as Dorothy came into the kitchen. "I'm stiffening up sitting here. I think I'll just take me a walk outside."

Brad got to his feet, but she just waved him away and walked slowly down the hall, the thump of her cane marking her progress. They heard the front door and Brad sank back into his chair.

"So, what can I do for you?" he asked.

"Nothing," Dorothy said. "I'm here to report what I did for you. Sold your house."

"Already?" He felt disappointed, though that made no sense. It was what he wanted. Now there'd be no ties when he left. "That's great."

"To Toto," she said.

"Toto bought the house?" Brad was overcome with an un-expected surge of jealousy. "What's he going to do with it?"

Dorothy made a face. "Fix it up and resell it, he says. Thinks he can make a big profit."

"That doesn't seem like him. Somehow I never thought he cared about money."

"Who knows what he cares about?" Dorothy snapped, then took a deep breath. Her smile looked rather forced, but he wasn't one to criticize. "Anyway, the good news is that I'll be leaving for Paris soon. Bank account is healthy, so there's noth-ing to keep me here."

He looked around at the kitchen which had never been part of his home, and never would be. Just as the town had never been a part of him and never would be. "I'm just about done here, too. Still game to fly over together?"

"Sure, why not?" Her eyes held a worried, lost look, but her voice was bright. "When?"

"Soon as possible."

She pulled her cell phone out of her purse. "Let's see when that is. No sense in lallygagging around here." She dialed a number—the travel agency, it turned out—talked for a few minutes, then looked up at him. "A midnight flight out of O'Hare on Monday? We can leave right after Penny's poetry reading."

"Perfect." Three days to finish packing things up and then a drive into Chicago.

Toto was sitting in front of the dryer, watching his clothes spin around. Junior had better things to do, of course. He was sleeping in the Laundromat's front window in the sun. But then, Junior didn't know that their dreams had all been shat-tered.

"Lordy, but you are hard to find."

Toto looked up. Aunty Em was thumping down the row of dryers to where he sat. He jumped to his feet.

"Something wrong, ma'am?" he asked. He was off duty, but that was only a technicality.

"Everything's wrong." She sank into the molded plastic chair next to him with a weary sigh. "I've got bad news."

Junior had woken up and trotted over to say hello. Toto figured the news couldn't be all that bad if she was taking time to pet the dog, but still his stomach tied itself up in a knot.

Finally she leaned back in her chair. "Dorothy's going to Paris," she told him.

He felt the tension ease out of him. "I know. She told me."

"And you're letting her?"

"It's not a matter of letting," he tried to explain. "It's what she wants to do. She wouldn't be happy here if her heart's over there."

"Who said anything about her heart?" Aunty Em snapped. "I don't think you know diddly about her heart these days."

Toto just kept quiet. Aunty Em was a good-hearted lady and it wasn't his place to argue with her. His momma had taught him respect. And besides, he did too know about Dorothy's heart. He had seen the light in her eyes when she talked about Paris.

"Well, that's neither here nor there," Aunty Em mumbled to herself, and fixed him with a piercing glance. "Did you also know that she's leaving Monday?"

"Monday?" That was so soon. But maybe it was better that way.

"And with Brad?"

Toto just stared at Aunty Em. He'd thought his heart was too numb to feel anything else, but he had been wrong. It was broken already, but now the pieces were being stomped underfoot and ground up into tiny bits.

"With Brad?" he repeated, his voice almost too weak to carry the awful words. No wonder Dorothy didn't want him. She had Brad. Handsome, mysterious Brad. "How did you find all this out? Did Dorothy tell you?"

"What difference does it make how I found it out?" Aunty Em snapped. "What are you gonna do about it?"

He just shook his head. "What is there to do?" he asked. "If that's what's going to make her happy..."

Junior whined as Aunty Em got to her feet. The disgusted look on her face softened as she patted the dog. "You know, Junior, I think you and I are the only ones in this whole town with any sense. So who's going to take some action, you or me?"

She started back toward the door, her cane thumping the death knell to Toto's dreams. Junior barked twice when she got to the door, but Toto just sat there, wondering how he could hurt so much.

Penny knew the weekend was only forty-eight hours long, but she could have sworn someone had slipped an extra week in. Time just seemed to stand still. Everywhere she went on Saturday, everyone told her about Brad and Dorothy leaving together.

She met the Jamisons at the hardware store. "I can't believe it," Mrs. Jamison said. "And to think Dorothy was your best friend."

"I'm sure there's nothing to it," Penny told her and went down another aisle in search of toggle bolts.

"Oh, you poor dear," the minister's wife said and enveloped Penny in a crushing hug.

"They're just friends," Penny said, and left without any of the things she'd come for. She skipped the grocery store, certain it would be a repeat of the hardware store, but did pull in at the gas station. She had to get gas, for one thing, and was certain that people were more stoic there. Ha!

"I sure am sorry," Mickey Juarez told her as they filled the cars at neighboring gas pumps. "Want me to check your oil for you?"

"Thanks anyway," Penny said. "I'm fine."

He nodded. "Yeah, probably best if you do it yourself," he said. "I hear keeping busy's best."

She just smiled and left. Leaving the whole town to talk

about how Brad had hurt her so badly that she couldn't even check her oil, no doubt.

"You should just go talk to him," Gran told her over dinner. "You two can still work this out."

"There's nothing to work out. This wasn't meant to be."

"Why?" the old woman asked. "Are we back to your ten languages rule?"

Penny hadn't thought of it, but it was true. Brad didn't speak ten languages, so he didn't qualify. She should be relieved. She could let him go and start over looking for her Mr. Right. "Why not? It's as good a criterion as any."

Sunday was no better. From all the mournful smiles she got at church, she would have sworn it was a funeral. When the hug brigade started after the service, Penny decided to spend the day at their tree field south of the tollway. She hadn't checked the fields since the storm last week and she was sure there'd be pruning and hacking and clearing that needed to be done in blissful solitude.

Well, it certainly turned out to be solitude, but she wasn't sure how blissful it was. Her thoughts were not the best of company.

Maybe she should go talk to Brad, she thought as she cleared some brush away from the gate. His leaving like this felt so wrong. Like things were unfinished.

But what did she have to say to him? That she forgave him?

Sure, like wrecking her dreams could be so easily—

She stopped, the gate half cleared. She had forgiven him!

The hurt was still there that she'd been uninvited, but that was more ego than anything else. And she was conscious of a deep sense of disappointment that she still hadn't made him proud of her, but she was also profoundly aware of the fact that he had been right. She had been trying for something beyond her reach. Something that would always be beyond her reach, but did that mean she had no value? That she wasn't smart?

She looked out over the gate at the rolling acres and acres of trees and bushes and evergreens. She had bought this property two years ago from a Valparaiso nursery that was going out of business. She had had the capital and the credit to snap it up at a bargain price. A price that was a steal when you considered the value of the plants already here. That had been something. And though she hated to compare herself to her father, it hadn't been something he would have been able to accomplish.

Brad was right. She did have a lot to be proud of. And she had to be smart to have done all that she'd done.

She finished clearing the gate and pulled it open, then drove the truck along the dirt road that roamed the acreage. It really didn't matter if she wasn't given some academic honor, she told herself. And it didn't matter that Brad had never been proud of her.

Except that it did. And that didn't make sense. She hadn't seen him for eighteen years and might never see him again. So, why did his lack of faith in her hurt? It wasn't as if she loved him.

Oh, criminy. She screeched to a halt and laid her forehead on the steering wheel. Of all the gosh darn idiotic things to do, she had to go and fall in love with Brad Corrigan again!

No, it wasn't *again*. This was a real love, a forever love. An adult love.

Except that he was all wrong for her. They had nothing in common. He didn't speak ten languages. And although she might give up her dream of academic honor, she was not giving up her ten-language criterion. She needed some sensible way to judge if a man was right for her. If she left it up to her silly heart, it would pick Brad who was leaving and had never meant to stay.

That decided, Penny spent the rest of the afternoon hacking and cutting and working up a sweat that washed away all thoughts of Brad Corrigan. When it was getting too dark to see, she packed things up, but vowed her love for Brad would stay here in the deserted tree lot.

Gran came out onto the back porch when Penny drove into the yard. "Brad was by this afternoon," she said.

"Oh?" Penny just went into the kitchen bathroom to wash up, almost not wanting to know why Brad had been here. If he'd suddenly discovered he loved her and knew ten languages he would have come out to the field. Gran had known where she was.

Gran followed her to the bathroom door. "He wanted to say goodbye."

"Oh." Penny'd thought they'd said everything that had needed to be said. He sure didn't need to know of her recent discoveries. She soaped up her hands and face, and then rinsed with cool water but didn't feel any more refreshed. Maybe it was because she couldn't wash off what was really bothering her.

Maybe he did have a right to know she was no longer angry at him. But she could drop him a note to that effect. Dorothy's real estate firm had to have an address to forward the money from the house sale. While she was at it, she would drop a note to that Oz conference committee and apologize for the whole mess. Formally withdraw her abstract and wish them all well.

"I told him you were counting on him coming to the poetry reading tomorrow," Gran added. "He might not be able to stay for the whole thing, but he promised he'd be there."

The poetry reading! Lordy, she'd forgotten all about that. It seemed such a total waste of time now, but since it was all set up, she supposed there wasn't much she could do but participate as planned. Not that she wanted Brad there.

"You should have told him not to bother," Penny drawled.

The old woman just shrugged and turned away. "It'll give you a chance to say goodbye," she said. "And it'll mean someone'll be there for you. I might be a little late."

Penny came out of the bathroom with a frown. "How come?"

Gran was standing at the open refrigerator and glanced over at Penny. "Uh, Marilyn wants to have an extra physical therapy session tomorrow after dinner. I figured I could do it and then get her to drop me off at Sam's."

Penny stopped. "I could have sworn Marilyn has a senior's exercise class in Valparaiso on Monday evenings."

Gran began pulling containers out of the refrigerator. "Oh, yeah. She used to. But it got canceled for this Monday. Want some chicken chow mein or tuna salad?"

A bad feeling was growing in Penny's stomach and it wasn't from hunger. "Gran, what's going on?"

Gran looked over with a bright smile. "Going on? I'm fixing you some dinner."

"Forget dinner and come clean."

Gran looked confused, then annoyed, then she sat down at the kitchen table with an exasperated sigh. "I don't see what the fuss is if I want to go into town for a little bit. Maybe I have a gentleman friend I want to visit."

"I'd be delighted if that was the case," Penny said. "Now, let's have it. The truth, this time."

Gran glared, and frowned and tried a pitiful look, but then just leaned back with a grunt of resignation. "I kind of left something at Brad's and need to go get it back."

Penny sat down across from her. "That's it?" she asked. "Why didn't you just tell Brad? He would have brought it back out, or he'd give it to someone in town to hold for us."

Gran just fidgeted with the place mat she'd left out for Penny. "Well, it's not that simple...."

"What do you mean?" The bad feeling had crept into Penny's throat, making her voice all squeaky. "Just what did you leave there?"

Gran just looked at her, then smiled. "Some bugs."

"Some bugs? What in the world were you—" Penny took a deep breath and laid her head on her arms on the table. If it wasn't one thing, it was another. She lifted her head and looked at Gran. "Brad didn't tell you about his plans, did he? You bugged his house and overheard them."

"Well, somebody had to find out what was going on," Gran snapped. "You've turned into a stubborn lump who's feeling sorry for herself and Toto just moans about how Dorothy has to follow her dreams. But I really want my bugs back. Not to mention the fact that Toto bought the house and I'd rather if he didn't find them.''

''Since they're illegal?''

Gran looked offended. ''Since I paid good money for them.'' She shrugged. ''And since they have my name on them.''

Penny sat up at that. ''Your name on them! What in the world did you put your name on them for?''

''So they'd get returned if I lost them,'' Gran explained, then grimaced.. ''I can see that that wasn't a very smart idea, though. Now when Toto finds them, he'll know they're mine.''

''I doubt that he'll arrest you.''

''I'm not afraid of the big house.'' But a bit of doubt had crept into Gran's voice.

''Okay, I'll get them.'' Penny closed her eyes. She was living a never-ending nightmare. ''But I really am not up to seeing Brad just now.''

''Who said you have to see him?'' Gran said and got to her feet. ''He's staying at some motel by the tollway. Let me get you my lock picks.''

Chapter Fourteen

Brad had given up on the idea of sleep as long as he was in Chesterton. Uncle Hal's house was haunted. The crickets were too noisy. The night was too dark. Penny was too close.

He rolled over, punched his pillow a few times and stared at the shadows dancing on his far wall. Had his uncle lain awake in this bed, staring at that wall and dreaming of what would never be?

The shadows of leaves swayed in the breeze. The drapes moved back and forth. He closed his eyes and he saw Penny, soft and loving and so very gentle. The air left the room, and the temperature rose. His heart began to race.

He rolled onto his back, opening his eyes. He should have just stayed in the motel, instead of spending the past few nights here. It's not as if this place meant anything to him.

A soft rustle of leaves came in through the open window, and the sound of occasional distant traffic. The neighbor's dog started to bark, then quieted after a moment.

Maybe he should just get up and go through some more of

those boxes. He'd never realized what a pack rat Uncle Hal had been and going through some more boxes tonight would mean fewer unsorted boxes to ship to his place in L.A. Not that he was finding much—

He stopped and listened. There it was again. A creak. Like the noise the boards on the porch made when you stepped on them. Was someone out there?

He waited but the only sounds he heard were the normal night ones. Maybe it had been a squirrel or a cat. This was Chesterton, after all. Nobody snuck around and—

He sat up. There was an odd scratching noise coming from below his window. From the back porch. He slipped out of bed and pulled on a pair of running shorts, then moved silently across the floor to the window. He couldn't see anything out of place in the yard, but the porch roof blocked his view of the door. Then he clearly heard a soft click.

Someone was breaking in.

Damn. This happened in L.A., not Chesterton. He lived in a secure building there, with an elaborate security system. He didn't have a thing here. Including anything worth stealing except for a few personal items up here in the bedroom. But nobody was getting that far. He reached for his cell phone to call the police, but put it down, picking up his flashlight instead. Then he crept out of the room and down the stairs.

He could hear someone moving around in the kitchen. There was nothing in the kitchen, but a little bit of furniture and the kitchen appliances. The large appliances. This couldn't be a serious burglar. It had to be a kid.

He eased down the hall, then stopped. For a split second he thought he'd caught a whiff of a soft flowery scent. Lordy, even now, he couldn't get Penny out of his mind.

He quickened his steps, as if he could outrun all thought of her, then stopped in the kitchen doorway. He could see a figure near the table. A tall figure, tall and slight and moving with Penny's grace.

This was insane. Even burglars looked like Penny to him. He reached into the room and hit the light switch. The room filled with light and for a split second he couldn't see. Then he could.

"Penny?" he asked.

She looked startled. She looked scared. She looked so damn beautiful, even in some ridiculous burglar outfit of black shorts and T-shirt and a black baseball cap, it was all he could do not to take her in his arms and make mad passionate love to her right here.

"Brad?" Her voice was a squeak. "I thought you were staying at a motel. Gran said you were."

"They turned the power on so I moved in here."

"Oh."

It had only been a few days since he'd seen her, but she looked thinner. Sadder. And he had done that to her with his stupid meddling. "What are you doing here?"

She looked around as if she had forgotten where she was for a moment. "Oh, Gran left something here the other day and asked me to get it."

"Why didn't she just tell me?" Then he frowned. "And why did you come in the middle of the night?"

If catching her in the kitchen had made her ill at ease, his question had doubled it. "Uh…"

"No, you don't have to tell me," he said quickly, reality stabbing him hard. He walked over to the sink, and leaned against the counter as he stared out at the night. But all he saw was his own reflection in the window over the sink. "I know. You didn't want to see me."

"No, it wasn't—"

He turned, torn even more by her attempt to protect his feelings. "You don't have to pretend," he assured her. "But in another day, I'll be gone and you won't be troubled by me anymore.

"Gran said you were leaving tomorrow," she stated. "That you and Dorothy are leaving together."

He nodded. "I promised to attend a conference in Paris and since she was going to Paris, too…" He shrugged. "I suppose everybody read their own interpretation into that."

"You know how the town is."

"Well, I just wanted you to know that there wasn't anything to it."

She tried to smile but gave up and just nodded. "Thanks."

Had he killed her smile? Lordy, he hoped not. "I expect there'll be a lot of talk when we leave the poetry reading together but you can set them straight."

"You don't have to come, you know. I'm not even sure why we're having it anymore."

The wistful note in her voice tore his heart apart. "No, I want to come. I wouldn't miss it for the world."

She made a face. "Suit yourself," she said. "Well, I'd better get going."

But he didn't want her to leave. He wanted just one more moment of the two of them. One more moment to remember. "Did you find what you were looking for? I can help you look."

"Thanks. I got it." She held up something flat and metallic, but she stopped, turning back to him after only a step. "Uh, I'm actually glad you were here. I wanted to tell you it's okay about the seminar stuff."

Her voice was low and raw with pain. Her eyes couldn't seem to meet his. She looked like a fragile flower that had been stepped on. He had never felt so low and worthless.

"No, it's not. I should have stayed out of it."

She turned as if even the peripheral sight of him was too much. "I know why you did it and it's okay. You were only trying to help."

"But I didn't."

"We all do things that backfire. Like my extra sandwiches."

"There was nothing wrong with that," he said. Another nail in his coffin. Was there no end to the hurt he'd caused her? "I overreacted. I appreciated those sandwiches more than you'll ever know. You kept me from going hungry."

She looked back at him then. Her face so still and dispirited. "And you tried to keep me from being hurt by the truth."

"What truth?" Her words made no sense to him, but then

all he knew was the need to hold her. To kiss those ruby lips. To taste her tenderness.

"That I'm just not smart enough to do some of the things I wanted."

"What?" He was loosened from his need to hold her, shaken free by confusion. But the urgency to enfold her in his arms swept in again, stronger, more intense. As if touching her could make her feel the truth in his heart. "That wasn't it at all."

But she just shook her head at him, her smile sad and knowing. "It's okay. Really it is. I knew you thought I was dumb back when we were kids—"

"I did not," he cried. "I was so crazy about you I couldn't talk."

She laughed, and it was the sound of raindrops on a forest bed. Soft and silvery. But it was also the sound of goodbye somehow.

"Things were probably doomed between us from the start this time around," she said. "We both were so locked into who the other was back years ago, we forgot to take a good look at who we are now. Or at least, I did."

"Why won't you believe me?" he snapped. "I thought about you all the time. I worked those long hours just to be close to you. I chased away any other guys who wanted to come over and see you. I never thought you were dumb."

She didn't believe him. He could see it in her eyes and the quiver of her smile. But she just reached up and took off her hat, shaking her soft blond hair onto her shoulders like a golden curtain. With a quick smile at the hat, she tossed it over to him.

He caught it, a reflex action, but just stared at her.

"Keep it," she said softly. "One day you'll have someplace to hang it."

He glanced down at it, at the bright yellow road embroidered on the front along with dancing red letters. Follow the Yellow Brick Road. If only it was that simple.

"I wish I could," he told her. "But I think I must be a

Quadling or a Winkie or even a Hammer-Head. There are no yellow brick roads for me.''

Penny stopped, her hand on the doorknob as she turned slowly around. ''You must be what?'' she asked, staring at him as if he'd been speaking a foreign language.

''You know,'' he said. ''A Quadling, a Winkie, a Hammer-Head. Different creatures in the land of Oz.''

''Right, sure.'' She seemed to shake herself, though her confused look seemed to stay in place. ''Your knowing them just took me by surprise.''

''Hey, I know all sorts of silly little things,'' he replied.

''I never realized it,'' she said, her eyes taking on a strange glint. ''I never thought about it that way.''

Thought about what, what way? But he didn't ask, just stood there watching her.

''So, I'll see you at the poetry reading?'' she asked. ''This isn't really goodbye.''

It would be easier if it was, but he wasn't going to go the easy route. ''No, I'll see you tomorrow.''

''Great.'' With a fleeting smile, she hurried out the door.

He went after her into the night, not wanting her to leave, only to see her slipping past the garage and down the alley. At the sound of his steps on the porch, the dog next door started barking, alerting the neighborhood to danger. Where was that dog this past week, Brad thought, when he'd needed warning?

''Oh, shut up!'' Brad snapped at him, then sank onto the porch steps.

He'd thought he'd hurt Penny this past week with his stupid meddling, but he'd actually been hurting her all along. His great and wonderful caring had done nothing but harm. Watching her leave he realized that he loved her. Had loved her for years, actually. Yet she was better off without him. When he left, she would be well rid of him.

Well rid of him maybe, but still having to carry the burden that he'd given her. If only there was a way to make her believe that he'd done all this out of caring, not pity.

If only...

A movement in the trees caused him to turn and there in the low branches of the maple tree, he saw it.

A birdhouse.

''Penny?'' Gran called up the back stairs. ''Shouldn't we be going?''

''In a minute.''

Penny was only half-dressed as she sat on her bed, her notebook lying open in front of her. The poetry reading was set to start in fifteen minutes and she wasn't ready. But how could she be ready when her whole world had tumbled upside down only eighteen hours ago?

She didn't even have time to figure out if she was smart to realize it at last, or dumb to not have realized it sooner. All she knew was that she had a lifetime of happiness to fight for. And the only guarantee she could make for the evening was that Brad Corrigan was not getting out of town easily.

She read over her poem one last time, then glanced at the clock. It was now or never. She folded up her poem and went over to her dresser. She'd put her makeup on earlier—rosy red cheeks and star-speckled eyes-so she just pulled on her flannel shirt and jeans, then grabbed up her straw hat. Her poem went in her pocket and boots on her feet. She took a last look at herself in the mirror and smiled.

She did make a damn good scarecrow.

Brad pulled his rental car up next to Penny's truck in the Sam's Place parking lot, then hoisted the box from his trunk and slid it into the back of the pickup. It had taken him all day and lots of digging in his memory to try to come up with some of the nursery's frequent customers back then, but unbelievably he had found all eight of the birdhouses. All he'd had to do then was loosen the tops and number them, so Penny could read the poem in order.

Once she did that, she would believe that he had done everything out of love for her, not because he thought she was dumb. He would have set her free of that demon hopefully forever. And then he would be the only one haunted.

"About time you got here," Dorothy said.

Brad turned. Dorothy was walking over from the bar's porch, a carry-on suitcase in one hand and a larger bag in the other.

"Hey, let me take those."

She shook her head as she put them down by his car. "There's two more over by the building. How about if you get them? I'll toss these into your trunk."

"Great. We'll be all ready to go after the reading, then." He wished they were gone already. How could he see Penny one more time, knowing it would be the last?

"You know, you ought to be staying here," Dorothy told him as he loaded her other two bags.

"Let's not go there again. It's over. Through. Done with." He slammed the car trunk closed and then walked in silence into the bar. For two people who were on the way to adventure and excitement in a few hours, they were pretty damn glum.

"It sure sounds noisy," Dorothy said as they went down the hall.

"Maybe there's a party in the bar," Brad suggested.

But as they rounded the corner, they could hear that the laughter and talking was coming from the meeting room. People had spilled out into the hallway, but all of them were straining to see inside.

"Quite a turnout," Brad said. He was glad for Penny's sake. Maybe this would make her feel better.

"I'll say."

They stopped at the back of the crowd. Dorothy looked ready to push her way in, but Brad wondered if he should bother. There were so many people in the room, Penny wouldn't even notice if he was here or not.

But then Heather came through the crowd, all smiles when she saw them, and hugged both Dorothy and Brad. "I'm so glad you both could make it. Come on. We've got a spot inside saved for you."

Brad went first to open a path, but it wasn't necessary. The crowd parted like the Red Sea to let them through.

Brad just looked around at the smiling faces of the towns-people. The Jamisons and Nancy Abbott and Matt Harris. Mickey Juarez and the Kirby brothers. Mr. Mayberry and the Clevingers. An uneasy feeling grew in his stomach, but he could hardly back out. Heather led them to some empty chairs off to one side. Aunty Em was already there and smiled at them.

"I am so jubilant you have all joined us this evening." Alex was up at a podium at the front of the room, addressing the crowd. "We have pledged to recite poems by various area po-ets, but I believe we'll commence with Penny Donnelly. So, if she would come forward…"

There was a murmur from the back of the room and Brad turned. He remembered how beautiful she'd looked at the last reading, her hair as bright as the sun, her eyes all aglow. Could he bear to see that radiance again? But there was Penny sud-denly—and she was dressed as a scarecrow!

What was this? Anger coursed through him. Was someone trying to make fun of her? But she was laughing as she greeted people. The smile she sent his way held more joy than he'd ever seen. Joy and something else. Something that filled his heart with hope, and at the same time, scared the hell out of him.

Then she was up in the front of the room and her smile held only welcome. "Hi, everybody. Thanks for coming." She glanced down at her costume with a grin. "This probably isn't what you expected to see up here reading poems tonight, but it's what you're getting, so relax and enjoy."

Alex stepped aside from the podium and Penny settled her-self there, after giving him a warm smile—that set Brad's teeth on edge with jealousy. Lordy, this evening had better pass quickly.

"You're probably wondering why I'm dressed this way," Penny said. "Well, you see, very recently someone told me I had made a great Scarecrow. At the time, I found this pretty discouraging because we all know the Scarecrow is dumb.''

Jeez, was she on that kick again? He almost told her to stop, but just clamped his lips shut. He folded his arms over his chest, as if that would keep him seated and quiet as Penny went on.

''But last night I reread *The Wizard of Oz* and I discovered something—the Scarecrow wasn't dumb at all. He only thought he was dumb.''

Brad began to relax a bit. Her voice radiated laughter and joy and some of it seeped behind his reserve.

''The Wizard knew better,'' she continued. ''Well, I found my own Wizard—Brad—and he set me straight, too.''

Everyone turned to look at him—to smile at him—but he was just watching Penny. Did she really believe what she was saying? There was something different about her. A new confidence. A new feeling of freedom.

''So anyway, this is my 'come clean' night,'' she said. ''I'm here to be honest and confess I'm a C student at Midwest.''

As if anyone really cared about her grade point average. There was no shocked outcry, no one stood up and left. Brad let a small smile onto his lips, his happiness growing along with her confidence.

She went on. ''And that I'm not going to be speaking at the Oz conference.''

Her smile fell. If she was going to be honest, so was he. ''That conference thing was my fault,'' Brad pointed out loudly. ''Not yours.''

She just grinned at him, her eyes brimming with emotion that touched him even at this distance. ''Brad likes to believe it's his fault,'' she said. ''Because he tried to buy me a spot to speak at the conference, which is, of course, the absolute sweetest thing anyone ever did for me.''

There was something in her gaze that made him strong, that swept away his reticence. Or maybe it was his conscience that just wouldn't let him off the hook so easily. ''It was criminal meddling,'' he stated as he got to his feet. ''I had no right to interfere.''

''Trying to give someone what they think is their heart's desire is criminal?'' she asked. Her voice was lower and her eyes were locked with his. ''No, it was loving and generous.''

His mind knew there were people all around them, that they were fifteen feet apart in the middle of a crowded room, yet his heart saw only her. As much as it felt as if he were basking in her sunshine, he couldn't have her looking at him like that. After all the hurt he'd caused her, he didn't deserve it.

''You would have been better off if I hadn't come back,'' he said.

''But I'd still be reaching for impossibly silly goals.''

''They weren't silly. I never said they were.''

''You two wanna be alone?'' someone called out.

''Just ignore us.''

''I think they already are.''

The time, the place, the reality came back to Brad in a rush and he looked around him. People were all smiling but his heart closed back up. Tightened with the unplanned opening. Penny just smiled at him and it eased some of the tension in him as he sat slowly back down.

''Maybe it's time for my poem,'' she said and unfolded a piece of paper.

I'm only a scarecrow
And not all that smart
So what do I know?
Where can I start?

I knew I was dumb,
And not at all wise,
But I wanted to see
Pride in everyone's eyes.

If I got a degree
In a big brainy field

Success would mean
Dumbness concealed.

Someone did tell me
I was far from a fool,
And I was quite wrong
To measure brains by that rule.

But I didn't listen,
I didn't want to hear,
I needed glory and acclaim
To be the star one year.

My friend foresaw disaster,
He predicted the doom,
Though he tried to save me
My attempts ended in gloom.

Though from ruin and wreckage,
A truth I did learn,
And repeat it each night,
In my heart it is burned.

I am who I am,
Sometimes smart, sometimes not,
But pride is earned by being good,
Not for the awards you've got.

So I'd like to tell him,
When push comes to shove,
The only thing that matters
Is that you are loved.

"And that you know ten languages, of course," she added.
There was laughter and applause as she stepped away from
the podium. Both Heather and Dorothy hugged her as she came
to sit next to Aunty Em, but Brad was just still.

"So, what do you think?" Aunty Em asked, nudging him
in the ribs. "She's a pretty special lady, don't you think?"

But he'd always thought she was special. Tonight hadn't changed that. What he hadn't realized until now was that she was ten million times smarter than him. Love was the only thing that mattered.

But he didn't have her ten damn languages.

"Brad." Penny was leaning across Aunty Em to touch his arm. "Can we talk before you leave? It's important."

He nodded, but his heart kept echoing her words. Before he left. In just an hour or so he'd be going. How many languages could he learn in sixty minutes?

"Our next poet is a young man from…"

He barely heard Alex's introduction of the next speaker. Okay, maybe he wasn't the one for Penny. His lack of languages proved that. But he could give her something before he left. He could publicly assure her and everyone that he never thought she was dumb. If she had thought that had been behind his actions, then so did most of the town. And she deserved better than that.

He got to his feet and edged toward the aisle.

"Brad?" Penny whispered.

"Where're you going?" Dorothy wanted to know.

"I'll be right back," he murmured as he turned into the aisle.

People were giving him strange looks, but he just smiled. He'd get that box from Penny's truck and be right back. He had a poem to read, too.

Once out in the hallway, he broke into a half run, then was out the back door and hurrying across the parking lot. So what if the poem revealed his feelings to everyone here? What was the worst they would do? Laugh? After tonight he'd never see them again anyway, so what difference did that make? Nothing compared to opening himself up for Penny.

He got to Penny's truck and pulled open the door at the back of the cab. Or tried to. The latch wouldn't turn. He tried again, harder this time thinking it was stuck, but it wasn't. It was locked. How the hell could it be locked when he had just opened it?

"What are you doing?" Penny snapped.

He spun around. Penny—a worried look on her scarecrow face—had come out after him. And so had just about everyone else. Dorothy, Heather. Alex. Most of the poetry-reading crowd. Even Aunty Em was there, pushing her way through the others, and looking like she was ready to use her cane on him.

"Just where do you think you're going, young man?" she demanded.

He just stared at her, at Penny and everyone, and shook his head. "I came out to get something. I was coming right back in."

"Looked like he was leaving to me," someone muttered.

"Running off after Penny's nice poem, too."

Brad sighed and tugged at the handle again. "I just need to get this box out of here," he said. "But the thing's locked."

"It can't be locked," Penny said and came over to try herself. "I never lock it." She couldn't budge it, either.

"Maybe I did somehow when I put the box in." It was the only thing he could think of. "Use your key."

She glared at him. "I don't have a key for it. Dad lost it ages ago. That's why I never lock it."

"Oh, for pity's sake," Aunty Em muttered and came over to the truck. She dug in her purse for a moment, then pulled out some long thin tools.

"Lock picks?" Brad marveled. "You really come prepared."

"Ain't got time for a biscuit run," she said.

He just laughed. "No, I guess not."

She poked one of the tools into the lock. A few little turns on her part and then she had the back open. "Now make it good, smart boy."

Smart boy? He hadn't felt all that smart lately, but just pulled the box out of the back and set it on the ground. Everyone was watching, some eager, some bored. Penny's eyes were wary and that did in whatever remnants of reticence were lingering in his heart.

"I know I wasn't scheduled for this evening," he said. "But

I have a poem to read, too. I wrote it ages ago. Eighteen years ago to be exact.'' He pulled the first birdhouse out of the box.

''A birdhouse?'' Aunty Em snapped. ''You got a box of birdhouses?''

''Yep.'' He pulled the loosened top off. ''But these are special ones.''

''I remember them,'' Penny said slowly. ''You brought those over the night before you moved.''

''These are them?'' Dorothy pulled back the flap on the box to look.

''Just wait,'' he ordered, and put the flap back down. ''These things have been lying around for the past eighteen years. You didn't read them when you had the chance, so now we're doing it my way.''

''Read them?'' someone asked. ''How do you read a birdhouse?''

''There was something inside them,'' Penny said. ''I remember the tops were loose.''

He took a deep breath, turned over the roof of the first birdhouse and read. '''No matter the kind, the size or the hue, these flowers all tell of my feelings for you.'''

''What flowers?'' someone asked.

He held up the birdhouse roof so everyone could see he'd painted flowers on the inside.

''Aw,'' someone sighed.

He handed the first roof to Penny, all wide-eyed and silent, then took the next birdhouse out. '''Yellow acacia and cowslip bouquets, masses of calla in vibrant arrays.''' He handed that roof over also. She just stared down at the lines surrounded by his feeble attempts to paint the individual flowers.

''Oh, isn't that sweet?'' someone said.

''What's it mean?'' someone else wanted to know.

He went on to the third birdhouse. '''Cudweed and peach blossom, and a strawberry tree...'''

The fourth. '''Myrtle and rose and wood sorrel for thee.'''

''Cudweed? What's that?'' someone asked.

''Shut up, will you?'' Aunty Em snapped.

The fifth. "'But now it's a daisy I have to present.'"

The sixth. "'And with meadow saffron I must be content.'"

The seventh. "'I wish volkamenia will forever find you...'"

The eighth. "'But when night's curtain falls, a zinnia or two.'"

He handed Penny the last of the roofs. "So anyway—"

"But what does it mean?" Heather asked, looking over Penny's shoulder at the poem. "It's just a lot of flower names."

But Penny didn't seem to be listening. Her eyes looked ready to overflow with tears as she looked at him. Her gaze was so deep, so steady, he thought she was trying to read into his soul. But she still would only see one language there.

"Eighteen years is a long time," she said softly.

He nodded. "But it's still true, every word of it."

"Not every word," she said, dumping the pile of roofs into Dorothy's arms. "We can do without daisies."

"Why would anyone do without daisies?" Heather asked. "They're nice."

Penny just took a step closer to him. "And if we do without daisies, we don't need the zinnias."

"I guess not." His heart was pounding so loud everyone must have been able to hear it. Did she know what she was saying?

"And then the meadow saffron can certainly go." Her eyes locked with his, she came closer still.

Maybe she did. Or maybe those were just some flowers she didn't like. "That's it?" he asked.

When she shook her head, his heart wanted to stop. "I think we should dump the acacia and just stick to myrtle and roses."

He dared to breathe again, a slow smile on his lips and in his heart as he opened his arms to her. She was there in his embrace before he had time to think, and he was complete once more.

"Alex, what the hell was all this about?" Dorothy asked.

"I suspect the flowers all have meanings," he said.

"It's a language," Aunty Em said. Her voice had a quaver

in it and she wiped at her eyes. "Don't remember all of it but daisies are for farewell, and myrtle and rose are for love."

"A language," Dorothy cried.

But Brad just shook his head, his arms holding Penny but his heart heavy once more. "But it only makes two. I'm still eight short."

Penny pulled back from him with a grin. "Are you kidding? You just don't know how to count. What was the business about the biscuit run with Gran?"

"It means a useless trip. It's from some detective novel."

"Private investigator language," Penny said.

"And there was the square dancing," Dorothy said. "He talked about do-si-doing."

"Square dance language," Heather counted.

Penny's hold on him tightened. "And last night, you talked about the Quadlings and Winkies."

"Oz language," someone shouted.

"Hey, he talked to me about the weather once," someone from the crowd called out. "Storm squalls off the lake, tornado alley and lake effect snow. Hoosier weather language."

"Computer networking has its own language," Alex added.

"So does poetry when it comes right down to it," Heather said.

"So we're up to eight," Penny told him. "Do we keep counting?"

Brad just shook his head, his heart so happy he thought it would burst. "It doesn't matter. Will you have me?"

"Only for forever."

Chapter Fifteen

"Sorry to be dropping out at the last minute like this," Brad told Dorothy. "We could still drive you to the airport if you want."

Dorothy just laughed and heard it echo across the now-deserted parking lot. "No, you guys stay here and be happy. I can drive there on my own." Thank goodness, it was getting dark out and no one could really see her. She had a feeling the disappointment in her heart had to be on her face. But it had nothing to do with Penny and Brad. "I'm just so glad that you two decided to reconcile in public so we could all share it."

Penny grinned. "Anything to keep the town entertained." Her smile faded. "I just wish you weren't still going to Paris."

"Hey, we all have our dreams," Dorothy said. Toto hadn't even showed up to say goodbye. Showed how far off from reality her dreams were.

"Toto's a fool," Heather said.

But Dorothy just laughed. Who was to say who the fool was? At least Penny's crowd had gone back into the bar and they were able to say their goodbyes in private. "Remember our club, The Bridal Circle? I was going to find a prince and live in a palace. These are just my first steps along that road."

She stopped and looked at Brad and Penny, and sighed. "Well, you guys stay in touch, will you? And if you're ever in the neighborhood…" She blinked back a sudden rush of tears.

"Be happy, you hear?" Brad said. He hugged her, and then gave her the keys to his rental car.

Suddenly a huge, hairy monster flew across the parking lot and practically jumped into Dorothy's arms. Junior.

Dorothy bent down, putting her arms around the dog. "Oh, Junior, you take care of Toto now, you hear?" she whispered into his fur, then straightened up. The only Toto here to say goodbye was the furry one. This was just the fitting end to a lousy week. A lousy year. A lousy thirteen years. She was wise to leave.

"Well, this is it," she said.

Junior woofed as with a bright smile, she got into the car and rolled down the window.

"Junior's telling you not to go," Brad said.

Dorothy just laughed and started the motor. "You understand him? Dog language." She smiled at Penny. "Add that to his list."

Penny nodded, slipping her arm through Brad's. "We'll reach ten before the night's over."

Dorothy waved and put the car in gear. If she didn't go now, she'd be crying too hard to ever leave. With a spurt of determination, she pulled out of the lot and onto the road. In her rearview mirror, she saw Penny, Brad and Junior watching her leave.

Then she turned her eyes ahead. That's where they'd stay, too, focused on her future, not her past.

The parking lot was silent. Brad supposed they ought to go back inside for the rest of the poetry reading, but he was just as happy standing here, his arm around Penny and no one but

Junior around. Brad couldn't believe how things had turned out tonight.

He turned, pulling Penny into his arms. "What do you say we—"

He stopped as a police car careered into the lot, lights flashing. Toto screeched to a stop next to them.

"Where is she?" he cried. "I got tied up on a call."

Penny let go of Brad and leaned down to talk to Toto. "She just left, but she's driving Brad's rental car—a red Taurus. If you hurry, you can catch up with her."

With a wave, Toto was off, speeding down the road after Dorothy. Junior trotted to the edge of the parking lot, watching the car race away. Penny sighed and took Brad's hand in hers.

He could feel her worries. "He should catch up with her in a few minutes," Brad told her.

"I guess," she said, still staring down the road. "But why did he wait until the last minute?"

"Maybe he didn't really think she would go. Or maybe he didn't think he could ask her to stay."

She turned to face him. "Speaking of asking to stay, are you sure you don't need to go to that conference in Paris?"

"I'm not going anywhere without you," he said. "If you want to come with me, we can go."

"Me, in Paris?" Her voice sounded awed at the idea. "I've got to think about that."

"Well, while you're thinking, I've got something for you," he said, and led her over to her truck. Opening the back, he reached into his suitcase and pulled out the yellow brick road hat she'd given him.

"You were taking that with you?" she asked. "That's so sweet."

He took her scarecrow hat off her head and replaced it with the yellow brick road cap. She frowned at him, and took it back off.

"I gave it to you."

"Because home is where I hang my hat. I know." He put

it back on her head. "And this is where I want to hang my hat. Because wherever you are, that's home for me."

"Oh, Brad," she said with a sigh and reached up to meet his lips with hers. But she pulled away before he could slip his arms around her. "You know what that is?"

He wanted to hold her. He wanted to feel her body next to his and around his and forever his. "Frustration?" he asked.

She just laughed. "It's your tenth language," she said. "The language of love."

Epilogue

Dear Ms. Donnelly:

Thank you for your letter. The committee read your explanation of the events leading up to the withdrawal of our invitation with interest. Of greater interest to us all, though, was your eloquent description of the Oz festival in your town. You painted a vivid picture of the blending of tradition and today's culture and made it clear that the century-old story does have pertinence in today's world.

If you are still willing, we would very much like to have you present a talk on the relevance of the Oz story in today's society to our conference. It would be both a pleasure and an honor to have you. We were fortunate to catch your appearance on the Olivia Collins show and know you are indeed an articulate speaker.

We are looking forward to hearing from you.

Professor Michael Bennett

Dear Professor Bennett:

I'd be glad to speak at your conference. How many tickets can I get? I think half the town wants to come.

Penny Donnelly

* * * * *

*Don't miss Andrea Edwards's
next emotional love story,
SECRET AGENT GROOM, in
THE BRIDAL CIRCLE miniseries,
available August 1999, only from
Silhouette Special Edition.*

Silhouette ® SPECIAL EDITION ®

presents THE BRIDAL CIRCLE, a brand-new miniseries honoring friendship, family and love...

by

Andrea Edwards

They dreamed of marrying and leaving their small town behind—but soon discovered there's no place like home for true love!

IF I ONLY HAD A...HUSBAND (May '99)

Penny Donnelly had tried desperately to forget charming millionaire Brad Corrigan. But her heart had a memory—and a will—of its own. And Penny's heart was set on Brad becoming her husband....

SECRET AGENT GROOM (August '99)

When shy-but-sexy Heather Mahoney bumbles onto secret agent Alex Waterstone's undercover mission, the only way to protect the innocent beauty is to claim her as his lady love. Will Heather carry out her own secret agenda and claim Alex as her groom?

PREGNANT & PRACTICALLY MARRIED (November '99)

Pregnant Karin Spencer had suddenly lost her memory and *gained* a pretend fiancé. Though their match was make-believe, Jed McCarron was her dream man. Could this bronco-bustin' cowboy give up his rodeo days for family ways?

Available at your favorite retail outlet.